"No," Avery said. " _____ what I need is a job, and this one s___ the line."

Logan finished his coffee. At one time, he'd been a good judge of character. Now he didn't trust his own instincts. He didn't think she'd lied, but there were secrets shifting around in those gray eyes, and her expression was just too bland. But what did it matter? All he wanted was to be left alone. He had the feeling Avery Jensen was looking for the same.

"We'd best get some things straight," he said. "Haven has its busybodies. They're going to make a lot out of a beautiful, single woman living on a ranch with a widower." He paused. "There are people in town who are going to talk about me. I don't give a damn what they say, but you might."

The corner of Avery's mouth tipped slightly upward and she said, "I don't put much stock in gossip. But just so I won't be surprised or shocked—what am I likely to hear?"

"That I'm responsible for my wife's and son's deaths. And that I benefited by getting an ungodly amount of insurance money." He shoved back his chair and stood. "They're right on both counts."

ABOUT THE AUTHOR

Evelyn A. Crowe worked for twelve years as a media director in an advertising company before turning her hand to writing in 1983. Her decision to change careers was certainly a stroke of good fortune for Harlequin readers. Evelyn's best-selling books are favorites around the world.

Books by Evelyn A. Crowe

HARLEQUIN SUPERROMANCE
186—MOMENT OF MADNESS
233—FINAL PAYMENT
262—TWICE SHY
294—A WILD WIND
362—WORD OF HONOR
570—REUNITED
646—LEGACY OF FEAR
667—FATHERS & OTHER STRANGERS
704—A FAMILY OF HIS OWN
745—SO HARD TO FORGET

Don't miss any of our special offers. Write to us at the following address for information on our newest releases.

Harlequin Reader Service
U.S.: 3010 Walden Ave., P.O. Box 1325, Buffalo, NY 14269
Canadian: P.O. Box 609, Fort Erie, Ont. L2A 5X3

SAFE
HAVEN
Evelyn A. Crowe

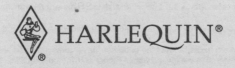

HARLEQUIN®

TORONTO • NEW YORK • LONDON
AMSTERDAM • PARIS • SYDNEY • HAMBURG
STOCKHOLM • ATHENS • TOKYO • MILAN • MADRID
PRAGUE • WARSAW • BUDAPEST • AUCKLAND

ISBN 0-373-70850-5

SAFE HAVEN

SAFE
HAVEN

CHAPTER ONE

THE TEXAS SPRING MORNING was pristine and breath-takingly beautiful, the air intoxicating with its scents of freshly mowed grass and newly tilled earth. But-terflies flitted over the fields. Rolling green hills were splashed with the jewel-like hues of wildflowers.

The setting was picture-perfect—except for the blacktop highway, an ugly tear in the landscape. It was also a dangerous stretch of highway, a deadly couple of miles that twisted and dipped and rose.

The purity of the morning and the cathedral silence was suddenly shattered by sounds of an ancient truck, which emitted a rooster tail of blue smoke as it rolled to a stop. The grinding of the brakes startled nearby birds from their perch in the trees.

A young woman, tall and shapely, climbed out of the passenger side of the truck. As she closed the door, a soft breeze teased her black hair around her face and made the hem of her dress flutter. She hoisted a suitcase from the bed of the truck and waved her thanks to the old man she'd hitched a ride from.

Avery Jensen watched the truck until it disappeared around a bend in the highway. She took a steadying breath to bolster her courage and turned to face the ornate wrought-iron sign arched high over the lane entrance. Her exhausting trip was almost at an end.

Despite her eagerness to finish it, she hesitated,

knowing that when she walked under that arch she would truly be cut off from her world as she'd known it. She'd be a new person. If she could have given herself a whole new identity, Avery admitted, she would have. But that was illegal, and she couldn't afford any run-ins with the law. She'd had enough of those.

Her life had been torn apart and turned inside out. She was scarred and bruised. She'd survived, but the price had been high. Once, not too long ago, she'd had it all. A beautiful home. Family and friends. She'd had a career, a position in society. She'd had power, money and the respect of her peers. She'd even had a fiancé. Now all she had was herself.

For the first time it hit her: she was free. She was safe. Avery laughed. She'd found a safe haven—Haven, Texas, that is—and it beat the hell out of the home she'd had for the past eight months.

She picked up her suitcase. Everything she owned was in it, none of it old. There was nothing to tie her to the past, nothing to remind her of what she'd endured. Nothing to openly declare she'd been a fool. The heaviness of the case was a pleasant reminder that she was carrying her life with her. It felt damn good to realize she was leaving everything else behind.

Her resolve firmly set, she straightened to her full five foot eight, lifted her chin and walked under the archway of the Circle M ranch. She'd been told the owner was Logan Monahan, who raised cattle and quarter horses.

Once she was through the gate and actually on the property, her steps faltered. She was so far from Seattle it felt like another world. But that was what she wanted. Avery adjusted the shoulder strap of her bulging purse, switched the suitcase to her other hand and started walking again.

It didn't take long for the thicket of overhanging tree limbs to thin out enough for her to see how far she had to walk. She gasped in dismay. The lane snaked for several hundred yards over the rolling land toward a grove of cottonwood trees on the crest of a hill, where she knew, from the detailed directions she'd been given, the ranch house was.

She was stronger now. She could handle anything. Gripping the heavy bag firmly, she put one foot in front of the other. On both sides of the lane, barbed-wire fences sectioned off green rolling pastures. Cattle and horses munched on the lush grass, their tails swishing lackadaisically back and forth, batting flies.

By the time Avery reached the house, she was out of breath and perspiring heavily. Too exhausted to really admire the two-story Victorian house, she did get a quick impression of butter-yellow walls, hunter-green shutters at the windows and a front porch that extended the width of the structure. The thump and bump of her case against the steps and her heavy breathing were the only sounds until she collapsed on the top step with a loud groan. Her arms were twitching with strain and her leg muscles ached. She cursed whoever had messed up and neglected to collect her at the bus station, hoping it wasn't an omen of things to come.

After taking a few minutes to regroup, Avery struggled to her feet. She straightened the sleeveless denim dress and tried to smooth out some of the wrinkles, then pressed the doorbell. As she waited, she attempted to put some order to her hair, then waited some more. On the fourth try of the bell, with still no answer, she glanced around, a little nonplussed.

"Dammit, someone was supposed to be here," she grumbled, and made a decision to go looking. She left all her belongings on the porch and wandered around to the side of the house. She gazed about and noticed the neglect evident in the flower beds, lawn and house. Gingerly, she stepped over an extension ladder lying on its side, as well as various tools carelessly scattered on the ground. Upon closer inspection she discovered that the side of the house had been scraped down, as if being readied for a new coat of paint.

She rounded a corner to the back and shaded her eyes to see rail fences and several other buildings. One was a small, one-story version of the main house. Its porch was shaded by blooming wisteria vines desperately in need of pruning. From the location of a truck and other machinery, she figured that two of the buildings were garages of some sort.

Despite the warmth of the sun, she shivered. The whole place was eerily quiet, as if everyone had just disappeared. Still, it awarded her the luxury of looking around and studying everything.

The last building puzzled her. It was a huge, square, redbrick structure with a slate roof and few windows. She looked from the Victorian house to the buildings again and realized what it was that nagged at her. While everything else seemed run-down, the redbrick building was modern and well kept, expensive looking. Though she knew little about ranch life, she figured it was the barn. Maybe she'd find someone there.

She'd just skirted the big truck, which was half-filled with hay bales, when she heard the sound of running water. She checked her pace, and it was then she saw him. Maybe it had been too long since she'd been so close to so much testosterone, but the sight of him made her tingle with nervous energy.

He was solidly built and naked to the waist, his tight, sun-faded jeans riding low on his hips. Bent forward with the hose held above him, he let a stream of water wash over his dark head and upper body.

Avery felt her heart slam against her ribs as she watched the water slide over his muscular shoulders and roll across his broad back, then trickle to his narrow waist and soak the waistband of his jeans.

She was transfixed by the way his muscles rippled under the tanned skin. Then he dropped the hose, straightened to what appeared to be at least six-four, and ran his fingers through his hair. Lifting her eyes from the knotted stomach muscles to his face, she bit her lip. He was not a pretty man. His nose was hawkish, his cheekbones high and sharp. His jaw, while strong, looked unrelenting. His chin and cheeks were lightly scarred from what she assumed was adolescent acne. His eyes were large and light brown, the color of autumn leaves, yet distant somehow. The only remotely soft feature that hinted at any flexibility was his wide mouth with its well-defined lips. At the moment they were held in a stern line.

A breathy sigh trembled across her own lips. He wasn't handsome, not by her standards. But there was an aura of strength and pride about him. He was, she thought, the sexiest man she'd ever laid eyes on.

"Are you going to stand there staring," he snapped, "or are you going to throw me that towel?"

She jumped, every nerve in her body alive with

embarrassment. "I'm sorry," she mumbled, grabbing the towel from the truck bed she was standing beside and pitching it to him. He plucked it from the air and began drying his hair, chest and stomach, never once taking those eyes off her.

"You want to tell me what you're doing here?"

His voice was deep and smoky soft. Her own voice was stuck somewhere in her throat. Suddenly he smiled, and the appearance of a dimple in his right cheek was enough to jolt her out of her trance. "I'm Avery Jensen," she told him.

He waited. When she didn't continue, he returned to his task of drying off, and gave his hair another rough rub before pitching the towel into the back of the truck. "Is that supposed to mean something to me?"

If she could have, she would have kicked herself for acting like a dimwit. "I guess not if you don't recognize it. I'm looking for Logan Monahan."

"You got him."

"What?"

"I'm Logan Monahan."

To cover her confusion, she stuck out her hand. "I'm pleased to meet you, Mr. Logan. I thought you were going to pick me up at the bus station this morning. When you didn't show up, I tried to call, but no one answered."

He was looking at her as if she was crazy. When he took a few steps toward her, she felt threatened. Reflex made her drop her hand and step back before she realized he was simply reaching for his shirt hanging on the corner of the tailgate.

She tried not to watch the way his muscles moved

under the smooth skin as he slipped it on. She swallowed. "Mr. Wilson gave me a ride."

Logan nodded. "He's a neighbor. You say I was supposed to pick you up at the bus station today?"

"Three hours ago, actually," she said, and barely managed to keep the irritation out of her voice.

"Me? Logan Monahan?"

She was becoming impatient with his questions. "That's right. You did hire me, after all."

"Did I?" Logan knew he was making her nervous, but he didn't give a damn. His first impression was that she was a strikingly beautiful young woman, with her long, jet-black hair and clear gray eyes. Maybe eleven or twelve years his junior—twenty-eight, or younger. She carried herself proudly, shoulders straight and her full breasts thrust out.

A closer look made him scowl. Although her skin was a beautiful milky-white, there wasn't a drop of color in her cheeks. She looked strained, exhausted. The kissable mouth seemed to tremble. She appeared too thin and a bit wired, as if she were running on air and sheer guts.

"Oh, hell," he grumbled under his breath. She resembled a wounded animal. All his life he had tried to fix what was hurt. He hadn't always managed, though.

"I hired you?" he asked again.

Avery felt light-headed, but there was no way she was going to end up a fainting female—not in front of this man. With a hand that shook, she reached for the truck's tailgate and sat.

"I believe your specifications were very exact," she said, "and I was the only one to fit the job description. You needed someone with computer savvy and bookkeeping skills, a no-frills cook, a general dogsbody to do light housekeeping, even-tempered and easy on the eye.''

''You mean I didn't demand a strong back and good teeth, too?'' Logan propped one worn boot on the side of the tailgate and gave her a long, amused look. She tried to hide her quick smile by ducking her head.

''Denise didn't mention those.''

''But you fit the bill otherwise?''

She steeled herself. ''Yes, indeed, and feel free to call Denise if you want to double-check my qualifications.'' Oh, she was qualified, all right. She just couldn't back up any of her qualifications. The only one willing to vouch for her was Denise Kirk, and they'd been best friends since they were ten. Denise would lie, cheat and steal for her. Fortunately, so far her friend had only had to lie.

Logan laughed. Then he said, ''I think I see my father's hand in this. He's Logan Monahan, Senior. Mac to his friends and enemies. He has a few other names I won't mention—they're for when he sticks his nose where it doesn't belong, which happens to be most of the time.''

A heavy sick feeling settled in her stomach like a brick. ''You mean I came to the wrong place? Your father hired me?''

''No and yes. And no again. Oh, hell.'' He raked his fingers through his hair. ''I don't need any help.''

She'd come so far, traveled by bus, of all things. She'd borrowed money from Denise for clothes and the ticket, and now it appeared she didn't have a job. She didn't even have the money to buy a return ticket. If she wasn't so determined to keep from falling apart in front of this man, she would have thrown up all over his boots.

Anything she might have said fled from her mind when a vehicle suddenly appeared around the corner of the barn and skidded to a stop beside the truck. Avery scrambled off the tailgate and jumped back from the cloud of dust and sprayed gravel that pinged against the truck. Unfortunately she backed into Logan Monahan. He placed his hands on her shoulders to steady her as they watched a young woman vault from the driver's side.

"Dammit, Jessie," Logan snapped. "You know better than to drive like that. Are you trying to kill yourself or me?"

Avery had the sudden sensation of being drilled clean through by a pair of knife-sharp, green eyes. Just as quickly, she was apparently dismissed as inconsequential, for the girl, Jessie, suddenly had eyes only for the man towering behind her. Avery figured her best bet was to keep quiet and let the little drama play itself out.

Jessie, she noted, couldn't have been more than twenty. She reminded Avery of her own sister at that age, all brashness and swagger. The girl was beautiful, tall and slim, with an abundance of strawberry-blond hair, but it didn't take much to see she was also spoiled and used to getting her way.

"I heard in town that Gus brought a woman out here, and Mac told me you'd hired a housekeeper. You really didn't need to do that, Logan."

Logan's hands were still on Avery's shoulders, which she was all too aware of. She suddenly felt she was being used as a shield. Why, she wasn't sure, though she sensed Logan was in some distress. She stuck out her hand. "Hi, I'm Avery Jensen."

"Oh, yeah. Hi," Jessie said, rudely ignoring the extended hand. "Really, Logan, if you needed help, you should have asked me." She glanced at Avery. "I'd be happy to drive you back to the bus station, and I'm sure Logan or Mac would compensate you for your time and inconvenience, but you see—"

"Shut up, Jessie. You don't run things around here. The woman's here and I'm going to give her a try."

"But, Logan—"

"Drop it, Jess." He waited as an older man climbed slowly from the truck. "Dad, I take it this is the young lady you stood up this morning."

Mac Monahan dusted his hands on his thighs, pulled off his Stetson, then stuck out a hand to Avery. "I can't tell you how sorry I am. I could have sworn that woman from the agency told me you'd be arriving *tomorrow* morning on the bus."

"It's okay," Avery said. "Really it is. I managed."

Mac laughed and turned a fierce scowl on his son. "You see, here's a gal who thinks for herself. Took the bull by the horns and got out here on her own. Why don't you let go of her, Logan? You're holding on like she's a fence post or something."

Logan jerked his hand off her shoulders and took a step back. It was apparent to Avery that he was furious with his father.

"You old coot," Logan grumbled. "You manipulated this little scene."

"Logan, you don't need a housekeeper." The seductive tone in Jessie's voice didn't disguise the whine.

"Hush, gal," Mac said. "This is Logan's call."

Logan gave a rough bark of laughter. "How kind of you, Dad," he said, "for allowing me to run my life."

Avery cringed inside. It hadn't taken long for her to realize what was going on. At another time or place, she would have excused herself and been out of there in a second. Then again, if she'd been smart and less trusting, she'd never have gotten herself into this mess in the first place. Since walking away wasn't an option, she had to endure being talked over, while the young woman shot dagger looks at her.

"I guess I'd better show Avery her living quarters," Logan said wearily.

"No!" Jessie shouted, and looked ready to stomp her foot in a fit of temper.

With his son's words, Mac perked up. "Great. Was that your gear I saw on the porch, Miss Avery? I'll go fetch it."

She didn't know what had happened, but everything abruptly changed. Logan had hold of her arm now and she was being forcibly led away. "Just the one suitcase and my purse," she said over her shoulder. "Thank you, Mr. Logan."

"Everyone calls me Mac, honey."

"Come along, Miss Avery," Logan said. "My father is too damn pleased with himself as it is to have you batting your pretty eyes at him. Now, I've had a long night and hard morning. Maybe I'll be able to hold a more intelligent conversation after some rest."

She didn't want to rock the boat of good fortune, so clamped her mouth against any notion of a tart comeback. She went with him silently and obediently, managing another quick glance over her shoulder to see that Jessie was following them at a discreet distance. From the look on the young woman's face, Avery had made an enemy. It was easy to see that Jessie was besotted with Logan Monahan. *Poor dear,* Avery thought. She knew all too well that feeling. Look where it had gotten her.

When they arrived at the one-story Victorian, Avery couldn't restrain a grin as Logan gave an irritable swat at the vines that tickled the side of his face. "I'd be willing to bet my father had the place cleaned out," he grumbled.

"He does seem like the take-charge type."

Logan laughed. "He's a pest, and when he gets a burr under his seat, it's best to let him have his way—for a while." Logan placed his hand on the doorknob and looked at her. "Don't get too comfortable. I'm a hard man to please."

"From your father's specific requirements, I figured that out for myself." She decided he probably didn't respond well to sass, and bit her lip.

Logan opened the door and pushed it wide. Avery squeezed past him, making sure she kept her gaze straight ahead and not focused on the exposed skin peeking from his unbuttoned shirt. "Oh, it's wonderful!" she said and meant it. There was a small living room furnished with a comfortable chintz sofa and an overstuffed chair. The tiny kitchen was separated from it by a counter that would serve as a table. She walked around the room, then opened the only other door and found a furnished bedroom and bath. "This will do just fine."

Logan, in fact, hadn't been near the house in two years. The walls suddenly closed in around him and he had to will himself not to turn and run. Maybe the place was too small for his new housekeeper. He thought of the big house with its five spacious bedrooms and large modern bathrooms and felt like an ogre. "This was originally built as a mother-in-law house. You don't have to—"

He broke off as Jessie let the screen door slam behind her. "Logan," she whispered. "Please."

He held up his hand for her to stop, then gazed past her. "Get the door for Mac, Jess." His heart was racing like that of a cornered wild animal. He leaned against the wall, making it look as if he was just getting out of his father's way, when all the time he was using the support to keep from falling over.

"Are you all right, Mr. Monahan?"

He'd lost track of time fighting the memories and hadn't seen his father drag the suitcase into the bedroom, nor had he noticed that Avery had been watching him. "Logan," he said. "We're an informal bunch. I'm sure in a couple of days you'll find other names for me."

"You're probably right," Avery said seriously, but her lips twitched.

Logan didn't actually smile, but the corners of his eyes crinkled. "By the way, who's Denise?"

Logan's question coming out of the blue took Avery off guard. She replied, "Denise Kirk. She runs an employment placement agency in Houston. She's also a friend." She'd called Denise from the bus station in Haven, but planned to call her again. Her old friend would enjoy her predicament and all the drama.

"Do you mean to tell me that my father had to advertise all the way to Houston before finding someone to fill the position?" Logan laughed with real pleasure.

Jessie watched them with a scowl. Mac elbowed

her and winked, and she jumped and rushed forward. "Why don't you go rest, Logan, and take Mac back to the house with you? I'll help Avery unpack and get settled in, then I'll bring her up to the house and show her around." Her lips twisted in a false smile as the men agreed and disappeared. She turned to Avery. "He doesn't really need any help, you know. It's just that Mac likes to have things his way and he thinks Logan needs someone."

"Sounds like a concerned father to me." Avery knew the girl was just itching for a scene or an argument, and she wasn't about to accommodate her. She walked into the kitchen and started opening the cabinets, familiarizing herself with her new surroundings. It was definitely a change from her former residence.

"Mac's concerned, but Logan can take care of himself, and I'm always around to help. We're very close." She picked up a pillow from the sofa and fluffed it.

Followed by Jessie, Avery headed for the bedroom. She was entertained by the girl's jealousy and childish attempts to warn her off, but she could have told Jessie a thing or two about men, and Logan Monahan in particular. She'd seen the way he looked at Jessie. There was nothing in his eyes but controlled amusement. Certainly, there was nothing remotely sexual.

She opened her suitcase and began putting away her belongings under the young woman's watchful gaze. It was hard to miss the swift lack of interest; she realized her clothes weren't up to Jessie's standards. Some of them even brought a sneer. Still, she could feel those angry, cat-green eyes boring into her, following as she moved around the room.

"Logan's not interested in women, you know."

Avery bit her lip, finished hanging up one of her cotton dresses, then gave Jessie her full attention. "You mean he's gay? That doesn't bother me."

"God, no. He's not gay. I meant, he's still mourning Becky."

Avery decided she might as well ask and save Jessie the effort of finding another way to tell her. "Who's Becky?"

The turbulent gaze directed at her was a shock. She saw torment, an emotion far too heavy for one so young. The struggle to keep the pain at bay was evident in the way Jessie held herself so straight and stiff.

"Rebecca Middleton Monahan, his wife. My sister." She cleared her throat, then swallowed hard. "They were madly, passionately in love. She's dead."

"I'm sorry," Avery said, pretending not to hear the anguish in the girl's voice. She sensed that Jessie, under normal circumstances, would never talk to a stranger about her sister. But something other than her being hired to work for Logan had triggered Jessie's highly charged state. All Avery could do was wait, seemingly not noticing, while the young woman composed herself.

"They were childhood sweethearts, you know," Jessie finally added. My sister waited for Logan to finish college so they could get married."

Avery had a sudden desire to put her arms around Jessie. Memories of a different time and place, of a younger girl, of heartbreak and misery, flooded back. She could have told Jessie that with time the pain would lessen.

Instead, Avery sat on the side of the bed, one hand squeezing the material of her dress. She was swamped by a wave of compassion and sorrow as it all came rushing back. She missed her friends, her job and her family. She missed laughing, and the secure feeling of being home. Texas was not Seattle. Logan was not her fiancé, and Jessie was not her sister, Emma. For her own sanity, Avery couldn't afford to look back. She'd had to learn to be hard and unyielding for so long that any show of tenderness almost took her breath away.

The exacting lessons and self-preservation were powerful teachers. She'd made a promise to herself that no matter where she went or whom she met, she couldn't afford to get involved. She would keep to herself, never ask questions unless they pertained to her job, and stay out of people's personal lives. Most important of all, she would keep her mouth shut.

"What happened to Becky?" Avery asked. *So much for promises,* she thought wryly.

Jessie shrugged, got off the end of the bed and began to roam the small room, touching everything. "She and Jamie were killed in a car crash." She tapped her fist to her chest as if she was having trouble getting the next words out. "It happened at the entrance to the ranch. She pulled out in front of an eighteen-wheeler."

Jessie slid her fingers over the smooth wood of the bureau, then stopped in front of the mirror, where she straightened her bangs and tucked a strand of hair behind her ear. She checked the condition of her pink lipstick, then her eyes met Avery's.

Her pose struck a too-familiar cord. Avery recognized the desperate actions of a person trying to disguise her feelings but still needing to talk. "Who's Jamie?" she asked.

"Their son. My nephew. He was killed, too."

Avery could think of nothing appropriate to say, nothing that would ease the hurt. She watched as Jessie angrily wiped away the tears from her cheeks with the back of a hand. Avery almost caved in and went to her, but suddenly their gazes clashed and she stopped in time. It didn't take much to see that, for her own reasons, Jessie had made up her mind to hate her. She, Avery, was an outsider, an intruder in Logan's life.

Jessie started to leave, then paused by the door to say, "I wouldn't unpack everything if I were you. You won't be here that long." She gave the dress Avery was holding a contemptuous glance. "When you're through, you'd better come up to the house." The parting remark was said like the lady of the manor to a lowly servant. Avery gritted her teeth.

The girl's lightning shift from heartbreak to arrogance puzzled her. With a shiver of foreboding, she thought maybe she *should* leave. There were too many dark currents under all that civilized surface, and too many raw emotions barely cloaked by strained smiles. But where would she go? With a sigh, she unhurriedly put away the rest of her belongings. As she did so, she realized something. She'd become a fighter, and she wasn't going to be so easy to dismiss.

Before leaving the little house, she hesitated, taking the time to look around. This was her home now and the only one she was likely to have. All she had to do to stay was simply discover a way to get along with Logan Monahan.

CHAPTER TWO

AVERY FOLLOWED the well-worn path leading to the back door of the main house. The shade from the trees and the lazy breeze cut the noonday heat, cooling her skin and filling the air with the scent of honeysuckle.

She was a city girl, had never been on a ranch, but even so, she'd seen enough Westerns—movies and television shows—to realize something was wrong with the picture. The sun was shining. Birds were singing happily. She could even hear the rustle of trees in the wind. Somewhere far away she thought she heard the mournful bellow of a cow. The big brick building she thought was a barn appeared to be in perfect condition, but why the neglect everywhere else? The mystery was intriguing enough to ease her jumpy nerves and queasy stomach.

Avery mounted the steps of the porch, and as she drew closer to the door, she could hear raised voices. She hesitated before knocking. It was then that she recalled another nagging question. Except for the people in the house, the place seemed deserted. She would have thought a ranch would be a hive of activity.

Walking into the middle of a family argument wasn't an appealing prospect. She'd done that too many times in her previous life and knew the pitfalls and the likelihood of getting sucked into taking sides.

Curiosity got the better of her, however, and she tried
to eavesdrop, but the rumble of voices on the other
side of the solid door proved impossible to understand. She'd raised her hand to knock when the door
was yanked open. Jessie pushed past her, followed by
Mac at a more sedate pace.

"Don't mind my son's bark," Mac said to Avery,
loudly enough for everyone to hear. "It's way worse
than his bite, and he don't mean nothing by it." He
patted Avery on the shoulder, winked, then lowered
his voice. "And don't let him bully you. He's dang
good at that."

She smiled in gratitude, closed the door, then gathered her courage to face the lion in his den. The
kitchen was spacious and wonderfully modern, obviously planned by someone who loved to spend a
great deal of time there. Logan was seated at an antique oak table, his chair tilted backward, his hands
locked behind his head as he stared at the ceiling. She
couldn't help noticing that he still hadn't buttoned his
shirt.

Her line of thought shook her. She stomped on the
mental brakes. For a long time she'd managed to bottle up that part of her, and this wasn't the time to
uncork it. There was too much at stake.

"Pull up a chair, Avery, and let's have a chat."
Logan sighed wearily and closed his eyes. Avery took
a chair opposite him. "It seems easier to go along
with the program than fight my father," he said, "so
I guess you stay." He dropped his hands from behind
his head, settled the chair in an upright position and
met her gaze across the table. "Let's start off on the
right foot and get something straight between us. I
can't abide mothering.

"Dad tells me you can handle a computer. That's great, 'cause I'm terrible at it." He rubbed his face and tried to concentrate. "He says you can keep books, do invoices, pay bills and generally make everything in the office run smoothly, so I can work. As for the cooking and housekeeping—" he shrugged "—I have a woman who comes in two days a week to clean. Sometimes she'll cook a ham or a roast for me. But mostly I've been fixing my own meals when I can, or eating in town. So if you'll just handle my meals, I think that'll do. We'll see how it works as we go along."

"What about your father and Jessie?"

Logan frowned. "What do you—?" Then he realized what she meant and grinned. "They don't live here, thank God. Jess stays on her father's ranch with her brother. As for Dad, he divides his time between his house in town and the farm."

She didn't intend to involve herself in any personal conversations, and figured that keeping their association on a business footing was best. She needed to be efficient. Most of all she had to make herself irreplaceable. "That all sounds fine to me. You look exhausted, though. Have you eaten?" She pushed her chair back.

"You're mothering me."

"No, I work for you, Mr. Monahan. You just told me part of my job is to cook your meals. You also said your morning was long and hard. Mine was, too. It's almost lunchtime and I'm hungry. I just assumed…" She let the unfinished statement dangle between them, and waited.

Avery was too logical for his sluggish brain to come up with a fitting retort. "I thought we'd

agreed—none of this mister business. Just Logan."
He managed a strained smile. "A sandwich and a
Coke will be fine, thank you. After that I'm going to
rest for a couple of hours, so you might as well finish
settling in."

It didn't take long to find everything she needed.
His cleaning woman had baked a ham, and Avery
quickly had his sandwich on the table. He was almost
finished when she sat down. He didn't try to hide the
fact that he was watching her. It made her nervous,
but she'd learned the hard way to hide her feelings.

"How old are you?" Logan asked, genuinely puzzled. She handled herself like a mature woman.

"Twenty-eight," she said, then dabbed at the corner of her mouth and took a sip of her own Coke. "Is
my age a problem?"

"None I can think of just now." There was something that still didn't seem right, but Logan gave up.
He didn't feel like playing games with her. He folded
his napkin and rose from the table. "Your first official
duty is to answer the phone and take messages."

AS HE CLIMBED the stairs to his bedroom, Logan wondered where he'd gotten the notion that she was playing games. Was that what she was about? He couldn't
put his finger on it, but there was more to Avery Jensen than she allowed him or the world to see. He'd
have to give it some thought when he wasn't one of
the walking dead.

By the time he reached the landing, he felt like a
man twice his age. As he passed one of the closed
bedroom doors, he paused and stepped back. He put
his hand on the cut-crystal doorknob and noticed how
cold it felt. A familiar sense of foreboding settled be-

tween his shoulder blades. As much as he wanted to walk away, he couldn't. He twisted the knob and opened the door.

He couldn't force himself to take that step over the threshold, though, so he simply stood there. His son's room was as silent as a tomb. It was also empty. Every piece of furniture, all the toys and posters had been taken away, but Jamie's presence hadn't been erased. Even the faint musty smell hadn't obliterated that special child scent that was Jamie's own.

For a moment Logan thought the pain in his chest would destroy him. He wished it would, and thus end the dreams and the awful longing. Sometimes when he closed his eyes he could still feel small arms wrapped tightly around his neck and hear the bubbly giggling in his ear. At last he pulled the door shut and continued down the hall, his heart filled with tears he could no longer shed.

AVERY LISTENED to the muffled footsteps overhead, the opening and shutting of doors, the rush of water in the old pipes, and knew he was taking a shower. Folding her arms on the table, she lowered her head and breathed deeply. More than anything she longed to relax, let go and cry from sheer relief. She'd done it. Her life was about to begin anew. This time, she vowed, she wasn't going to screw up.

With that thought firmly in mind, she got to her feet. First she cleaned the kitchen and then studied the contents of the refrigerator, freezer and pantry so she could plan dinner. Then she decided to acquaint herself with the first floor of the house.

It didn't take more than a few rooms to see that someone had expensive taste and a flare for decorating. There were antiques mixed with chintz, lace and leather. Still lifes and nineteenth-century portraits were artfully mixed with Oriental paintings, and all were cunningly arranged with a few fine pieces of Western art. Eclectic taste, to be sure and it worked, but Avery's first thought was that the display was the work of someone who liked change but was loath to let go of the past.

Avery was very observant, and she realized there was something out of place here, too. Expensive area rugs covered the beautiful hardwood floors, and she noticed impressions in the nap of the wool where furniture once had stood. The room was obviously missing some major pieces.

Wandering back toward the rear of the house, across the hall from the kitchen, she found the office. It was full of the usual things—file cabinets, a computer, printer, a phone and fax machine. The desk appeared to be an antique. An effort had been made to bring some sort of order to the desktop—it had a clean, white pad of paper, an in-and-out tray and a brass pencil-and-pen holder. It was obvious this room was Logan's territory and he'd furnished it. Here and there were items that showed a feminine influence— a cut-crystal vase full of dried flowers, a delicate china dish of potpourri.

But like the rest of the house, something was lacking here, too. As Avery was about to leave the room, she spotted boxes stacked haphazardly in a corner. A couple of them were open, and she saw the edges of picture frames. Her boss was either moving in or moving out. Puzzles—the house seemed full of them.

When the telephone rang, Avery flinched, still startled by the almost forgotten sound. She hesitated, then picked up the receiver, a little unsure how to answer. "Monahan's," she said, and recognized the surprise in the long silence that followed.

"Who is this?" a male voice demanded rudely.

"Avery Jensen. Mr. Monahan's unavailable at the moment—may I take a message?" There was another lengthy pause. As she waited, she frantically searched the stacked papers on the desk for something to write with, found a stubby pencil, then tore off a scrap of paper from the unblemished notepad. "Hello?"

"Yeah, this is Tanner. Tell Logan Molly's gone down on me again and if he doesn't get here quick, I'm going to have to put her out of her misery."

The phone clicked in her ear so abruptly she wondered if she'd just received an obscene telephone call. With the blank bit of paper in one hand and the pencil in the other, she walked to the bottom of the staircase and called Logan's name. The second floor seemed to be his personal domain, his space when he was home, and she was reluctant to invade it. Then she realized how ridiculous she was being and sprinted to the top landing.

As she made her way down the hall, she noticed all the closed doors. She was tempted to stop and inspect each one. "Don't do it, Avery," she warned herself under her breath. "Keep your mouth shut and your nose out of his business." She kept walking toward the door directly in front of her. It had to be the room situated directly over the kitchen and office, where she'd heard most of the sounds.

She knocked and called his name, then waited a moment before doing so again. The doors in the old house were solid, and even pressing her ear against this one, she couldn't tell whether or not he'd heard.

She'd raised her fist to give it another good pounding when the door was suddenly yanked open.

"What?"

Her gaze flicked over him, taking in every detail of the towel wrapped loosely around his hips, his damp skin and long muscular legs. She also noted the expression of frustration and anger on his face. It flustered her, made her stumble over her explanation. "Some—someone named Tanner called."

She looked down at the blank piece of paper in her hand as if it would help, but saw entirely too much of her employer around the edges. Her eyes bounced back up to his face. She struggled to keep her gaze steadily fixed on an imaginary spot in the center of his forehead. "He said Molly went down on him and..." Her voice trailed away.

Ordinarily Avery didn't blush, but now she felt the heat rising in her cheeks and couldn't stop it. All her concentration was fixed on relaying the message and keeping her eyes from darting where they shouldn't.

Logan watched fire stain her pale skin and gave a rough bark of laughter. "That got your attention, didn't it?" He hooked the towel in his hand around his neck. "Did Tanner say anything else?"

"Only that he was going to put her out of her misery if you didn't come quick."

Logan glanced over his shoulder at the big bed. He sighed. "I'd better get over there." He started to turn away, then stopped. "By the way, Molly's a horse and down with colic."

Avery was as nervous as a cat. But she managed a nonchalant shrug and forced herself to calmly turn and walk away.

Logan watched her, his eyes narrow and his jaw

tight. She was a cool one. Too calm, too cool and much too collected. She hadn't even cracked a smile.

Avery vanished down the stairs and out the front door, her heart pounding like a racehorse's at the starting gate. Once back in her quarters, she leaned against the door to catch her breath, amazed by the way her hands shook.

After a desperate search of the kitchen for tea bags and a juggling act with a teapot, she almost dropped everything when there was a window-rattling pounding at her door.

Logan was standing on the porch holding some keys. "I locked up the big house, so you'll need these to get in."

She didn't think she was crazy, but he seemed incredibly agitated. "What time will you be back?"

He barely stopped from snapping at her. "I don't know—maybe in a couple hours. Maybe not, but make yourself at home. Unpack, look around, and if you need me, there's a list of numbers by the phone in the kitchen." He turned to go. "If I'm late, just leave me something to eat in the oven."

She stood on the porch, watching him, and realized the truck he was driving was different from the pickup she'd seen earlier. This was white and one of those paneled things, with double doors that opened at the rear. And on the side of the truck was stenciled in black letters Monahan's Veterinary Clinic.

As the sound of the truck dwindled away and she was suddenly left in silence, she smiled. "A vet," she said under her breath, and wondered if Denise knew. Avery had only been told her new employer lived on a ranch and raised horses.

Logan had suggested she look around, make herself

at home, and she intended to do just that. But first she had to call Denise and tell her the news.

"So how bad can a man be if he administers to sick and injured animals, Dee?" Avery asked when she'd dialed her friend's number. "Not very." She laughed.

"It's good to hear you laugh, Avery. I take it you'll keep me up to date on the mystery?"

"Yes, but, Dee, I don't know how often I can call. I mean, I don't know his work schedule yet. I'll call when I can."

"Sure. First see how the wind blows."

"Thank you, Dee."

"For what?"

"Everything. Especially your trust in me." The lump in Avery's throat kept her from saying more than a strangled goodbye. She blamed her weepiness on exhaustion. She'd get an early night tonight.

AVERY SAT BOLT UPRIGHT in bed, her heart banging furiously against her chest, her nightshirt damp with perspiration. Confused and disoriented, she fought for breath as she tried to figure out where she was and what had awakened her. She listened to the night and in the utter silence remembered where she was. She squeezed her eyes closed as relief washed through her.

It was funny, really. For eight months, twenty-four hours a day, she'd heard nothing but noise. Every minute of every day had been filled with sounds. She would lie awake at night and pray for just a moment of this sort of silence.

Her wish had been more than answered, but crazy as it was, the quiet had kept her from falling asleep until well after midnight. Maybe it was a nightmare, already forgotten, that had startled her awake. As she tried to shake off the residue of fear, she glanced at the travel clock on the bedside table and groaned.

Five o'clock and she was wide awake. She knew she'd never go back to sleep. The craving for freshly made hot coffee was far more appealing than wrestling with the covers for a few more hours.

Just as she was about to climb out of bed, something thudded against the side of the house, next to her bedroom window. Avery froze, straining to identify the sound, waiting to see if it would come again. When nothing happened, she exhaled, then laughed as she realized she'd actually been holding her breath. It must have been a wild animal of some sort, or maybe the wind blowing something against the house. She threw back the covers, swung her legs to the floor and reached for the lamp.

With her back turned to the window, she didn't see the shadow slide past it or the way a pair of eyes watched her every move. As the glow of the lamplight chased the darkness to the corners of the bedroom, the figure stepped back and was swiftly swallowed up by the night.

DAWN DIDN'T SCARE the demons away. Still sluggish with sleep, Logan was halfway down the stairs when he smelled coffee. He froze, one foot suspended, praying it had all been a nightmare and he'd walk into the kitchen to find Becky sipping her first cup of coffee, Jamie talking a mile a minute, his upper lip covered by a milk mustache. Logan would hear that sweet childish laughter as he reached over and wiped his son's mouth....

But he knew it was all in his head. He set his foot on the next step, then the next, until he could do it without having to tell himself to move, to think and to talk. Mornings were the worst part of his days, he thought. Then there were the nights.

"Good morning," Logan said as he picked up the newspaper, pulled out the chair and sat down. When he looked at Avery, he was shocked. Yesterday she'd been a tall woman, her body shapeless in a shapeless dress. As she filled his cup, he scowled, then pushed away the cream and sugar. Today she was wearing jeans that still had that new stiffness and creases from being folded. The white cotton shirt, neatly tucked in at the waist, had to be right off the rack. She was all brand-spanking-new. He hadn't missed the lovely way she was put together, either—the small waist, rounded hips and full breasts that pushed against her shirt. She had a woman's figure, a refreshing oddity nowadays from the clothes hangers he usually saw. Logan lowered his gaze and took a sip of coffee. He didn't miss the sparkling clean sneakers.

"Thanks for leaving dinner." He opened the newspaper and shook it out. "Did you take a look around? You weren't scared staying out here alone, were you?"

Avery was standing by the kitchen counter. She glanced over her shoulder and figured by the way his face was buried in the newspaper that he was just making polite talk. "I walked around enough to get the lay of the place. Do you want your eggs scrambled or fried?"

"Scrambled with a little grated cheese in them would be good." He watched her over the top of the paper, the way she moved so easily around his kitchen, finding everything she needed. This morning her hair was pulled back into a ponytail and her pale skin had a little more color. But her gray eyes were dark and storm ridden.

"I sat on the fence for a while and watched the horses in the field."

"Paddock."

She set a plate of hot biscuits on the table. "They're beautiful. I hope you don't mind, but I looked around inside the barn." She'd been delighted at what she'd discovered when she'd entered that enormous brick building. The smells and sights were all so foreign and new to her. Strange objects hung from doors and hooks.

There had been horses, too, and she'd been lulled into relaxing by the warmth of life, scents and sounds. One horse in particular had drawn her with friendly eyes and soft noises. She'd sat on a bale of hay outside the animal's stall and talked until she'd nearly fallen asleep.

"They're all big babies and love the attention," Logan said. "Feel free to go in there anytime."

She felt his eyes on her back as she scrambled the eggs and heated the slices of ham in another skillet. "I didn't know you were a veterinarian. Is your clinic in town?"

"I've given up my clients at the clinic. My brother handles everything now."

It wasn't what he'd said, but the icy snap in his voice that indicated another closed door. He didn't enlighten her further, and his expression made Avery change the subject. She placed his breakfast in front of him and took her seat across the table.

After he'd taken a few bites, she spoke. "I hope

you don't expect anything fancy for your meals. I stay fairly close to the basics.''

''Basic will do fine. I'm not picky and I'll eat just about anything except green peas.''

A small smile touched her mouth. ''Green peas. I'll remember that.'' The ice seemed to have been broken and she ventured, ''I saw the office yesterday and wondered if you wanted me to start setting it up. It looks very disorganized.''

''That's an understatement. And yes, please, start there. The manual on the special software I use for keeping records on the horses and cattle is in one of those boxes. You know, I consider myself a fairly intelligent man. I can understand complex chemistry formulas, but this manual…hell, it's like reading Greek. So far I've managed to screw up everything I've entered. There's a three-ring binder in the desk drawer with all the data. Then there's the accounting program. I'm a little better at that, but I've been lax lately and there's a box of receipts, bills and invoices to be posted. You think you can handle it?''

Her smile was a little wider this time. ''Fortunately I read Greek.'' She recognized the flash of amusement in his eyes. She liked the way the skin crinkled at their corners when he smiled. ''Who's Tanner? Did you get there before he put Molly out of her misery?''

''Tanner's my brother.''

''The other veterinarian?''

''No, that's Pierce. Tanner's our kid brother. He has a place down the road, but he's always hanging around here. You'll meet him soon enough. Molly's fine. Tanner would sooner shoot himself than that horse. She had a bad case of colic, but we got her through the worst of it. I'll have to keep an eye on her, though, because we haven't pinpointed what made her sick. Bad feed more than likely.''

Logan amazed himself with his long-winded explanation. He must be more desperate for company than he'd thought, to be talking about his cases with a stranger. Hell, Becky had hated him bringing his work home, especially details of some of the more gruesome cases. He glanced at the clock, surprised by the time, and set about finishing breakfast.

Avery's powers of observation had worked beautifully for her. She mentally tallied how much she'd learned about Logan without asking an endless stream of questions. He was a widower. His wife and son had been killed in a car accident. He was a veterinarian who'd given up his town practice. Obviously he wasn't retiring, but setting up business from his home. It didn't take much to guess that his loss had changed his life and been the deciding factor in his choice, though it wasn't entirely clear why. He had a father who cared and worried about him. Also a sister-in-law who was madly in love with him.

Logan laid his silverware on his now clean plate and reached for his coffee. He'd permitted her game to go on long enough. ''You're not from around here—Texas, I mean. Where are you from, Avery?''

One thing Denise had drilled into her was if she lied, keep it simple and close to the truth. ''Seattle.''

The answer startled a rusty laugh from Logan. ''That's a hell of a distance to go to find me some help. My father outdid himself this time.''

''Actually, a friend of Denise's has a placement agency in San Antonio, and she told her about the outrageous qualifications some rancher had. After they shared a good laugh, Denise told her she had just the person.''

''So you were living in Houston?''

''That's right.'' She wondered if two weeks' residency allowed her to claim Houston as home. At any rate it served her purpose.

Logan touched his shirt pocket for a pack of cigarettes. It was empty. Of course. He'd given up smoking. His mood darkened. ''What or who are you running from, Avery Jensen?''

''I beg your pardon?'' It was as if her heart had suddenly jumped into her throat. She swallowed painfully.

''You heard me. When a woman with your looks and obvious education decides to hide away on a ranch in a small Texas town, there's something wrong. Is it an abusive husband you're running from, or was he unfaithful?''

''No, no. I'm not married.'' She made herself meet him stare for stare.

''A boyfriend?''

''No. Honestly, Logan—''

''Are you in trouble with the law?''

''No.'' She stopped herself before shifting her gaze away from his. ''I'm not in any trouble with the law and no one is looking for me. What I am is broke. What I need is a job, and this one suits me just fine.''

Logan finished his coffee. At one time—two years ago, to be exact—he'd been a good judge of character. Now he didn't trust his own gut instincts. He didn't think she'd lied, but there were secrets shifting around in those gray eyes, and that too-bland expression gave him pause.

What the hell did it matter? He certainly was in no

position to judge people. His needs were basic and few—nourishment to keep his body functioning, a clean house and clothes. He needed someone to take care of the everyday chores he no longer had the energy for. Most of all he needed to be left alone. Logan had a feeling Avery Jensen was looking for the same things.

"We'd best get some things straight here and now," he said. "Haven is not considered a small town in terms of its population, but it has a small-town mentality. There's been a big infusion of wealthy people from San Antonio who, for whatever reason—status maybe—decided they wanted a ranch and picked Haven as the location. The only problem is they've brought the city with them, and the pecking order here now has two levels—the rich country-club set and the local social hierarchy.

"Both sides have their busybodies. They're going to make a lot out of a beautiful, young, single woman living out here with a widower. If you plan to stay or make friends, you'll have to deal with them on your own. Don't expect me to help, and I'd appreciate it if you'd keep me out of your conversations." He paused. "There are people in town who are going to talk about me. I don't give a damn what they say, but you might."

The corners of Avery's mouth tipped slightly upward and she said, "I don't take much stock in gossip. But just so I won't be surprised or shocked, what sort of things am I likely to hear?"

"That I'm responsible for my wife and son's death. That I benefitted by getting an ungodly amount of insurance money." He shoved back his chair and stared down at her upturned face. "They're right on both counts."

CHAPTER THREE

LOGAN'S WORDS left her speechless. And just as she was picking her chin up off the floor, she caught a tiny glimmer of satisfaction on his face and a lingering impression that he was entirely too pleased with himself over her reaction. As if he was deliberately trying to shake her up. Well, he'd certainly succeeded.

Before she could recover enough to comment, Logan turned and left the kitchen. Had he meant what he'd said? Had he really been responsible for his wife and son's deaths? The sound of the front door shutting noisily behind him snapped her from her reverie. She'd just seen a side to Logan Monahan she must never lose sight of. The man was nobody's fool.

With the warning firmly implanted in her mind, Avery set to work cleaning the kitchen. The only sounds were of her own making. Sounds that were normal, everyday noises to anyone else, she treasured. Water running into the sink, the clink of dishes, the slap of the mop on the kitchen floor. Even the sound of her own humming.

When the kitchen was spotless, Avery stood back, admired her work and smiled. Who would have thought that in less than a year she could take so much pride in menial work? It certainly wasn't something she'd ever excelled at before. Eight months didn't seem like such a long time for so many changes, but for her it had been a lifetime. She'd learned a lot about herself and her abilities. She was stronger than she'd imagined. She was wiser, yes, but cynical and distrustful of everyone. And she'd come to realize she was a poor judge of people. But she was free and that was all that mattered—that and her job. She knew she'd do whatever it took to keep this job and her freedom.

The light housework gave her a chance to spend much of the morning roaming the big house, duster in hand, peeking behind closed doors, more mystified then ever by the lack of furnishings. All the upstairs bedrooms, except for Logan's, were empty. The barren rooms made her uneasy. There was a sadness about them, and they made her shiver as if someone had walked over her grave.

Her inspection of Logan's room told her little about the man other than he was neater than any male she'd ever known. Certainly tidier than her slovenly brother and even her fastidious father. Logan made his bed, picked up his clothes and placed them in the hamper. He even left the bathroom sink sparkling clean.

As she headed downstairs, she realized Logan Monahan didn't really need anyone to take care of him. Then why was his father so insistent? A more disturbing thought was why had Logan agreed she could stay?

She worried at the edges of the question until something else struck her about what was missing in the house—the usual array of family photographs. The walls and dressertops were bare of pictures, nor were there any belongings or reminders of his wife or child. The house was as impersonal as a hotel. If he was responsible for their deaths, as he said, did that explain it somehow?

Don't try to figure it out. Mind your own business and don't get involved. She remembered the warning she'd given herself; she was prepared to follow it as if it was set in stone. With that thought in mind she continued with her morning work.

When she finally stepped into the office, her interest in working for Logan was stirred. Like yesterday, the desk was a chaos of papers, unopened letters and bills. Her eyes actually brightened at the overflowing boxes of files just waiting to be organized. At last her hungry gaze came to rest on the pillar of computer manuals perched rather precariously on the edge of the desk. Yes, she'd enjoy this work, and she'd be good at it.

She inhaled the scent of leather, stale coffee and books—all the essences an office should have. To her the scents were as intoxicating as French perfume. Once, not so long ago, her world had been centered in just such an office, a world of power and position, a world of people who looked up to her and listened to her advice as if she were a goddess. She caressed the top of the monitor as she rounded the desk, and didn't even mind that her fingers came away dusty. Her heartbeat accelerated as she settled in the big leather chair, leaned her head back and closed her eyes. Logan may not need her pitiful domestic talents, but he needed her office help.

The shrill ringing of the telephone jolted her upright. She'd been far away in a daydream of a happier time; she'd thought she could actually smell the leather of her executive chair. She'd have sworn she heard her secretary's laughter and her father's deep rumbling voice.

The phone shrilled again and reflexively she picked it up and said, "Yes, Margaret?" She caught herself, then said, "Monahan ranch." The caller would think she was the village idiot. When there was no answering voice, she repeated her greeting.

Still nothing but silence. Just as she was about to hang up, she heard the distinct sound of fast breathing. She felt a creeping sensation, as if something clammy was crawling over her skin. Inexplicably, she knew this call wasn't a childish prank, but something more insidious.

Nevertheless, she tried again. "This is the Monahan ranch. Who's there?" She used an angry tone, hoping to banish her fear that someone already knew about her.

"Hang up."

The male voice charged with authority didn't come from the receiver but from the doorway, and three things happened at once. Avery gave an ear-piercing scream. The phone clattered to the floor. And as she jerked to her feet, she knocked the stack of computer books off the corner of the desk.

The stranger filling the doorway clamped his hands over his ears and backed away slightly. "Hey. I'm family."

She took a few deep breaths to calm herself. "So do you usually just waltz in without knocking or letting anyone know you're coming? You scared the living daylights out of me." He looked a lot like her boss, but was taller—at least six-seven—and whereas Logan was solid and muscular, this man was lean and stringy. She eyed him warily.

"I'm Tanner, darlin', Logan's youngest brother. And I've never knocked before and don't intend to start now. You must be Avery—the burr in Jessie's craw, new grist for the gossip mill and the reason Dad's walking around with a grin the Cheshire cat would envy. And yes, I use to play pro basketball."

"I didn't ask."

"But you wanted to."

"No," she lied, "it never crossed my mind." He was charming, handsome and obviously having entirely too much fun at her expense. Avery tried to keep him in her line of vision as she began picking up the fallen manuals. "You called yesterday, didn't you."

He nodded and grinned. "Yep. I was surprised when Logan the Bear didn't answer."

"Logan the Bear?"

Tanner laughed, a delicious sound of pure amusement. "You got it, sweetheart. He has other pet names—as do we all. But that's for another day. You can see I'm harmless, though, so why don't you stand up and let me get a good look at you?"

"Harmless" was not a term that fitted this man. His charm, she sensed, could be most dangerous. And where Logan's eyes were light brown, Tanner's were black, lively and full of mischief. Even though she had to bite her tongue to keep from asking a dozen questions, one slipped out. "Why did you order me to hang up?"

"It was an obscene call, wasn't it?"

"I don't know." She shrugged. "No one said anything." As she restacked the manuals on the desk, she continued to watch him, but he didn't seem inclined to do more than drape himself in the doorway. "What makes you think the call was obscene?"

"You were angry. Your cheeks were on fire, and those big gray eyes were kind of iced over." He straightened. "We've all gotten a few of those calls. It seems to go with the territory of being a main topic of conversation in this town. Don't let them bother you. It's just kids and their nonsense."

Avery had always had a kind of radar for trouble. She didn't know Tanner well enough to tell him her own feelings about the caller. She finished stacking the books, pretending not to see the way he looked her over, but she was painfully aware of the warmth that stained her cheeks. The absurdity of it almost made her smile. She'd blushed more in the past twenty-four hours than she had in the past five years, all brought on by Monahan men.

"Where's Logan, by the way?" Tanner glanced at his watch. "It's a bit early, but my stomach tells me it's lunchtime."

"Damn," Avery said as she rounded the desk and almost knocked the books off again. "I forgot about lunch." Tanner didn't move and she was forced to stand and wait.

"Let me ring the barn," Tanner said. "That's where he spends most of his time—where he hides from the world."

Tanner stepped around her, picked up the phone and punched in a number. He gave her a wink. "Don't worry about lunch. I'll fix it." He stopped her protest by motioning for her to be silent. "Hey, Logan. How about coming up to the house? I'm starving."

Tanner knew the kitchen far better than she did.

She realized all too quickly she was only in his way. Finally, after they'd bumped into each other twice, he guided her to a chair and gently but firmly pushed her into it. All she could do was watch as he gathered items from the refrigerator and set to work. What Logan would think when he saw his brother taking over her duties, she couldn't say. She decided the best thing to do, however, was keep her mouth shut and be still.

"Have you ever had a grilled cheese sandwich Texas-style?"

Avery shook her head, amused and a little miffed at just how efficiently Tanner moved around the kitchen.

"You're in for a treat. Mind you, it's not often I make these for anyone but Logan. So don't get any ideas about making them yourself just because it's my brother's favorite meal."

She grinned. "I wouldn't dream of it."

"Good."

She kept a straight face, though she had to work at it, as he pulled a loaf of bread from the freezer, then held it close to his body as if trying to keep Avery from seeing it. Then she realized why. He was thawing it just enough to separate the extra-thick slices.

Just as Tanner was carving slabs off a block of cheese, Logan walked in. Avery had been so captivated and amused by Tanner's running dialogue about everything and nothing that she'd forgotten to keep her guard up. Logan's eyes found hers and held her gaze for a long moment, as if searching for an answer to something. She was the first to look away.

Logan hung his Stetson on the hat rack, and his

gaze shifted to Tanner, who was busy at the counter.
"I see you've met Peewee."

Avery felt more than saw Tanner bristle at the
name, and didn't know whether to move out of the
way or laugh when he carelessly tossed a wrapped
stick of butter at Logan.

Logan plucked the butter smoothly from the air,
unwrapped it and handed it back to Tanner.

"I hope you've washed your hands," Tanner said,
then glanced at Avery, his black eyes dancing with
laughter. "You do know that half the time a vet is up
to his elbows in—"

"Mind your manners, little brother, at least until
she knows you better." Logan opened a cabinet,
pulled out a blender, then looked at Avery. "We tend
to make chocolate malts at lunchtime—especially for
washing down Tanner's clunkers—so you'd best get
the vanilla ice cream out of the freezer. There's a jar
of malt in the pantry."

And that was how it started—Logan and Tanner
treating her as if they'd known her for years, sending
her scurrying around the kitchen fetching, carrying
and measuring while Tanner explained the highlights
of his methods for making the "world's best" Texas-
style grilled cheese sandwiches. Logan, too, was dil-
igent about explaining the art of concocting his
"prizewinning" extra-thick malts. Of course, both
explanations were going on at the same time, and any
questions she might have asked were hopelessly lost
in the cacophony.

At last the meal was ready. She picked up half of
her monster sandwich and raised it to her mouth, then
paused. The brothers waited, their amused gazes on
her. She realized they were waiting for her praise. She

eyed Tanner, then Logan over the top, deliberately stretching out the moment.

"I can feel my arteries clogging already," she said.

Finally she took a bite. Logan and Tanner leaned forward as warm soft cheese oozed from the sides of the crispy-brown toast. Avery closed her eyes and slowly chewed. She swallowed and looked at Tanner. "Bigger is better," she said with a smile. She meant it. The sandwich was wonderful.

"Now try the malt," Logan urged.

She wiped her greasy fingers on her napkin, reached for the frosty glass and took a huge gulp. It was thick and entirely too cold. Immediately she paid for her gluttony, but even though a knife-sharp pain shot through her head, she grinned and managed a hoarse, "Heavenly."

"Brain-freeze." Logan laughed and picked up his own sandwich. "Happens every time."

Avery hadn't thought she could finish the sandwich. But not only did she clean her plate, she tilted her glass until every last drop was drained. With a sigh of contentment, she set the glass down, then realized Logan was staring at her. A flash of heat colored her cheeks.

Logan ignored the awkward moment and asked, "Have you tackled the office yet?"

Tanner butted in without giving her a chance to answer. "Avery had one of those calls."

The smile died and Logan's eyes hardened. "How bad was it?"

"She said—"

This time Avery cut him off. "I can speak for myself, thank you. And I never said it was an obscene call. *You* did. All I heard was breathing." For some reason she couldn't bring herself to tell Logan that the call made her uneasy.

"Well, just so you're prepared, you'll get a few. The whole family has. The calls run the gambit of heavy breathing to outright threats."

"Have you reported them to the police?"

Logan and Tanner shared a hard look, then Logan said, "Ross Middleton is the sheriff of Haven. He was my wife's brother. He's not willing to give much credence or time to crank calls."

"I wonder why," Tanner said sarcastically. "I know, I know, you don't want to discuss it."

Avery was mystified. She watched as Tanner picked up his dirty dishes and dumped them in the sink. "I'm out of here, folks," he said. "Thanks for lunch. Avery, it was good to meet you." He opened the door, then stopped. "I'm bringing Molly over later, Logan. So don't do one of your famous disappearing acts, okay?" He waved and left, leaving a growing silence behind.

Avery gazed around at the chaos in the kitchen with a sinking feeling. How had it happened? She'd been enjoying herself so much she'd forgotten to notice what a mess the two men had made.

"Did you make any headway in the office?"

"I was just about to start when your brother came in."

Logan had been pleased to see that wounded look disappear from Avery's eyes when he and Tanner had been cooking and generally acting silly. But now it was back, and it reminded him of an animal that couldn't tell him where it hurt.

Cruelty in any form saddened him and made him angry. He'd devoted most of his life administering to defenseless creatures that had borne the brunt of human rage and brutality. Who had hurt her?

He was good at diagnosing what ailed his patients, good at figuring out the puzzles. Avery was a different matter, though. He'd have to find out about her pain another way.

Logan had not forgotten his parting remark that morning. He knew she must be wondering. "Why don't I help you clear up this mess and we can talk? I'll try to answer any questions you have."

Avery realized she had a hundred questions, but none she was willing to risk asking. *Stick to business,* she reminded herself. The last thing she wanted or needed was to get involved in Logan's life.

Together they carried the dirty dishes to the sink, and as she began filling the dishwasher, she noticed him watching her. His eyes no longer seemed distant. They had a gentle, knowing look, as if he perhaps saw far too much. An icy finger of unease ran down her spine. She wanted to keep her past to herself, hidden away so she'd never have to face the shame of what had happened to her.

Her nerves must have been more frayed than she'd thought, for unthinkingly she said the first thing that popped into her head. "Why is the house so empty? It's obvious there was furniture. I mean, there are indentations in some of the rugs and I was..." Her voice trailed away. She couldn't believe she'd actually asked.

Logan barely managed to keep from smiling. He was aware that she'd dropped her guard, but now it was back in place. She was obviously trying to ignore the way he was staring as she busied herself by filling the sink with soapy water to scrub the cast-iron skillet and the blender. He liked the way she moved, the sway of her hips, the graceful hand gestures.

He leaned his backside against the edge of the counter, crossed his arms over his chest and said, "All the missing furniture belonged to my wife, to Becky's family. They're heirlooms from Becky's mother, who wanted them back after the accident. There wasn't any reason to kick up a fuss. I never particularly cared for them in the first place. They always had a musty smell I disliked."

"And there was no reason to replace them?"

"Not with just me living here." He changed the subject to her. He still wanted to understand about her past. "I hope you called your family and let them know you arrived safely. Where did you say you were from?"

"Seattle. And I don't have anyone there anymore. I called Denise last night."

"Denise, the friend in Houston? The one who got you this job?" Logan glanced around the kitchen. "I don't know if she did you a favor or not. Just wait until you tackle the office." He was intrigued by her smile, as if her lips were unused to the movement.

Avery found that the turn the conversation had taken was making her edgy, so she headed off any further questions with another of her own. "I thought from what you said yesterday that you no longer had a practice, but from what I saw in the office, you seem to be in business."

"Confusing, isn't it. There's a saying in my work—once a veterinarian, always a veterinarian. It's true. I have patients I've treated for years. Their own-ers aren't willing to go to anyone else, even my brother. They refuse to let me retire and they call here day and night.''

"And you don't turn them down, do you," she said softly. Warmth coursed through her. Maybe the world did have people you could believe in. For all Logan's initial indifference and the aura of mystery, he was a caring, sensitive man. Then the warm feeling cooled. What did she know about people? Hadn't she learned, the hard way, that her judgment couldn't be trusted?

He watched her attack the dirty skillet with zeal and a wire scrub brush. Her abrupt silence baffled him. He waited for Avery's next question, because weren't women, in general, notorious truth seekers? Secrets drove them nuts and led to a cross-examination worthy of the CIA. But Avery didn't fit that mold, seemed loath to put a voice to her curiosity.

All of a sudden, he understood. Conversation, with questions and answers, was a two-way street. By asking, she would leave herself open to being quizzed. That was the last thing she wanted.

As Avery scrubbed, unaware of Logan's thoughts, she allowed herself to dream a little, to slip back into familiar territory. "You'll need me to set up your books as a small-business venture," she said. "And of course you'll want invoicing and billing. What about inventory? I mean, you use supplies and stuff, right?" She didn't have a clue what a veterinarian required, but figured his needs were closely in line with those of a medical doctor. A vet was a doctor, after all. "And you'll need tax depreciation on your equipment. Oh, and a profit-and-loss statement."

She turned her head and looked at Logan. Omigod. Had she said too much, given something away?

"That sounds about right to me." Logan's suspicions were confirmed. She was well educated. Laypeople didn't throw around terms like profit-and-loss statements and tax depreciation.

But Avery, excited by the prospect of getting involved in something she loved, forgot about discretion. Just as she started to tell Logan some of her plans, the kitchen door swung open. Hair flying, hands full of paper sacks, voice loud and laughing, Jessie Middleton blew into the kitchen like a whirlwind. She was scantily dressed in short shorts and a tank top that left little to the imagination.

The fact that she was being ignored made Avery bite her lip. Obviously Jessie thought that by pretending not to see the interloper, Avery would simply disappear. Well, Jessie was in for a shock. Bad manners didn't faze Avery in the least. The less she was lured into this family and its problems, the better off she'd be. But becoming invisible didn't seem to work with Logan. He was standing directly behind her, and as she started to move away, he stopped her with a hand on her shoulder.

Jessie kept her gaze on Logan's face as she began pulling plastic containers from one of the bags. "I brought lunch. Your favorites, Logan. I talked Louise into making chili. She used Becky's recipe." She darted a cutting look at Avery. "You always said Becky was the best cook in the world and her chili was worth its weight in gold—" she giggled "—or did you say it was worth its weight in hot peppers? Anyway, I thought it would be a treat. Do you have any beer? Oh, and I stopped off at the café just in time. Maebell was taking blackberry cobblers out of the oven. You know how stingy she is about using her stockpile of fresh berries, but when I told her it was for you, well, she couldn't say no. She never forgot how much Jamie and you loved her cobblers, and the blackberry was his very favorite in the whole world. You ought to stop by the café, Logan. She misses Jamie like we all do.''

Jessie juggled the deep-dish cobbler pan like a hot potato, then quickly set it on the table. ''I'll get the plates,'' she said.

''I'm sorry, Jess,'' he answered, his apology laced with kindness, ''but we've eaten.'' He made an effort to continue to smile. The mention of his son opened that deep hole in his heart again, like a fresh wound. He tightened his grip on Avery's shoulder.

''But, Logan, it's not even twelve-thirty yet! You never eat before twelve-thirty.''

''Tanner stopped by and made sandwiches for us.''

''Grilled cheese?'' Jessie asked. ''He fixed his grilled cheese sandwiches?'' Her gaze swung to Avery, as if to confirm her worst fears, then back to Logan. ''And you made malts?''

Apparently Logan had hurt her feelings. He walked over to Jessie, slipped an arm around her shoulders and gave her a brotherly hug. ''It was thoughtful of you to go to so much trouble and I appreciate it, Jess, really I do. But you should have checked first, honey.''

''I never had to check before.''

''How about storing this stuff in the fridge and I'll eat it tonight?''

It didn't take a genius to realize that as sure as the sun rose every morning, Jessie was going to blame her, Avery, for Logan's rejection. Avery had a feeling she was being dragged into something and she should turn tail and run as fast as possible. But where would she go?

Jessie threw barbed glances, full of loathing, at her as she pitched the food containers into the refrigerator and slammed the door. "I'll help you groom the horses, then."

Logan smiled and shook his head, "Thanks for offering, kitten, but the boys are here today. Besides, aren't you supposed to be in San Antonio this week making arrangements for Fiesta?" He glanced at Avery to explain. "Fiesta San Antonio is a big celebration held every year. And Jess is one of the duchesses."

Before Avery could comment on that, Jessie stormed out of the house, slamming the kitchen door. "She's in love with you, you know," Avery said instead.

"Nonsense. Jess is like a kid sister. Hell, she was a kid when Becky and I married. She spent more time here than with her parents in San Antonio." Avery's statement seemed to give him pause. "Okay, she's always had a schoolgirl crush on me, and she's just overprotective since Becky's death. I think she feels a need to take care of me. I just wish this possessiveness would run its course and she'd direct all those pent-up feelings toward someone else."

Men could be so dense sometimes, Avery thought. Or maybe he wasn't all that blind. She remembered, when she'd first arrived and again just a few moments ago, he'd used her like a shield against Jessie's advances. She sensed Logan was a man with too many problems on his plate and didn't know how to deal with them all at once. She certainly wasn't about to add to his troubles. "She's a little old for a schoolgirl crush, Logan."

Big mouth. What happened to her promise to keep her opinions to herself?

"She's immature and I feel sorry for her. She worshiped Becky, and my wife was the only Middleton who took much notice of Jess or who could handle her wildness. I think Jess has latched on to me as a way to deal with her grief. It'll pass with time."

Wildness was only one word Avery would use to describe Jessie. Others came more to mind, such as *spoiled* and *disturbed.* She recognized the signs and knew all too well where the young woman was headed if she didn't get some help. Avery could have told Logan a few things about the pitfalls of sticking his head in the sand. She'd done the same with her father and brother. Look what it had cost her.

"Your guilt won't do her any good, Logan."

"That sounds like the voice of experience."

"I see a lot of my brother in Jessie. I wish someone had recognized the signs." When she realized her slip, her hands shook. Avery quickly busied herself by drying the heavy cast-iron skillet.

He knew the second she withdrew back into herself, and he sighed. Hell, he had enough worries of his own. Taking on a stranger's problems was beyond him. "You know, Avery, you can't run forever. Believe me, I've tried, and I promise you it'll catch up with you. If you're in some sort of trouble, I might be able to help."

She turned, ready to deny that she needed anyone, much less his assistance. Their eyes met and held, and the words caught in her throat. At an earlier time in her life she would have been thrilled to have a man look at her the way Logan looked at her. Things were different now, though. She couldn't afford to believe in anyone, much less trust herself.

Logan didn't look away from the shifting emotions in Avery's lovely gray eyes. Having a good-looking, desirable woman underfoot perhaps wasn't such a good idea, he mused. After all, he'd only agreed to the crazy scheme to shut his father up and keep him from interfering any further in his life, but that was before Logan had felt the novelty of desire zing through his veins. He halfheartedly cursed himself for being weak. "Whatever you're running from, Haven's the right place to get lost. Nothing much happens here."

Suddenly the kitchen door slammed open against the wall and a lanky teenage boy, arms waving like flags, eyes round with fear, skidded to a stop just inside. "Doc, come quick! Something's wrong with the horses. They're all really sick."

"If this is one of your jokes, Benton, so help me…" But Logan was moving, and his threat lacked any anger as he saw how pale and scared the boy was. He grabbed his hat, then turned to Avery. "How are you around horses?"

"I don't know. Except for yesterday, the closest I've ever been to one was the television."

Her answer made him give a quick bark of laughter. He motioned for her to join him. "I might need you."

The thought of being needed, even wanted, was all the impetus Avery required. She took off after Logan.

CHAPTER FOUR

THE AFTERNOON SUN was high overhead. There wasn't even a breath of wind. The shock of stepping from the sweet coolness of the house into the heat of the day was like walking into an inferno. Avery's limbs felt leaden, sweat promptly dampened her forehead and it was an effort to keep up with Logan.

She saw the boy, Benton, disappearing into the dark hole of the open barn doors. Who was he? she wondered, then remembered Logan's saying to Jessie something about the boys being there today.

Once inside, she shivered as the breeze created by the overhead fans touched her damp skin. Four teenage boys were lined up outside a stall. When they saw Logan, they silently stepped aside to let him enter.

Logan recognized the pungent odor of sickness. From the sound of Allspice's labored breathing, the horse was close to death. He hunkered down beside the animal and felt his pulse.

"What happened here?" he asked the boys.

They all hung back except Benton. His voice cracked with emotion. "We were just feeding them like we've always done, Doc."

Avery stood there, horrified, as she looked at the horse, crumpled in the hay. His beautiful red-brown coat was slick with sweat. She wanted to clamp her hands over her ears with each rattling breath. "How sick is he, Logan? Can you give him something?"

Logan didn't answer, but moved from stall to stall, evaluating each horse's condition and listening to Benton.

"You know Allspice, Doc. He always has to be first or he kicks the stall. And he's a glutton. But by the time we fed the others, Allspice was like that."

"The feed?"

One of the other boys spoke up. "That was the first thing we thought of, Doc. Maybe it had soured. We took it away from all of them, but they'd eaten some—not as much as Allspice, but..." His voice trailed away in anguish.

Logan headed toward a row of feed bins against the far wall. He reached in, brought a handful up to his nose and sniffed. "It's tainted," he said. "Tom, empty the bins into those metal trash cans, then take it to the storeroom, lock the door and bring me the key. Under no circumstances are any of you to use any feed from that room." He glanced at Avery.

"What can I do to help?" she asked.

"Come with me."

Avery followed him toward the front of the barn, then through a green door, which he unlocked. She got a quick view of a small waiting room before she trailed him down a hall to another world, an environment of spotless stainless steel, high, glass-fronted cabinets with neat rows of labeled bottles. They passed through a set of double glass doors, and Logan stopped beside an examining table.

"I need you to call Tanner and tell him not to bring Molly here." He pointed to a typed list of phone numbers taped to the wall as he stuffed vials of medicine and syringes into his shirt pockets. "If you can't reach Tanner at home, try his cell phone. After you talk to him, call Dad and tell him to get in touch with Pierce. When you finish, come find me."

He was barely out the door when she had Tanner on the phone. In an economy of words, and because she had no idea what had happened to the animals, she was curt with Tanner, but softened when he offered to call Mac and Pierce. As she talked, she had a chance to look around the office. There was an array of confusing items: instruments in glass drawers; tables on wheels which held colored bottles; what looked like a pressure cooker of some sort.

Remembering Logan's orders, Avery gave one quick glance at the photograph of a child on the wall, then headed out. She found Logan kneeling beside Allspice, stroking the quivering horse's neck and talking softly to him. She saw an empty vial and syringe.

"Is he going to be all right?"

Logan didn't answer. She waited for what seemed forever, watching him tenderly care for the sick horse. When Logan finally looked up, she realized the harsh breathing had stopped.

Avery blinked back sudden tears. Not only for the horse, but for the pain in Logan's eyes.

"Do you still want to help?" he asked.

"Yes," she whispered.

"It won't be easy, and if you've got a weak stomach, you better say so now."

"I'll be okay and I'll do whatever you say." She glanced at the motionless animal and had to ask, "Are they all going to die?"

"Not if I have anything to say about it." His tone held grim determination.

Something about Logan changed, like light shifting across his face. She could have sworn she caught a glimpse of rage, just under the surface and ready to boil over.

AVERY GRIPPED Possum's lead as she walked the dainty dappled-gray mare around and around the paddock. She'd learned from watching two of the boys, also walking horses, how to hold the lead rope close to the side of the animal's face so she could pet her and talk to her. Raul was walking King Moe, a black stallion too ill to be ornery, the boy said, and Tony was walking Hopalong, a pretty, light brown horse with a white tail and mane.

She discovered a lot about the boys as they walked. They were working for Logan without pay as punishment for getting into trouble at school. From the way they cared for the horses, she didn't think they minded their punishment. She would have learned more, but the increasing heat, worry and the struggle to keep the horses on their feet and walking soon took all her energy.

She lost track of time or how long she'd been walking until Logan came out, shoved a wide-brimmed straw cowboy hat on her head and handed her a bottle of water, insisting she drink some now. Then he clasped her chin in his hand and searched her face. He smiled as he said, "Your nose and cheeks are turning pink. Keep the hat pulled low."

She was perfectly still and gazed steadily into his eyes. "I'm okay."

Logan nodded and reluctantly dropped his hand. He was impressed that she didn't complain or want to quit because she was tired, dirty and hot. "If you feel dizzy or nauseated at all, don't be ashamed to speak up." He busied himself examining Possum. "You don't have to prove anything to those kids. Believe me, you're not tougher than they are just because you're older."

"You don't have to rub it in," she mumbled softly, but not so softly he didn't hear.

He hid a grin as he pulled a full syringe from his shirt pocket. "Those kids are used to working in the heat." He gave Possum a shot.

"How are the other horses, Logan?"

"Mac's Lady isn't going to make it, but Dad's not ready to let go of her yet."

He saw her eyes fill with tears. "What happened?" she asked. "Have you found out what made them sick?"

The truth could send her running to Haven to jump on the first available bus. He glanced at her again. Disheveled and tired, she still managed to look tempting. And strong. Nevertheless he sidestepped her question. "Pierce's taking samples of the feed to be analyzed."

"Do you have any ideas?" she asked.

Strong *and* persistent. He sighed. "There's little doubt that they were poisoned."

"Oh, no! Surely you're wrong. Who would do something like that? And why?"

Logan shrugged, unwilling to put words to his demons.

Avery caught sight of Raul and Tony inching closer, their youthful curiosity aroused enough that caution was forgotten. She tried to keep her gaze on Logan so the boys wouldn't feel as if they were suspects. But she sensed a change in Raul's and Tony's demeanor.

Raul's stiff stance radiated outrage. Black eyes narrowed and shimmered like polished rock. The jerk of his head and the defiant flip of his long ponytail were further outward signs of anger. "Doc, we didn't..." For all his bravado, words failed him.

Tony looked scared sick and seemed unable to say anything at all.

Logan glanced around. "I never thought you did, Raul."

"But Sheriff Middleton will, won't he?"

Tony found his voice. "I swear, Doc."

Logan began examining the other two horses. "Let me handle the sheriff."

"But—" Raul began.

"Raul, I've seen you with the horses. Whatever your problems at home or school, I know that it isn't in any of you to hurt an animal." Whatever had almost killed off his stock was far more sophisticated than anything a bunch of teenage boys could come up with. Logan patted each horse, pleased to see the medicine and attention were working. "Keep them moving, boys. Don't let them cool down yet."

"They're scared and worried," Avery said, when the two youths had led their charges away.

"I know. No matter what we find out, there will always be those who believe the kids had something to do with this mess."

Avery cringed. "The stigma never goes away, no matter how innocent you are."

Logan didn't comment on her statement, but tucked the tidbit of information away to mull over later.

"Give a holler when you've had enough, and someone will spell you."

Avery returned to circling the paddock with Possum. The only real relief in the long afternoon heat came when they stopped and allowed the horses to drink. After she and the boys hosed down the sweat-soaked animals, they took advantage of the cool water themselves and indulged in a friendly water fight. Afterward, the boys loosened up enough talk about themselves. Their crimes were so typical of teenage boys that she laughed. But it seemed parents, teachers and the law of Haven, Texas, kept a careful and collective watch on their young people. As Avery resumed walking Possum, she secretly admired their efforts.

"Are you sleepwalking or daydreaming?"

Startled, Avery jerked to a stop. "Hi, Mr. Monahan."

"I thought we'd agreed you'd call me Mac."

Whatever she was about to say was drowned out by the roar of an engine. "What's that?"

"Tanner finally got the tractor running. He's going to bury those poor horses."

"I'm sorry Mac's Lady didn't make it."

"She was a fine quarter horse. Logan trained her and Tanner rode her at the rodeos before he bought Molly." Mac waved at the boys, then pulled off his hat, scrubbed at his lined face and sighed loud and long. "This is a sad day, I tell you, when someone's so evil they take their hate out on defenseless animals."

"Does anyone have any idea who would do such an awful thing?"

Mac's lips thinned and the expression in his hooded

eyes looked downright deadly. He shook his head. "Ain't got a clue. 'Course, you might ask Logan that same question." He paused. "Who knows, he might just tell you. But the boy's being his typical close-mouthed self with us."

They walked side by side around the paddock, silent, both listening to the clamor of the tractor. Eventually the noise faded away to a faint rumble, and Mac took the lead rope from Avery. "I hope all this hasn't scared you. I mean, you ain't leaving, are you?"

The question brought an immediate response, one she didn't have to consider. "No." Where would she go? She would have loved to ask Mac why he'd been so determined to hire someone to take care of Logan, when it was as obvious as the nose on his face that Logan was capable of looking after himself.

"Why don't you take a breather? I'll stay with Possum." When she hesitated, he said, "Go on, get out of this heat. You might check with Logan and see if he needs you for anything else."

Avery stopped just inside the barn door to let her eyes adjust to the darkened interior. She savored the coolness for a moment, then made a face as she caught a strong scent of disinfectant. As she moved past the line of empty stalls, the smell became sharper until it stung her nose and made her eyes water. She halted near the open doors of the two stalls where the horses had died, and saw Benton and Tom, outfitted with rubber boots and face masks, scrubbing the floors.

Just then she heard the deep tones of men's voices coming from the direction of Logan's barn office. Though she couldn't make out the words, she could hear the anger. As she rushed around the corner on her way there to ask Logan if there was anything else she could do, she realized her mistake. Sound traveled oddly in the barn and she'd misjudged where the voices were coming from.

She blundered into a solid body and was thrown off balance. Her hat tumbled from her head. As she struggled to right herself, the man whipped around to catch her. In that awkward and embarrassing couple of seconds, as she tried to regain her footing and apologize, she spotted the silver, five-pointed star pinned to his shirt. The shock of seeing a policeman stopped her cold. When she was finally able to breathe, she strangled on her own air and disguised her fear and nervousness with a coughing fit.

The distraction afforded her time to recover her wits. Obviously the man with the badge was the sheriff Logan had mentioned earlier. But the distraction also cost her. Now she had the concerned solicitation of *three* men focused on her. Waving them away, she recovered and forced herself to smile. But like a guilty criminal, she couldn't bring herself to hold the sheriff's steadfast gaze. Instead, she stared at the other man standing beside Logan.

He had to be the brother she hadn't yet met—Pierce. He had the family's good looks, though he wasn't as tall as Tanner, nor as muscular as Logan. His eyes were hazel instead of brown or black, and they lacked the compassion and passion of Logan's, the fire and flirtation of Tanner's. But his gaze held something that startled her. She recognized the look of someone living in his own personal hell. Her mirror reflected the same expression every morning before she was able to hide it.

Logan stepped into the growing silence. "Avery, this is Sheriff Middleton—Ross." He grasped Avery's elbow and half turned her. "And this is my brother Pierce. He's the middle brother."

"You're the hired girl from Houston?" Ross asked, studying Avery intently.

Avery was relieved that he scooped up her hat and held it out to her. It gave her somewhere to look besides his eyes. *Take the hat, Avery, before he thinks you're brain damaged or that you've got something to hide.* "Thank you," she said softly as she held the straw cowboy hat in both hands, barely stopping herself from tearing it into tiny shreds. She stood perfectly still under the sheriff's piercing green gaze.

"It's a little hotter here then around the coast. Takes some getting use to. You don't sound much like you're from Houston. Where 'bouts in the city did you live?"

"Come on, Ross," Logan grumbled good-naturedly, "you take your job too damn seriously. Avery has no earthly reason to kill off my stock. Instead of standing here shooting the bull with us and overworking your brain, you might take that sample you insisted on having to the lab."

Ross laughed, then flipped a half-full specimen bottle in the air and neatly caught it. "You better have a closer look at those kids, Logan. I've warned you about taking juveniles in. My sister hated them here, you know."

"Yes, Ross. She told me enough times and so did you. But I didn't agree with Becky or you then, and I haven't changed my mind. I'll tell you this just once more. Despite all the trouble they've gotten up to, Ross, those four young men would never deliberately hurt an animal. Not even if they had a reason to hate me, which they don't.''

''If you say so.'' Ross touched the tip of his hat, looking at Avery. ''You be careful, you hear?'' He gave Logan and Pierce a kind of arrogant salute as he strolled away. Pierce called after Ross and followed him out of the barn.

Avery had observed the interchange and was confused by the mixed signals, wondering if it was a man thing and she'd just imagined it. But she had a strong feeling that Logan, and perhaps Pierce, didn't have much use for Ross. And the sheriff was a puzzle. He didn't seem much fazed by the urgency of the situation.

She suddenly had a headache and said the first thing that popped into her mind. ''The gene pool isn't too deep here in Haven, is it?'' Logan stared at her. ''Well, there's no doubt that Jessie and Ross are related in more ways than one—as are you Monahans.''

Logan threw back his head and laughed. He must have needed such a release after all the tension and horror of the day. He caught sight of Tanner approaching. ''Little brother thinks I've lost my mind, Avery. Maybe he's right.'' He shook his head.

''I saw Pierce before he left,'' Tanner told him. ''He said to tell you he was going to take a specimen to another lab in San Antonio rather than wait to hear what Ross has to say. He's got a couple of calls to make before he can leave, but more than likely he'll head out this evening. He also said to tell you he'll call just as soon as he gets the results.''

Whatever Logan was about to say was cut off by the sharp sound of tires skidding on the gravel driveway and the repeated blast of a car horn.

Logan froze and was pitched back in time. He could clearly hear the scream of brakes, the sound of metal twisting around metal. He thought he could feel the vibration of the impact shimmying through his body. The knife-sharp pain of his memories seldom left him, and he'd often thought that his own death would have been preferable to living through what came next....

He felt Tanner touch his shoulder. Mercifully, the nightmare ended, and both men set off at a run for the barn door.

Avery still wondered at Logan's reaction to the sound of the car. What hell had he relived? Could it have been his wife and son's accident? She hurried from the barn herself, only to be pulled up short as a young black woman and what appeared to be her daughter rushed toward Logan. The child had something wrapped in a pink blanket cradled in her arms. She was crying so hard she could barely talk.

"Doc Logan," the child finally managed to gulp as she held out the blanket. "Sugar's hurt bad."

The mother stepped forward. She wasn't in much better shape than her daughter. "One of the neighbor's dogs attacked Sugar when she and Annie were in the front yard."

"Did the dog bite Annie, Rosemary?"

"No, thank heavens."

Logan went down on his knees. He didn't try to take the injured animal from the child's arms, but gently folded the blanket back to reveal a small poodle, the white woolly fur stained with blood.

"I'm sorry, Logan, but Annie wouldn't hear of taking Sugar to anyone else. She insisted we bring her here."

Annie gave a hiccupping sob. "Jamie always said you were Dr. Dolittle—you talked to sick animals and made them feel better. Please make Sugar better, Doc Logan." She hiccupped again. *"Please."*

The mention of Jamie's name twisted the knife of pain in Logan. As hard as he tried to cut himself off from all reminders of Jamie, his son's friends weren't going to allow him that little luxury.

"Annie," he said, "Sugar and I need two very important things. First, you must be brave. Second, you have to let me hold Sugar." He met the child's gaze, swallowing visibly around the lump in his throat. "You and your mom can come to my office and wait while I examine her. But I can't help her if I can't see where she's hurt, Annie."

Reluctantly the child loosened her grip, but at the last moment, she lost her courage and refused to let go. Staring up at Logan, she whispered so only he could hear, "Please don't let Sugar die. I—I—need her."

He never made promises. But as he gazed down into Annie's tear-filled, imploring eyes, all his resolve melted away. "I won't."

She let go of Sugar. Logan strode quickly into the barn, all his concentration on the injured animal.

Avery watched as the woman grabbed her daughter's arm to keep her from running after Logan. The two seemed lost, shocked by what had happened. Annie turned her face into her mother's stomach, wrapped her arms around her waist and sobbed anew.

Careful not to startle her, Avery put her own arm around the woman's shoulders for comfort. "Rosemary, isn't it?"

"What? Yes, Rosemary Chapman."

"Why don't you and Annie come with me?" Avery glanced at Tanner for help.

"I'll go check on the boys," he volunteered, "and the horses."

Obviously Tanner was quite happy to turn two emotional females over to her. "Come on, Rosemary, Annie. We'll go to Logan's office and wait while he fixes Sugar up. How does that sound?"

They were beyond caring where they went or who took them. Avery opened the same green door Logan had taken her through earlier. She led the pair into the waiting room.

Once they were seated, Rosemary put her arm around her daughter, then looked up and said, "You're Avery, aren't you?" Rosemary smiled wanly at her look of surprise. "Don't be shocked. News travels fast in Haven, and I was at Maebell's café when Jessie Middleton came in."

Avery was a little in awe. While Rosemary was talking to her, she'd managed to calm Annie down enough that the exhausted child rested her head in her mother's lap and Rosemary soothingly stroked her hair.

"Don't be turned off by the gossip, Avery. Five years ago Haven was desperate for a third doctor on their hospital staff. My husband decided we needed to get out of the city. After all this time of him treating their ailments and listening to their personal troubles, we still haven't been totally accepted. Of course, the fact that we're black might have something to do with it."

For a moment Avery was shocked. Surely Rosemary was wrong, but then again, this was a small town.... When she saw Rosemary's dark eyes sparkling with wry amusement, she said, "I wonder what they have to say about me."

"I wouldn't worry about it. The Monahans swing a big stick in Haven, both personally and financially."

Annie was getting restless and beginning to fret and whine. Avery offered to go find Logan.

"Would you?" Rosemary asked.

Avery headed down the same hallway she had earlier. She passed Logan's office and saw what had been conspicuously missing at the big house. Awards, diplomas and family photographs were neatly arranged on the walls. Framed pictures were perched on the large oak desk.

Avery paused long enough to look at the ones of the young boy. She didn't need to be told it was Jamie. Except for the dark red hair and hazel eyes, the child looked a lot like Logan—the high cheekbones, well-shaped mouth. Her interest was drawn to one picture in particular—of a typical boy, all arms, legs and toothy smile, with his arm wrapped around a big black dog.

She was suddenly overcome with an uneasy feeling, as if she was peering too closely into Logan's personal pain. Hurrying on down the hall, she stopped at the door behind which she could hear Logan's voice.

She extended her hand toward the doorknob, then jumped back. She was utterly floored by the fact that she'd so easily recognized those soothing tones as Logan's and been drawn to the sound. *Damn!* She wasn't going to allow this to happen. Being attracted to her boss was totally unacceptable. She was a hopeless judge of character. Trusted too freely. Was dreadfully gullible. Blind to a fault, so that every emotion was suspect.

The bitter tirade of self-recrimination was what she needed to stiffen her spine. She gave the door a firm rap, then identified herself and waited.

Even after Logan had said she could come in, she hesitated, unsure what she'd find. Avery didn't think she could face Annie, much less have the courage to tell her that her beloved Sugar had gone to doggie heaven.

"It's okay, Avery," he called.

He must have guessed how cowardly she was. At last she screwed up her courage and slipped inside. The first thing she noticed was the chill of the room, immediately reminding her of a hospital operating room, which was, essentially, what this room was. She averted her eyes, suddenly feeling squeamish at the thought of seeing a lot of blood. In an effort to hide her nervousness, she blurted, "Why is it, I wonder, that men wearing masks are so fascinating?"

Logan chuckled. "The Zorro fixation of good triumphing over evil. Or maybe the Lone Ranger." He pulled the mask down around his neck.

"Wrong part of the face." She ventured a little closer to the table. The white bundle of fluff's sad little eyes were open and looking at her. "How's Sugar? Annie's terribly anxious." Avery murmured sweet nothings, then stroked the small head and received a doggy kiss on her hand. She fell in love.

Avery's baby talk to the dog seemed to amuse Logan. "She's going to be fine. A few stitches along her back were required—the wounds *looked* worse than they were. But sometimes the shock can kill them. Here, take the oxygen cup and hold it over her muzzle.'' Gently he pulled out the IV needle, swabbed the area, then snapped the latex gloves off. ''The oxygen, fluids and the shot I gave her will help her recover more quickly.''

He smiled at Avery. ''You're good with animals. I bet you had a houseful when you were Annie's age.''

Avery paid close attention to her task as she continued stroking Sugar. ''Actually, we didn't have any pets. My brother was allergic to almost everything that had fur or feathers. I think he even had an allergy to goldfish. But I'm more inclined to believe he just didn't want to share the attention he got as the baby of the family. Now that he has kids of his own, he's made sure they have a dog, and it never bothers his allergies.''

She fell silent for a moment, then a thought came to her. ''You know, I believe he gave the kids a dog for basically the same twisted reason. Herbie keeps them busy and out of his hair.'' She was so tired, she hadn't caught her slip.

Logan did, though, and was careful not to break whatever spell she was under. For a woman who was adamant that she had no family, she certainly seemed to have a brother, nephews or nieces, and more than likely a sister-in-law, plus a dog. What about a husband?

''You can take the oxygen away now,'' he said. ''I believe this little gal is ready to go home.'' He wrapped the dog back in her blanket. ''You want to get the door for me?''

A few minutes later Avery watched as he placed Sugar in Annie arms, then squatted at the child's level to explain everything he'd done, and the love, attention and medication Sugar would be needing for a couple of days.

A tearful but happy Annie looked at him adoringly and said, ''You're the best, Dr. Logan.'' Then she whispered, ''I miss Jamie.''

''Me, too,'' Logan said, his voice gruff with emotion.

''He'd be glad I brought Sugar here, wouldn't he?''

''Yes, Annie, he would. And you have your mom bring her back if you need to.''

He accepted Rosemary's thanks as Avery ushered Annie and her mother out of the office. Slowly he rose to his feet and sighed.

''Were they close friends?'' Avery asked.

Logan was a little startled by the question. The darkness of his thoughts retreated and he smiled. ''As close as any boy and girl can be at that age. Half the time he didn't want her hanging around with him and the guys, the other half he did.''

''We do have our uses.''

''A few…now and then.''

''What are you smiling about?'' she demanded, puzzled by what he found so amusing.

''Come with me.'' Logan grasped her arm and led her back to his office. Then he opened another door and pointed to her reflection in a full-length mirror.

Avery let out a shriek. Her clothes were rumpled and creased. Her shirt was filthy and half hanging out—the half she'd used to wipe sweat off her face. Her jeans were muddy, and her white, brand new tennis shoes were a suspicious brown. She was sure she knew what had dyed them that distinctive shade.

Her face and hair, however, made her burst out laughing. Her nose and cheeks were pink with sunburn, and there was a smear of dirt on her chin. Her black hair was almost beyond description. She had a ridge around her head where her hair had been plastered to her scalp—from the snug fit of the cowboy hat. But what had happened to her neat ponytail? One side of her hair was loose and stuck to the side of her head. "Oh, God. What must Rosemary have thought?"

"Probably that I'm working you too hard. Which is true. All that aside, you look ready to collapse." He gently pushed her into a chair and gave her a bottle of ice-cold water from the office refrigerator. "Drink."

"Doctor knows best?" Her hand hovered around her head. She didn't know what to start straightening first, so shrugged and gave up.

"You bet."

So thirsty she didn't have enough moisture in her mouth to spit, she did as he ordered.

"Have I thanked you for your help today?" he asked.

A few sips of the water did nothing to quench her thirst. Once she'd started drinking, she couldn't stop, and answered his question with a shake of her head.

"Thank you. You were great. Especially with the boys. They said you were cool. A 'real babe.' Don't laugh. That's high praise from those guys." He sat behind the desk, then made a show of looking for a key on his key chain. When he was sure he had Avery's attention, he unlocked the drawer and slowly eased it open.

Logan looked down at the contents, then at Avery. "My private stock."

Amused by the devilment in his eyes, she set the

now-empty bottle down and leaned forward to get a peek, but Logan blocked her view with his forearm.

"If I show you, you have to promise not to tell anyone, especially not Tanner."

She was intrigued, not so much about what he was hiding but at seeing another facet of the man. "I promise."

"Okay, choose what you want." One by one he began to line up a bag of M&M's, a Snickers bar, a Three Musketeers, an Almond Joy and the last one, a Moon Pie.

As Avery reached for the Almond Joy, she began to laugh. "You're a closet candy junkie?"

"Nonsense. I believe in the medicinal properties of a sugar fix when the body's overworked." He leaned back in his chair and peeled off the wrapper of the Moon Pie. "Junkie," he grumbled. "I'll have you know it's under control."

"Sure it is. That's why you've put them under lock and key." She was suddenly starving. Manners be damned. She gobbled the candy in seconds.

Logan grinned and eyed her with new respect. He used his fingertip to push the Snickers bar across the desk.

Avery hesitated only a moment before she reached for it. "I shouldn't. I really shouldn't. It'll go straight to my hips."

"And you have such nice hips." The words were spoken like a caress, and his eyelids drooped sleepily as if his imagination was working overtime. He tore open the bag of M&M's with his teeth.

"Said the big bad wolf to Riding Hood," Avery countered. She hadn't felt so lighthearted in a long time. It took a moment before she realized their banter had turned from good-natured joking into something else. She sensed the change in the air. There was a tightness in her chest. Even worse, she was sure her eyes mirrored the hunger and longing she felt for this man.

No! This was totally unacceptable. Her life was a shambles. Her past a disgrace. Her future grim. She absolutely could not afford to feel this attraction for Logan. But even as she struggled to deny its voice, her heart said otherwise.

CHAPTER FIVE

THE SPELL WAS SHATTERED by the voices of Tanner and the boys. They were coming closer. With a sweep of his hand, Logan cleaned the desktop of candy and locked the drawer, just in time.

Tanner pulled up short in the doorway and stared suspiciously at Logan and Avery. He opened his mouth to make a no doubt glib comment, but apparently changed his mind. Sniffing the air like a bloodhound, he said, "I smell chocolate." He eyed Logan, then Avery. "All our lives he's hidden the good stuff from me."

"That's because you have an insatiable sweet tooth and an addictive personality."

"Me?"

Avery laughed at Tanner's outraged expression.

"Help me out here, Avery." He sagged against the door frame. "I'm hypoglycemic and haven't eaten anything in hours."

Logan moved out from behind the desk, and as he passed Avery he clasped her shoulder. Before she could speak, the half-empty bag of M&M's slid down her chest and landed in her lap. She covered it with her hand.

Logan grasped Tanner's arm. "He's only mildly hypoglycemic, Avery, and candy is the *last* thing he should eat. He's also the biggest baby in Texas."

Logan began to usher Tanner out of the office. "Come along, little brother. I need to check on the horses, and Avery can stay here and rest."

Unwilling to leave Avery with a poor impression, Tanner resisted his brother's nudge, changed tactics and said, "The stalls are clean and spread with new hay. The boys are stabling the horses, then they're leaving. I've burned the remainder of that damn feed and am about to head over to Lawson's to pick you up some new feed."

"I'd rather you go to Bernstein's in Hamlet, if you don't mind." Logan gently shoved his sibling out.

She listened to the brothers banter until their voices died away. A rest suddenly seemed like a great idea. Avery pulled off her sneakers, settled back in the chair and propped her feet on the desk. She popped a candy in her mouth and looked around the office, taking in what she'd missed earlier. There were family photographs on the walls everywhere—pictures of people young and old. But as she glanced around, she couldn't find one of a girl that might resemble Jessie or Ross—Logan's wife, Becky. Avery popped another candy in her mouth and closed her eyes as she mulled over the mystery....

How long she'd dozed, she couldn't guess. Nor could she guess what had awakened her. But Avery had the eerie feeling of being watched, and it spooked her enough that, instead of opening her eyes completely, she peeked out from under her lashes.

Sitting like a sphinx on the edge of Logan's desk, next to her feet and entirely too close, was a huge cat. Was it even a domestic cat? It was certainly larger than any she'd ever seen. She guessed this animal had to weigh somewhere between thirty or forty pounds.

Taking into consideration the size and appearance, the battle-scarred and pugnacious face, Avery didn't think the gender could be anything else but male. Without a doubt he was also the ugliest cat she'd ever laid eyes on. His tiger-striped coat was a hideous rusty-orange mixed with dingy-white. His ears were oversize, and the tip of one had obviously been torn off in a fight, leaving it with a ragged edge. To add to his rather bizarre appearance, his face was peppered with black dots like freckles, and was crisscrossed with scars. His only claim to beauty were his eyes. They were a spectacular turquoise-blue, and they were fixed unblinkingly on her.

"Nice kitty, kitty." It was such a stupid thing to say to this fierce-looking beast that she almost laughed. The cat continued to stare. She felt the bag of candy in her hand and squeezed one out. The cat blinked. Avery placed the candy on the desk between his front paws and sat back.

"Well, well," she said as the massive feline snatched it up. "This place is full of chocolate junkies." One by one she fed him what was left. When they were all gone and he continued to stare at her, she gave him the empty bag to prove she wasn't holding out.

He moved quickly, and she couldn't do anything but freeze in fear as he set one foot, then another, on her legs and, with the casualness of a stroll, used her legs like a bridge. His solid weight settled in her lap and he stared into her eyes.

When he raised his paw, Avery flinched, but instead of the slash of claws, she received a pat on her cheek. Then he did the most amazing thing. He touched his nose to the same cheek as if kissing her, then curled up in her lap, closed his eyes and began purring like a truck engine.

"I see Casanova's introduced himself."

Avery looked over to see Logan at the doorway. She laughed. "What a fitting name. Do you know, I believe he tried to seduce me?"

"And did he succeed?" Logan asked. For someone who'd never had a pet, she seemed to have a way with animals.

"He stroked my cheek." She was both surprised and delighted. "Then he gave me a kiss. At least I think it was a kiss."

Logan was a little startled to see his cat in Avery's lap, too. Or was he? She seemed to have the oddest effect on males. His father, Tanner and the boys were all smitten. "Feel honored. He doesn't make friends lightly. Hell, he never makes friends at all. Just tolerates some of us. But you..." Casanova gave him a sleepy-eyed look, then Logan spotted the shredded candy wrapper. "Wait a minute. Did you give him my M&M's?"

"Give?" Her voice was incredulous. "It was hand over the candy or have my eyes scratched out." She was suddenly concerned she may have done something wrong. "Are cats not supposed to have chocolate? Will it hurt him?"

"For any other cat or dog, I'd say yes. But Casanova..." He shrugged. "I've seen what he eats sometimes and I can't say the chocolate would hurt him, but I'd rather you didn't give him any more."

Avery grinned. "I guess he has the Monahan sweet tooth." She watched the seriousness melt away from Logan's face and his eyes begin to twinkle. "What breed is he?" she asked.

Logan looked at Casanova. "There's no telling."
Envious of the cat, he plucked him from Avery's lap.
His reward for his efforts was a set of red welts on
the back of his hand. Logan dropped the cat and
looked first at his hand, then at Casanova.

Intrigued by the interchange between cat and man,
Avery wondered who would win their staring contest.
Casanova, obviously bored with both of them, stuck
his long fuzzy tail in the air, gave a rumbling meow
and marched out the door.

"He always does that." Logan shook his head with
disgust.

"Does what?"

"Has the last word." He started for the door and
motioned for Avery to follow. Once the office was
locked up tight, they walked out of the barn together.

"Logan, why do you have two offices? Wouldn't
it be easier for everything to be in one location?"

"Not really," he said. "I don't keep any files in
the barn office, and when I have to do billing or record keeping, it's usually done at the house." Logan
considered that to be enough of an explanation for the
moment. "I'm starving. How about you?"

The coolness of evening and the setting sun were
a pleasant surprise. The sky looked as if it was ablaze,
streaked bloodred and flaming orange. She was filthy
dirty and bone-tired but felt…wonderful. For the first
time in a year, she'd lost track of time and had managed to put her past behind her. The mention of food
made her realize she was ravenous, too.

As they neared the house, Logan glanced at his
watch. "A shower and clean clothes will do us both
wonders. I'll meet you in the kitchen in thirty

minutes.'' They separated, heading in opposite directions.

Even though her stomach was gnawing at her backbone, by the time she'd showered and washed her hair, Avery wanted nothing more than to crawl in bed. The fact that she had a bed to sleep in was an eye-opening reminder that she was hired help and not a guest. Logan wanted dinner.

She threw on a sundress, combed her damp hair back and raced out the door. As she entered the kitchen of the big house, she noted that the table was set and an incredible aroma filled the air. Now hunger overcame weariness.

''Sit down.'' Logan filled two bowls with chili and placed them on the table. ''I put a couple bottles of beer and mugs in the freezer. How about getting them out first?''

''Logan, I'm supposed to be fixing your dinner, not the other way around.'' Her words, even to her own ears, sounded hollow. She leaned over the steaming bowl and inhaled before heading for the freezer.

Logan joined her at the table, opened the beer and expertly poured hers so there was no head of foam. ''The way I figure it, you weren't hired for what you did today, so the least I can do is return the favor. Besides, you look about ready to fall on your face. As soon as you're finished, I want you to go get some sleep.''

Avery ducked her head to hide the sudden tears that filled her eyes. How long had it been since anyone had done anything nice for her? Afraid to look up and allow Logan to see how moved she was by the smallest crumb of kindness, she shoved a spoonful of chili in her mouth and swallowed. Then her head jerked up. Her eyes widened and her tears blurred the view of Logan's smile.

"Did I forget to warn you that it's a little hot? Take a sip of beer. It really doesn't help much, but it's cold and feels good."

She drank half her beer and gulped for air before she could talk. "Good heavens, what's in this stuff?" He didn't seem to be the least affected by it.

Logan laughed and pushed a basket of crackers across the table. "These'll help." He reached for a second basket and grabbed a handful of corn chips. "Personally, I like to add these to mine. Something Jamie hooked me on."

"He was able to eat this?" This was the first time she'd heard him mention his son. She was happy to see he didn't get that dark, hurt look just by saying his son's name.

"Sure. It was one of his favorites."

Avery followed Logan's lead and added chips to her bowl. After a couple more spoonfuls she had to admit the chili didn't seem quite as hot—or maybe her taste buds had been seared off. Either way, she settled down to do some real damage to her insides. After a second icy beer, she was definitely enjoying the food and the company.

"What does Tanner do for a living? He told me he played pro basketball, but he made it sound like it wasn't what he was doing now."

Logan mulled over his answer for a moment. "Tanner injured his knee the first year he played for the San Antonio Spurs. That ended his career. He bummed around for a couple of years, then decided to come back to Haven, did a little rodeoing and finally settled on working in the family business."

"He's a veterinarian?"

"Tanner? God, no." Out of habit, he'd been guarded with his explanations. Logan gave an oddly pleased laugh. She knew nothing at all about his family. "Monahan Farms raise and train quarter horses." She had no idea of the magnitude and prestige the Monahan name commanded in the horse world of champions.

"You raise them here?"

"No, Tanner lives on the home place, Monahan Farms, down the road about five miles. He and Dad breed and sell the horses. I train them after Pierce breaks them."

"How do you mean, break?"

"It's just an old term no one can let go of. Pierce is what's known as a horse whisperer. He has special talents where horses are concerned."

"I think I saw the movie. Do you whisper, too?"

Logan chuckled. "Yeah, we all do a little bit, but Pierce has a real gift. Dad says we inherited it from our great-great-grandmother, who was a Comanche Indian."

Looking at him now, Avery could easily see the heritage imprinted on his face. When she realized she was staring, taking an inventory of each feature, she self-consciously struggled for something to say, but ended up asking questions she had no business asking at all. "Why did you start the Circle M ranch? I mean, if you're the oldest, I'd have thought..."

"I bought the land when I was in college. After I married and Jamie came along, moving here seemed the right thing to do. Becky found the house somewhere outside of San Antonio and had it, plus the smaller mother-in-law house, moved here."

"You mean picked up and moved from one location to another? A house this size?"

"Mind-boggling, isn't it," Logan said. "It was a hundred-year-old house that had sat empty for at least ten years. They had to cut it in half, truck it here, then put it back together."

Avery wondered why she had the feeling that the house meant little to him.

By the time they were finished with the chili and Logan pulled the blackberry cobbler from the oven, she was completely relaxed and at ease. She watched him put a huge scoop of vanilla ice cream on each serving and groaned.

"This'll help you sleep."

"Sure it will. Like a sledgehammer between the eyes."

When she'd almost finished her dessert, he said. "You know, Avery, you really can trust me."

Her spoon stopped, suspended before her mouth, then slowly lowered. Suddenly she was full. "I don't know what you mean."

"Sure you do." He held up his hand when she started to speak again. "Just listen. A woman like you doesn't take a job like this unless you're running or hiding or both. And please don't insult my intelligence by denying it.

"This afternoon when you ran into Ross and realized he was the sheriff, you went white with fear. I believed you when you told me you weren't in trouble with the law—still do. But I have to tell you, you looked guilty as hell. Ross Middleton, despite the local-yokel impression he gives, is a smart man with the instincts of a hunter. He noticed your reaction and won't forget it. And when it suits him, he'll find out why you reacted that way.

"Now, I don't begin to know what happened to you. I just want you to know that no matter what or who you're hiding from, I'll help you any way I'm able to."

He resumed eating his dessert. When he glanced up, she was staring at him with a puzzled expression.

"Why?" she asked.

"Why would I help you?" Logan smiled. "Or why do I trust you?"

"Both."

"I don't know, Avery. Call it instinct or a gut feeling."

"I wish I could trust my gut feelings," she murmured.

"How about starting with me?"

She was more than a little tempted. But she was afraid.

"When you're ready, then," he said indifferently.

Relief washed over her like a warm, comforting wave. "Thank you."

"Just don't wait too long, Avery. Ross Middleton is a formidable adversary, and partly because of me, he won't let anything slide."

She didn't get a chance to question that cryptic remark because the back door swung open and Jessie stormed in. She stopped short when she saw the two of them together. Avery watched the struggle going on as the girl took in the remains of dinner and forced a smile.

"I just got back from San Antonio, and Ross told me about Allspice and Mac's Lady. How could something like that happen? I swear, Logan, you ought to horsewhip those boys.''

''Wait a minute, Jess. What the hell did Ross tell you?''

''That one of the boys might have accidentally, or maybe on purpose, spilled something like a pesticide in the grain. Or they could have left the feed bins open and the grain got moldy. He says you have to see now that you can't keep them here. If they're not just plain irresponsible, then they're dangerous.''

''Dammit, Jess!'' Logan raised his voice, something he never did with her. ''The boys had nothing to do with this. And I better not hear Ross or you repeating that story around town.''

Jessie's face crumpled and her pouty lips quivered. She looked ready to cry, and stubborn enough to want to argue at the same time.

Avery, without thinking of anything beyond the need to distract Jessie and keep Logan from getting any angrier, asked, ''Have you eaten dinner yet, Jessie? Or maybe you'd like some dessert?''

If looks could kill, she'd have had a knife through her heart. Avery realized her mistake as soon as the offer was out of her mouth. No one had ever accused her of being tactful, but she should have learned something in the past year.

She gathered the bowls, silverware and mugs from the table and carried them to the sink. And when, she wondered, had she appointed herself Logan's protector? He certainly didn't need her help. She cleaned the kitchen, listening to Jessie and Logan's conversation while pretending not to. It didn't take long to realize just how devious Jessie Middleton was. She talked about Becky, and when that didn't garner the reaction she wanted, Jessie turned the conversation to reminiscing about Jamie.

By the time Avery was finished in the kitchen, Logan's mood had turned dark and moody. Her hand itched to slap the girl's face. Jessie Middleton was far older and wiser than her years. She was manipulative, sly and selfish, and Avery wanted to scream at Logan for being so blind.

She closed the dishwasher door, proud she'd restrained herself from slamming it, turned it on and said good-night.

As she walked back to her house, she noted the full moon, the black velvet sky and the dazzling array of stars. But neither the beauty of the night nor the brisk breeze did much to cool her anger. With every step she berated herself. This wasn't her battle. Let Logan deal with Jessie any way he chose. By the time she put the key in the lock of her front door, she was in such a state that it took a moment to realize it was already open.

The unlocked-door policy that the Monahans lived by didn't apply to her. She was, after all, a city girl, and securing the door was an automatic reflex. That hers was not only unlocked but open gave her pause. Glancing back at the house, she wondered if Jessie had her own key. Had Jessie gone through her things while she and Logan ate dinner? Avery didn't have anything that spoiled brat would be interested in, nothing except... She rushed inside, and headed straight for the nightstand. She yanked the drawer all the way out, turned it over, then sat on the edge of the bed, sagging with relief. The thick envelope she'd taped to the back was still in place.

A quick check of the small house convinced her

that nothing of hers had been touched. Maybe, she thought, she'd been in such a hurry to join Logan that she'd simply forgotten to lock the door behind her. Or maybe she'd turned the key the wrong way.

Dressing for bed, Avery thought back over the day. Logan was sure that the horses had been poisoned. He'd been vehement in his defense of the boys, Benton, Tom, Raul and Tony. She'd asked him who would do such a horrible thing, but Logan had never answered her question.

She slipped into bed, pulled the covers up and turned off the light. Now, carefully reviewing the events of the day, she sensed more was happening on the ranch than met the eye. Something menacing.

Disgusted with herself for caring despite her promises not to, Avery punched her pillow. She was admittedly tired, but she must be worse off than she thought. Menacing, indeed. As if there was some evil force at work here. The strain of the last year must have been too much. She'd turned from levelheaded to fanciful. Avery closed her eyes…then screamed as something heavy landed on her legs.

Fumbling frantically for the bedside lamp, she almost knocked it over before she managed to turn it on. Casanova glared at her as if the light was an unwelcome intrusion. ''What are you doing in my bed? Better still, how did you get in?'' She didn't expect an answer, of course—he was, after all, a cat—but was shocked and amused when he rumbled something back, then stretched out across her legs and closed his eyes.

''Look here, Casanova, you might be the cat's meow around here, and I'll admit you're a charmer, but I sleep alone nowadays. Believe me, it's best this way—no complications, no heartache."

For all her bluster and fine words, Avery didn't have the courage to push him off. She sighed loudly and wiggled her legs, but Casanova didn't so much as twitch his tail. She switched off the light again and lay back, entirely too tired to fight.

LOGAN TUNED OUT Jessie's chatter as easily as he turned down the volume of a radio. He stood at the kitchen window, waiting and watching until Avery's lights went off. His father hadn't done him any favors bringing her here. Now he had to decide how he was going to make her leave.

Trouble had slithered back into his life. If today was any indication of how things would progress, he was sure events would get uglier. He shrugged off the notion that Avery's arrival had anything to do with the shattering of the calm that had prevailed for the past six or more months.

The thought of telling her she'd have to leave weighed heavily on his mind. Whatever Avery was running from, she had deliberately left everything behind. He was sure she didn't have much money and equally sure she had nowhere to go. Of course, he could offer her money or ask Tanner to let her work for him. But Logan had a feeling Avery was much too proud to take what she would most certainly see as charity. Besides, he knew Tanner, and the idea of Avery staying with him didn't sit well.

"Logan, did you hear a word I just said?"

He glanced over his shoulder, surprised to realize Jess was still there. "Go home, kitten. I'm beat." Manners be damned. Logan passed Jess without another word and headed upstairs. Until Avery's arrival, he had secretly been staying in the room over his office in the barn. At least he could sleep through the night there. As he passed Jamie's bedroom door, Logan's footsteps slowed. He wondered if his aversion for his home would ever heal.

FOR THE FIRST PART of the next morning, Avery worked diligently to make some headway in Logan's office. But all the frantic dusting, straightening and pushing boxes around couldn't make her shake the feeling that something wasn't right.

Logan had been unapproachable throughout breakfast, his conversation limited to one-word sentences. She had desperately wanted to make him laugh, or at least see him smile a little. But he was so grim, she couldn't bring herself to tell him about her roommate and bed partner.

She stared at the computer screen without really seeing it. Just before Logan had left the house, he'd told her he had errands to run, wouldn't be back for lunch and that she should make a list of groceries she needed and he'd pick them up. It was all so stiff and unfriendly, and when he'd left she'd had an empty feeling in the pit of her stomach.

But after a while, her attention became fixed on what she was looking at. Avery sat in growing fascination, then disbelief. She'd been trying to make sense out of what she'd found on the computer and in the boxes of files. Shaking her head now, she put aside her half-eaten tuna sandwich, then tapped a few keys. The computer screen changed and she choked, took a sip of Coke and studied the screen again. The figures hadn't changed. Logan had more than a million and a half dollars in, of all things, his checking account.

Her past training and education reared its head. She was outraged. It was criminal, a careless act of the foolhardy or the stupid. Only someone totally oblivious—or, she thought, a man who didn't care how much he had or what happened to it—would do this.

Avery couldn't sit still. And the room was suddenly too chilly for her liking. She unlocked the window and threw it open, then leaned out and inhaled the warm sweet air. She couldn't afford to let herself get wrapped up in Logan's business. Years of dealing with money, and the power of it, was too ingrained in her to ignore.

When she glanced over her shoulder, the figures hadn't changed. She told herself to forget it. All she was supposed to do was get his office set up and running smoothly. Curiosity was a luxury she couldn't afford. But it didn't stop her from wondering where that much cash had come from.

"Don't do this. Don't get involved. It'll never bring back what you've lost." Disgusted with herself, she said, "It's bad enough I'm constantly preaching to myself, but now I'm doing it out loud, too."

"You say something to me, Avery?"

She jerked back, banged her head on the window, then almost fell out as she twisted to see where the laughter was coming from. Glancing sideways, she followed the steps of a long extension ladder all the way to the top. "Benton, what are you doing up there?"

"We're going to repaint the house."

Avery looked around and blinked at the sight of the other three boys, each on a ladder propped against the house. Things were worse than she'd thought if all this activity and noise were going on and she was so absorbed she hadn't noticed.

"Doc wants the old paint scraped off first, and he said he needed us to stick close to the house today."

"Why aren't you in school?" She held her breath as the ladder shimmied when Benton leaned backward so he could see her better.

"Teachers' meeting today."

Anything else he might have offered was cut off when Raul yelled for him to quit goofing around. Avery rubbed the back of her head and returned to the desk. The figures on the screen still hadn't changed, but the whereabouts of her sandwich had. It was gone. Draped across the top of the monitor was a contented tomcat, looking at her with slitted, sleepy eyes. "You didn't even leave me a crumb?"

Casanova dangled one of his paws over the edge of the screen, held it out and stared at it as if casually inspecting his nails.

"Insolence suits you, but it won't get you dessert." That garnered his attention and he hopped off the monitor and pranced across the keyboard. Between laughter and horror, Avery watched the screen go crazy with the onslaught of commands. She plucked him up and put him in her lap.

"Gotcha. Now, since I don't have any candy, why don't you go catch a mouse or something?" He suddenly seemed more interested in the desk drawer than in anything she had to say. When he scratched the wood with his claws, she rolled her chair back. "Stop that, you silly cat." He took orders about as well as she expected, which was not at all. Finally, out of frustration, she yanked open the drawer.

"See? Nothing." But she was wrong. On top of a bag of M&M's and a Snickers bar was a handwritten note. "Just in case you get a sweet tooth today." The note was signed "Logan." Tears filled her eyes at the simple act of kindness.

Suddenly she was torn between crying and laughing as Casanova, ignoring the candy bar, swatted at the bag of M&M's until he captured it with his claws. He flipped the bag to the top of the desk, grabbed it between his teeth, then gave Avery a narrowed-eyed glare to make sure she wasn't going to try to take it away. In one leap, he was off the desk and out the window with the bag of M&M's in his mouth.

Avery unwrapped the candy bar and divided her attention between scrolling through the computer-system files and flipping the pages of the open file folder beside the keyboard. Figures at the bottom of one page captured her attention. Here was the explanation of the money: life insurance. Avery felt a chill of dread at what she'd found.

Logan's wife and son's deaths had brought him two million dollars.

CHAPTER SIX

WHAT WAS IT LOGAN had said? That she would hear stories, gossip that he'd received an ungodly amount of money when his wife and son were killed. There were people who believed he was responsible for their deaths. Logan's last words, before he'd walked out of the kitchen, had been something to the effect that they had been right.

But they were wrong.

No matter how much she distrusted her own instincts, she knew Logan didn't have it in him to deliberately hurt anyone, much less people he loved. She glanced around the office. The answers to many of her questions were in the boxes and papers; she knew it. All she had to do was find them.

Three hours later she sat surrounded by neatly organized stacks of files. As she sorted through one file, the hair on the back of her neck stood on end. She thumbed through a series of insurance-claim forms, surprised that Becky and Jamie had died only eighteen months ago. Three months after their death, Logan's barn had burned to the ground. She picked up the copy of the claim form. Besides the structure, an extensive assortment of equipment had been destroyed.

The construction on the new brick barn had been completed six months ago. Avery sorted out the bills and invoices for all the other expenses and the purchase of equipment and supplies. She totaled the cost, then leaned back in her chair, shocked and amazed. Half a million dollars for a barn? It seemed an outrageous sum. Then she reminded herself that it wasn't just a barn but a fully equipped veterinary facility. But why build one when he had access to the clinic in Haven?

About to give up for the day, she came across a long, disturbing letter cloaked in the mumbo-jumbo only insurance companies and lawyers use. Payment against the claim on the burned barn had been delayed indefinitely because the insurance investigator and the sheriff had determined that the cause of the fire was arson.

She was an expert at deciphering legal language, and this letter made her radar react. Hidden in the jargon, the insurance company was saying that, under the circumstances and until the person responsible for the fire was found and arrested, they would delay processing the claim.

There was something else that bothered her about the document—an insinuation that made her at first angry, then made her want to laugh. The insurance company and the sheriff thought Logan had deliberately set the fire. She could see how Logan might have raised a few eyebrows when he'd dropped the claim. But Logan Monahan wasn't a barn burner. He'd paid for his new barn with a portion of the life insurance money.

For a moment she stopped what she was doing and listened to the sounds of the kitchen door opening and closing. She'd made the boys sandwiches for lunch, and they'd been in and out all afternoon helping themselves to cold drinks from the refrigerator.

Avery stared at the file in her lap. A burned barn and now possibly poisoned horses? Why had Logan dropped the claim? She closed the file with a sigh, wishing she could ask him.

"What do you think you're doing?"

Avery nearly jumped out of her skin. Didn't anyone around the place knock? The file slipped from her hands and papers scattered on the floor as she glanced up. Jessie Middleton stared at her with those magnificent green eyes ablaze with hate. Avery sensed that one wrong word, one wrong move, and Jess would jump to the wrong side of that razor edge she'd been balancing on.

"Hello, Jessie," she said. "Logan wanted me to organize and set up his office."

"Why? He has an office in the barn."

Avery shrugged. "I didn't ask why."

"Of course not, you're just hired help."

As she reached down to pick up the papers, Avery kept her gaze on Jess. "He's not here—said he was going to town then run some errands." The girl was too still. Too watchful. "I don't think he'll be back until dinnertime."

Jessie moved farther into the office and folded her arms across her chest. With the desk between them, Avery figured if Jessie made a lunge for her, she could always jump backward and dive out the window.

"You won't get him, you know," Jess stated bluntly.

It was useless to pretend she didn't understand. "I don't want him."

Jessie's laugh was loud; her eyelids were half-closed and narrowed in anger. "You're a liar. I've seen the tight shirts you wear and the way you flaunt your big boobs, making him stare at you when you're not looking. He might lower himself to screw you, but he'll never love you. He'll never love anyone but my sister. Becky was his life, you know, and men like Logan don't get over that. Besides, Logan and I..." She shrugged and smiled.

Avery caught the none-too-subtle implication of what Jessie left unsaid. She thought she knew better than to aggravate a situation by antagonizing the girl. Yet something about Jessie got the better of her good intentions. Before she could stop, Avery blurted, "I didn't think you were the type to settle for being second best."

"What are you talking about?"

Taunting a cornered animal was not a good idea. Avery figured it was best to stop while she was ahead, but the next words popped out of her mouth. "You said Logan would never get over Becky. I'm sure you're right. So why would a young woman with your beauty and appeal, who could get any man she wanted, settle for living in your sister's shadow?"

Avery watched the meaning sink in and the confusion surface. Jessie reminded her so much of her brother that she felt a stab of pain. There was a constant battle going on between Jessie's twenty-year-old body and her immature mind. Avery gave a soulful sigh at the thought. She'd seen firsthand this type of internal war and knew that it made for an unstable personality. Even a dangerous one. She tried to feel sorry for Jessie, but memories of her own experience hardened her heart. The awkward moment passed, and she was saved from a venomous attack when Tanner appeared at the door.

"What are you two beauties doing?"

He was all smiles and breathless, as if he'd been in a hurry. She had the feeling he knew exactly what was happening and had come to head off trouble. Whatever Tanner's reasons, Avery was grateful for the interruption. It was fascinating how easily he cajoled Jessie from angry sulks to laughter. He escorted her so subtly from the office that Jessie wasn't aware she'd been evicted.

Avery propped her elbows on the desk and rested her chin in her hands. It wasn't long before Tanner returned. He carefully emptied a chair of files, pulled it up to the front of the desk and sat down.

"Did things get ugly?" he asked seriously, but his eyes twinkled.

"You're a real piece of work."

"Me? I rushed out here to save your pretty backside and you accuse me of... What're you accusing me of?"

"Enjoying yourself entirely too much. You probably thought—no, hoped—Jessie and I were tearing out each other's hair."

"Your accusation wounds me. Okay, flying female fists would have been the highlight of my week."

Avery didn't want to encourage him, but she couldn't stop herself from smiling. "She's a walking disaster just waiting to happen."

"Jessie's been like that all her life. Logan's the only one who could ever handle her or even took the time to care."

"What about her sister?"

"Becky stepped in only when it was convenient for Becky or made her look good."

Avery noticed the slight change in Tanner's voice when he mentioned his sister-in-law. It was time she got some answers and figured Tanner was the best place to start. "What brought you here in such a rush?"

"Logan." He leaned back in the chair and smiled. "We all live in dread around here when our father starts interfering in our lives. We usually live to regret it, too. But I must say, he's topped himself this time by bringing you here."

Asking questions was going to get her answers. Those answers would only make her want to ask more questions. And around and around she'd go—all involved in the Monahans' lives. Exactly what she'd wanted to stay away from.

"Why's that, Tanner?" Avery sighed in disgust. She never used to be so nosy. Or was it needy?

"Because, beautiful, I've seen him smile and I've heard him laugh more in the short time you've been here than I have in what seems like forever. He's almost like my brother again."

"And you think I've had something to do with this sea change?"

"'Nothing of him does fade, but suffer a sea change.'" He grinned. "Or something like that. Don't look so shocked. Did you think I was just a dumb jock or a bumpkin cowboy and never read Shakespeare?" He held up his hand. "Don't answer. But never doubt it, you are the cause of the change."

"No."

Tanner tilted his chair farther back on its legs and folded his hands behind his head. "You're either blind, being deliberately obtuse or fishing for compliments. And I don't think you're any of those things.''

She needed to head off the questions she knew were coming. ''Why are you here, Tanner? And don't give me one of your song-and-dance routines.''

''You're a tough cookie, cookie.''

He was a charming devil, despite the cutesy nicknames. ''And you're stalling.''

''Okay. Logan sent me. We were having lunch in town and Jessie found us. Logan doesn't want her hanging around the ranch so much. He thinks it's time she started to live her own life, cut the strings to us— that kind of thing. She needs to grow up.''

That was an understatement, Avery thought. ''Let me guess what happened. She offered to help out and Logan turned her down.'' Logan obviously saw more than Avery gave him credit for.

Tanner grinned. ''A *smart* cookie, too. She kept pushing, suggesting all kinds of things she could do around the place, but Logan wouldn't budge. She has this wild idea—''

''That I'm the reason for Logan's change of heart.''

''Yeah. Listen, Jess's a good girl. She's just highstrung and tends to blow things all out of proportion, but her heart's in the right place. Because of Becky and Jamie, she has this fixation on Logan right now.''

It wasn't Jessie's *heart* Avery was worried about, but what went on in her head. She didn't agree with Tanner, but he wasn't the right Monahan to talk to, and there lay the real problem. She had no intention of ever getting so involved that she'd give Logan serious advice.

"So you decided to follow Jessie and to check up on me?"

"No. Logan told me to follow Jessie and make sure you were okay. There's that look of surprise again," Tanner added. "We're a very close family. Though you couldn't tell it from appearances lately. No matter what we've done, Logan's cut himself off from everything and everyone. We've respected his need for solace and space." Tanner chuckled. "Well, Pierce has accepted Logan's boorish behavior and stayed away. Dad's more or less kept his distance."

"But not you?"

"Hell, no. I don't think brooding or being left alone is the answer. So I stay on his back and keep him busy bitching at me. Now that you're here...well, dear lady, what can I say but—"

Suddenly the front legs of Tanner's chair hit the floor with a crack as loud as a gunshot. He leaped to his feet and stared past her shoulder. It was a combination of raw nerves, reflex and his look of revulsion that made her jump up and swing around.

Casanova leaped from the windowsill, deposited a limp mouse on her desk, then sat like an unblinking sphinx. "Thank you, Giovanni." She tried to keep the tremble out of her voice. "Tanner, do something. Get it off the desk. Pick it up."

"His name's Casanova."

She couldn't take her gaze off the dead mouse. "Giovanni Jacopo Casanova de Seingalt. Yes, I know."

Tanner smiled but didn't take his eyes off the mouse, either. "Leave it to you to outdo me."

"Tanner. The mouse."

"No, no. Not me. No, ma'am. I don't touch those things."

"Tanner!"

She was torn between being sick and laughing hysterically.

He shook his head. "No. No way."

"Benton!" Avery yelled. "Raul? Tom? Tony?"

"They're gone. Left right after I got here."

"Well, what do we do now? Just stand here and stare at that disgusting thing?" She sensed rather than saw Tanner's slight movement toward the door. She tore her gaze from the mouse and the proud Casanova, who was licking a paw, and glared at Tanner. "Don't you dare even think about leaving me alone."

"But you and the cat seem to have developed a friendship if he's bringing you dinner. I thought I'd just leave you two to enjoy it."

"Very funny."

It was Casanova who broke the standoff between her and Tanner. His oversize ears twitched and his eyes narrowed to slits, then he leapt for the open window and was gone.

"He could at least have taken that thing with him," Tanner grumbled. He moved to leave again, thought better of it and glanced at Avery.

"That's right, leave me alone. I swear you're going to be sorry...." She realized that Casanova hadn't just abandoned his dinner but had heard something that perked his interest and had gone to investigate. "Be quiet, Tanner, and listen."

The kitchen door shut and she could make out the sound of bags being set on the table. Before she could comment, Tanner yelled for help.

Logan quickly took in the situation. He leaned

against the door frame, laughing. Casanova glided between his legs, jumped on the desk, picked up his prize catch, then positioned himself directly in front of Avery. Tanner's aversion to mice was legendary around the ranch. Well, Tanner obviously wasn't the only one.

Avery shuddered and squeezed her eyes shut. "Please, Logan, take it away."

Logan reached across the desk and picked Casanova up. The cat fought back, claws flying, but he found it harder to moan and hiss with his mouth stuffed with mouse. Logan pitched the cat and his prize out the window and shut it.

Avery sighed in relief, then moved to leave the room, but found Logan in her path. "I've got to get something to clean off the desk." She stared into Logan's eyes and swallowed. Hard.

His gaze was warm and laughing, his lips parted just enough to be an invitation.

"What have you done to my cat?" he asked.

She felt suddenly guilty. "Nothing. He's a thief, you know. He stole the bag of M&M's from the desk." She was close enough to feel the heat from his body and smell the fresh scent of the soap he used.

"Stole?" He'd never noticed until now just how milky and smooth her skin was. Her cheeks and the tip of her nose were still pink from the sun yesterday, and made her look absurdly innocent. "Don't feed him chocolate, okay?"

"Okay, but I didn't exactly give it to him. He just took it and I didn't dare try to take it back. Listen, I don't mind Casanova sleeping with me—and let me tell you, he's a snoring bed-hog—but I draw the line at sharing his dinner."

"Wait a minute," Logan said, his smile widening. "Casanova slept with you? When?"

"Last night. I have no idea how he got in."

Logan shook his head, a sweet kind of sadness in his gaze. Words failed him. Jamie had been the only human whose company Casanova had ever sought. And only on rare occasions, when there was a severe storm, would the cat sneak into the boy's bedroom.

"Did you miss him last night?" she asked. For some absurd reason the thought of the cat curled up next to Logan made her shaky in the knees.

"He only tolerates my presence, and he's certainly never slept with me." He studied the way the pupils of her eyes grew to wide, black-velvet circles when she was trying to hold back laughter. He steeled himself not to fall into their depths and shut out the rest of the world.

They had both forgotten Tanner and were startled, and a little embarrassed, as if they'd been caught in some intimacy, when he spoke. "You better watch yourself, Brother. The lady's dangerous. I swear, when she thought I was going to leave her alone with that mouse, she twisted her head around and glared at me like the girl in the movie *The Exorcist.*" He gave a dramatic shiver. "Her eyes all but froze my feet to the floor."

"Aha! Fear." Logan chuckled. "That's about the only thing that *would* keep you in the same room with a mouse." His gaze shifted back and forth between Tanner and Avery. "That, or the threat of reprisal when you least expect it."

Avery gave a guilty start of surprise, and Logan's smile grew, more with fascination than amusement. "Don't be shocked. You're obviously an old hand at the fine art of delayed retribution. You can only pull that sort of thing off within a family, though.'' He had unwittingly stolen the happiness from her eyes and wiped away her lovely smile.

The first blast of a car horn didn't alarm them.

Logan said, ''That'll be Dad. He caught up with me at the store and said—''

The horn didn't stop. It sounded as if Mac was leaning on it.

Logan moved first, quicker on his feet than Tanner. Avery reacted automatically and followed them out the back door. By the time she reached the bottom step of the porch, the two men were rounding the side of the house. For a moment she lost sight of them, then spotted them again, moving among the deep shadows of the old oak trees surrounding the garage.

When she caught up, Avery fully expected to see Mac Monahan being helped out of his truck. Instead, the three men were standing in the coolness of the garage. At their feet were smashed boxes and broken toys. She saw the damage to the wheels of a bright red bicycle, and it appeared as if someone in a fit of rage had stomped the spokes of the wheels until they were nothing more than broken wires.

Mac was on his cellular phone, and from his tone and language he wasn't a man to be denied. He demanded that Ross Middleton be found and sent to the ranch immediately. He snapped his phone shut and the sound echoed in the garage.

No one moved.

No one spoke.

Avery was breathless from running. She opened her mouth to ask a question, but stopped in time as she became aware of the awful silence. The tension was overpowering and the sheer strength of it frightened her. Afraid her raspy breathing might set everyone off in an explosion of raw emotions, she struggled to calm down.

The blatant vandalism puzzled her. It looked as if the only things touched were a few boxes of toys and the bicycle—Jamie's things. Her heart dropped to her toes. "Who would do this?" she whispered, barely aware she'd spoken aloud.

Mac scooped up a metal dump truck, the sides dented and the paint damaged. He glanced at Avery as if about to say something, but his attention was diverted by the sound of car tires on the gravel. Everyone turned to see Ross Middleton climb out of his car.

Mac looked at his wristwatch. "You must have been nearby."

The sheriff set his hat on his head and tipped the brim lower over his eyes. He settled the heavy gun belt in a more comfortable position around his expanding waist, then slammed the car door and strolled forward. "I was tying up some domestic problems again over at the Browns' place. What's the trouble here?"

Mac reached for Avery's arm and pulled her aside. Tanner stepped back, also, so Ross could get a good look at what had been done. The sheriff whistled, a high, cutting sound like fingernails on a blackboard. Avery gritted her teeth.

Ross squatted to get a closer look at the damage. He fingered a bright red piece of plastic. "Man. I'm sorry. This is just plain meanness."

Unable to look at Jamie's smashed belongings, Logan turned on his heel and, without a word to anyone, quickly left the garage.

Avery ached for him. She wanted to follow, and would have, but she felt Ross's gaze on her and stayed where she was. She couldn't afford to raise the sheriff's curiosity.

Mac and Tanner picked up the remains of the broken toys, and as Tanner dragged a large trash barrel across the room, Mac stood stock-still, gazing at the small crushed car in his hand. "Logan couldn't bear to look at these things," he said. "Told me to throw them all out. But I couldn't do it. I knew someday he'd regret not keeping some of the boy's cherished toys. So I packed them away and hid them here. Lordy, lordy, I just don't understand what's going on anymore. Who could do something like this?" He shrugged off the hand Ross had laid on his shoulder and crossed the garage to help Tanner.

"Poor old man," Ross said.

Avery blinked back tears, then suddenly realized she was alone with the one person she dreaded most. "Yes," she said, and searched for something to fill the silence. "They're devastated."

"Looks to me as if someone is systematically destroying everything Logan loves or values. I'd be really careful if I were you. The incident with the horses wasn't the first strange thing to happen around here."

She chewed her lip. "You mean the barn burning?"

"That and other things." He gave her a closer inspection, smiled, then grasped her arm and pulled her out of earshot of Mac and Tanner.

Avery couldn't explain the rush of panic she felt.

She didn't want this man touching her, and steeled herself not to flinch.

"Right after my sister and nephew were killed, Logan's clinic in town was broken into and vandalized. He and Pierce lost a lot of equipment, and some of their patients were turned loose. Then Jamie's dog, a beautiful black lab, disappeared. Everyone thought he might have run off, but who knows? Then the poisoning of the horses' feed and now this. I still think the problems could be placed at those boys' feet." He shrugged. "But what do I know? I'm just a hicktown sheriff."

Avery tried to smile, but her lips seemed frozen. The dumb, small-town sheriff cloak didn't hang well on his muscular shoulders. His green eyes were too sharp, seeing everything while he pretended to see nothing at all.

"I just don't understand how Logan—one man—can be the recipient of so much tragedy," the sheriff continued. "It's like an unknown force set in motion that no one can stop. You best watch your step."

"What do you mean?"

"From years of dealing with this sort of thing, little lady, I know that trouble has a way of escalating before it finally comes to a head. I'd hate seeing you pulled into this mess because you've got a good heart." He smiled and leaned closer. "You might consider employment elsewhere."

She couldn't stand still under those searching eyes, and without a thought she said, "Excuse me, I need to find Logan." But the sheriff didn't let go of her arm. Instead, he tightened his grip.

"Remember what I said, and if you need anything,

anything at all, just give me a call.'' He dropped his hand and she moved away.

There was only one place Logan would go. She turned in the direction of the barn. The shadows were lengthening and the breeze had kicked up, cooling her hot cheeks. As she stepped into the dimness of the building, she heard a horse whinny and headed toward the sound.

It was Possum, and Avery stopped outside the open stall for a moment. The mare snorted and nodded her head in recognition. Logan had his back to Avery as he groomed Possum, the brush moving rhythmically over the animal's coat. Avery didn't know what to say or do. All she knew was that he shouldn't be alone. She entered the stall and stood beside him, watching his beautiful hands, one following the other as he brushed, then stroked. It was a slow hypnotic movement like a caress, almost sensuous.

Logan had sensed Avery's presence long before she stopped outside the stall. She came up beside him, but didn't speak. Words of sympathy and comfort would have been meaningless. No one understood that the endless pain of losing Jamie was what kept him alive.

''Give me your hand,'' he said, and smiled when she stuck out her hand rather stiffly, as if suspicious of what he had in mind. Logan moved back a little from Possum's side and pulled Avery directly in front of him. He slipped the leather brush strap over her hand, then with one palm on her shoulder and the other on top of hers, he showed her the correct pressure and motion of grooming.

Every stroke brought his body in contact with hers. The light touching, the pulling away and the stroking motion made her heart pound and heat spread through her body. It seemed like the very room was holding its breath; certainly she was having trouble breathing. Her eyelids grew heavy and her limbs felt weak. She knew she was in deep trouble and fought the invasion of emotions. She couldn't afford to melt into a puddle of desire at Logan's feet. She wouldn't allow herself to.

Her urge to lean back and rest her head against his strong shoulder was almost overpowering. Dammit, she was only human and she yearned to feel alive again. But getting involved, even if only physically, meant a degree of honesty. In the heat of passion, secrets were revealed. What could she share? That she was a criminal?

Panic made her turn around, but instead of moving out of her way, Logan put both his arms around her. She gazed into his eyes and saw her own desire reflected back at her. Avery swallowed. This couldn't be happening. But it was, and suddenly all the fight drained out of her.

Logan gently pushed her up against Possum's side. She watched his head slowly lower and was almost breathless with anticipation. His mouth met hers. She closed her eyes and parted her lips, letting the kiss deepen. It was a lush, romantic kiss, both tender and sensual.

Logan abruptly pulled away and held her at arm's length. For a second she was disoriented, and struggled to gather her wits. She wanted to say something, anything, to end the awkward silence between them, but words failed her. He looked so serious, almost angry. All she could think was that Logan must feel he was betraying Becky's memory, and he must blame and hate her for his weakness.

For Logan, kissing Avery was like visiting his nightly dreams. Now everything had changed. If she stayed, she might be dragged into the middle of his own personal hell and end up a victim. Could he convince her to go? Could he scare her away?

Logan started to speak, stopped, then managed to say, "What would it take to make you leave here?"

He'd done the very thing he'd wanted to avoid— hurt her. She tried to mask it, but he knew he had. Logan let go of her shoulders, but grabbed her hands and held them. The vast barn seemed suddenly small and confined. He couldn't breathe. Logan dropped one of her hands and placed a finger across her lips. "Please don't say anything. Just come with me."

She was too embarrassed to utter a word, and his grip on her hand gave her little choice but to follow. They left the barn, crossed the paddock and headed down a well-worn path. Avery was too busy concentrating on where to put her feet to be concerned about where he was taking her.

Logan came to a halt, pointed ahead, then resumed pulling her along in that direction. Like a lamb being led to the slaughter, she didn't resist. Finally Logan stopped again, but this time he nodded to a stone bench.

The trek had left her breathless and she gratefully collapsed on it. They were beside a tree-lined pond, and the setting sun cast golden spears between the swaying limbs of the willows. As she caught her breath, she watched the flickering light bounce off the wind-ruffled surface of the water.

Enough time had passed for her to recover her dignity. She admitted she'd been a little wanton, even greedy. But who did Logan think he was in the first place, kissing her like that? The long rush down the path had given her time to cover her shame with injured outrage.

Logan sat down beside her. When he tried to take one of her hands, she pulled away. "I'll never apologize for that kiss," he said, "so don't ask me to. I meant it."

He'd stolen her anger with more than words. The truth was in his face, and it left Avery weak. "You want me to leave, don't you?"

"Yes. You've come at a bad time."

"And you don't want me here."

"That's right." Logan leaned forward, rested his elbows on his knees and stared at the ground between his feet. "If I give you enough money to start over somewhere, and one of my cars, will you take it?"

CHAPTER SEVEN

SHE INHALED DEEPLY before saying, "I don't take charity."

"That's a definite no, then?" His aim was to be charming and ease some of the damage. It wasn't working. "You've got entirely too much pride, Avery. More than what's good for you. And just for the record, the offer of money and a car wasn't a handout."

"Oh, sure," she snapped, then demanded, "What was it, then?" He looked so apologetic she couldn't stay angry. "Logan, I know you loved your son and your wife. That you have any sort of feeling for me doesn't diminish what you felt for her. You weren't being disloyal to Becky's memory just because you have needs."

"Needs?"

"Come on, Logan. You're too smart to play this game, and I'm too old to go along with it."

"Just a minute. You think I want you to leave because of Becky? And my offer of money is a way of salving my conscience for the kiss or any lustful thoughts I might have for you?"

"Something like that, yes." Put into words, it did sound lame. Still, she felt compelled to continue. "You don't have to worry. A moment's lapse doesn't mean anything."

Logan shook his head. The conversation had taken such a wide turn in the road. Explaining himself was a chore he seldom indulged in. "Avery, I worshiped Jamie. I don't think I'll ever get over losing that boy. He was my life. As for Becky…"

He met her gaze directly so she could see for herself the truth of what he was about to say. "The love we had for each other, if there ever was any, died a couple years before she did. In fact, we were planning to divorce."

Avery was at a loss for words. She'd been so sure his offer was based on a pang of conscience, that he felt he was somehow cheating on his wife. "Then why do you want me to leave?"

He sighed. "I thought things had calmed down. But I'm afraid trouble is about to rear its ugly head again. I don't want you here."

"I don't understand."

"I know, and I can't explain. Would you consider going to work for Tanner or Dad?"

"Are you firing me, Logan?"

"No. I wouldn't do that to you. Whatever you're running away from, it's scared you enough that you've given up everything important in your life. It takes a lot of guts and a powerful motive to do that. No, Avery, I won't throw you to the wolves."

Her inner voice, the one she seldom listened to lately, urged her to accept Logan's offer. Take the money and the car and get away as far and fast as she could. Some malicious and destructive force was at work behind the scenes at the Circle M ranch, and it scared her. *Take the money and run while you can, Avery.*

She shifted her gaze and stared out across the pond,

pretending to watch a few horses that had wandered down to drink. She steeled herself and refused to meet his eyes as she questioned his offer. "If you're not firing me, then I'm not leaving." She was as startled by her declaration as Logan was. "This sudden need to get rid of me has to do with what happened today and yesterday, doesn't it? The ruined toys, the sick horses."

"The *poisoned* horses," Logan corrected. "Pierce said the preliminary tests showed a particular fungus that needs certain uncommon circumstances to develop. It's rarely seen in the sort of feed we give the horses. And it's not just those incidents, Avery. There's more."

She remembered something the sheriff had said. "The vandalism at the clinic in town?"

Nodding, Logan said, "But it was more than vandalism. More like a deliberate sabotage of property. Before you came, a hole was cut in the back fence. Some wild horses that I'd had shipped from Montana got loose. It took Tanner and me three days to round them up and drive them over to Monahan Farms. Then there was a rash of gates deliberately left open so the cattle could wander out onto the highway. I nearly lost two cows."

The list of incidents made her queasy. She wondered what had happened that she didn't know about. Maybe she shouldn't be so quick to jump feet first into trouble. She could still take him up on his offer. But she said, "And there's the fire that destroyed the old barn and the disappearance of Jamie's dog."

Logan's faraway expression changed to a deep frown. "My, my, the mouse really rattled Tanner's cage. He has this habit of running off at the mouth when he's scared. Can't keep a secret worth a damn.''

"It wasn't your brother who told me. It was the sheriff.''

"Ah, now that figures. Did Ross say he thought Benton or one of the other boys was responsible? That man really has it in for those kids.''

"Yes. His hints pointed in that direction.''

"Do you believe him?''

"No, I don't.'' She turned in her seat to face him squarely. "What's going on, Logan? Who hates you so much?''

All of a sudden he seemed preoccupied, his attention elsewhere. Or was it his way of eluding her question? She was about to ask, but saw his interest was on a line of bushes at the edge of the pond. Something was making them quiver.

Avery wasn't sure what was happening until Casanova pranced out from under a bush with his tail pointing proudly at the sky. He came to a halt at her feet, dropped a dead lizard there and looked at her almost expectantly.

"What's with this cat?'' she whispered, afraid if she reacted the way she wanted to, which was to scream, she'd offend him. "Why does he think he has to bring me these...these grisly gifts?''

Logan chuckled. "I don't think they're gifts, more like a trade. He probably wants more M&M's.''

She gave the cat a fierce look and said, "Really, if you continue to bring me these presents, you'll spoil me.'' Casanova's only response was to bat the ill-fated lizard with his paw.

She cringed, but continued to talk to Casanova.

"No, really, I couldn't. It looks more to your taste than mine. You enjoy it."

She gave a start when Casanova leapt into her lap and began kneading her thigh. "Now what?"

Logan shook his head in amusement. "He thinks you're his mother. Just stroke him."

Avery did and in less than a minute, Casanova was sleeping. She looked at Logan. "Will you please remove that thing at my feet?" She turned her head while he picked the dead lizard up by the tail and deposited it in the brush.

She hadn't even noticed that the day had ended. The sun had set, and the moon hung so low and large in the sky it looked like it was being cradled by the treetops. As Logan returned and sat back down, she shivered. The breeze blowing off the water was damp and chilly.

"You're cold." Concerned, Logan started to get up again, but Avery grabbed his arm.

"You didn't answer my question," she said. "Who hates you so much?"

Instead of replying, Logan looked enviously at Casanova. "I wish I could sleep like that."

"Me, too." The cat was so relaxed he was limp, and his head hung at an impossible angle over her knees. "We can sit here all night and you can evade my question, but it won't stop me asking. Logan, if I won't leave and you won't fire me, then I guess I'm here to stay. Please let me help. I'm quite good at figuring out mysteries."

"Dammit, Avery, this isn't some story in a book. It's real, and though no one's been physically hurt, things could change in an instant."

He didn't know her very well, but was about to get

a taste of her stubborn nature. She refused to be swayed. "There are three things that can motivate this much emotion. Greed. Hate. Jealousy."

Logan nodded. "I…ah, hell. I don't know what to think anymore. I thought, no, hoped this crap was over. Now…"

"It's started again." Avery shivered once more. "How long has it been? When was the last incident before I arrived here?"

"Let's go back to the house."

"No." She would have stomped her feet in frustration, but forty pounds of dead weight had made her legs go to sleep. She shifted Casanova and cradled him in her arms like a baby. He moaned with pleasure.

"Lucky cat," Logan mumbled.

Avery smiled up at the moon. "And you can't evade my question with compliments."

"The last incident was the disappearance of Jamie's dog, Blackie. I don't remember how long ago— months, anyway. I put out fliers in Haven and a couple of surrounding towns. I called animal shelters and other vets, but there was nothing."

"Could someone passing through have stolen him?"

"Maybe. Labs are stolen all the time. But Blackie wouldn't have gone with a stranger. They'd have to drug him to get him in a car or truck. After a couple of weeks I didn't hold out much hope of finding him, but I couldn't give up looking.

"You see, Jamie and I trained Blackie from a puppy. At the time we first got him there was a rash of animal poisoning going round. I had to put a couple of dogs and cats down. So we made sure to train

Blackie to eat only from his bowl and never accept food from a stranger's hand.''

''So, if someone dog-napped him, would he have starved?''

''I honestly don't know. We trained him pretty well. Of course, we never tested him by starving him, either. And there were Jamie's friends, and children in general. Blackie never saw children as strangers.''

''Who in the family, besides you and Jamie—and I assume Becky—could feed him?'' Logan stared at her for so long she thought he wasn't going to answer.

''Everyone, if they used his bowl, and it was always in the kitchen. He'd take food from Tanner, Dad, Pierce and Jessie.'' Logan didn't like the way the conversation was going. ''If we were out of town, one of them would come over and take care of things.''

Casanova was getting heavier by the minute. Unceremoniously, Avery shoved the cat into Logan's arm. Casanova didn't appreciate being awakened so rudely. He hissed and lashed out at Logan, then vaulted to the ground and disappeared into the darkness.

Logan rubbed the fresh welts on his hand. ''Thanks.''

She remembered something. ''Did you tell the boys to stay close to the house today while you were gone?''

''Yes. After what happened to the horses, I didn't want to take any chances.''

''Do Tanner or your father have any ideas about what's going on?''

''Tanner's got a better grasp of the situation than Dad. But they're as much in the dark as I am.'' He headed off the question he saw in her eyes. "And before you ask, yeah, I sent my brother here today." He stood and held out his hand. "I smell rain in the air. We'd better get moving."

On the way back to the house, Avery mulled over how to broach a delicate subject. As the lights came into view, she gripped his hand harder and stopped. "I said there were three emotions that drive people to do crazy things—greed, hate and jealousy.

"You said you didn't know who hated you enough to hurt you. The sheriff said something that puzzled me, Logan. The acts of violence—retribution, he called them—seemed to be done by someone who was out to destroy everything you loved or held dear. I think he meant it like a punishment."

"They're doing a bang-up job of it," Logan muttered from between clenched teeth. "After each incident I waited for someone to show their hand. But there were long periods in between when I was lulled into a false sense of peace. The violence always comes out of nowhere and it's always aimed at me. The stakes seemed to have been raised since you arrived. For your own protection, I think you should leave." Logan abruptly dropped Avery's hand and walked on ahead.

"Wait. Have you considered Jessie?"

He swung around. "You're joking, aren't you?" But his voice lacked outrage. "You think it could be Jess?"

"I know you love her, Logan." It occurred to Avery she might be booted off the ranch yet if she didn't stop while she was ahead. She refused to let that deter her, however. "Listen, Jessie was here before the horses got sick. She was angry with your father for hiring me and hurt that you wanted to keep me here. And don't forget when she'd shown up with lunch, but you'd already eaten with me and Tanner. She must have felt very left out. Today, she came here while I was in the office. She was in a state. Tanner told me you saw her in town, and she was upset then. I don't know what pushed her buttons, but she came here spoiling for a fight.''

"What did she say?"

Now wasn't the time to repeat what Jessie had said, hinted at and insinuated. ''I don't think her mood swings are new to you. Let's just say she was in a nasty temper. If Tanner hadn't walked in, I think she would have flown into a rage. She left after a few words with your brother. What I'm saying, Logan, is that she had ample time to go to the garage.''

"Jess loved Jamie. She would never deliberately destroy his things.''

"But was she destroying Jamie's toys or was she striking back at you? No, Logan, don't say anything else, please. Think back carefully over everything that's happened around here. See if you can remember where Jessie was and what her mood was at the time.''

Logan walked across the lawn toward the house. Avery trailed silently behind. She figured she'd planted the seed to start him thinking and that was enough for now. When he held open the door, she moved to pass, then stopped. Logan shook his head as a warning, making her aware of the voices coming from the kitchen.

Tanner and Mac were far too busy sniping at each other, while they worked at fixing dinner and setting the table, to notice Avery's and Logan's entrance.

Avery felt it was an opportune moment to ask another question. "If you don't know who hates you, Logan, and you've ruled out jealousy, what about greed?"

"I'm the only one who benefited financially from Jamie and Becky's death."

THE EVENING STORM broke with a series of earth-shaking claps of thunder. Avery sat straight up in bed, kicking and fighting the tangle of covers and the weight of Casanova across her legs. The violence of the storm and being wrenched from a sound sleep made her heart hammer wildly. Her mouth was dry with fear. She hated storms. Obviously, from his moaning and the way he scrambled to get under the sheet, Casanova wasn't thrilled with them, either.

The curtains at the window were open enough for her to see jagged streaks of lightning rip the sky. The first ground strike was close enough that the thunder reverberated through her body. Then the bedroom was blasted with light so brilliant it left ghostly imprints on the inside of her eyelids. The fine hairs on her arms stood up from static electricity. She flinched with the next strike.

She threw back the covers and started to get up, then gasped. Casanova had attached himself to her thigh. When a deafening thunderclap shook the small house, his razor-sharp claws pierced her long night-shirt and dug into tender flesh. Turquoise eyes, wide and shiny, pleaded with her.

"You big baby," she said, "I'm just going to shut the curtains." Avery hissed with pain but managed to pull him free. He trembled and looked so pitiful she couldn't bring herself to put him down. Instead, she cradled him in her arms and stepped in front of the windows just as another streak of lightning forked the sky.

Avery yanked one side of the curtain closed. "One, one thousand. Two, one thousand..." In his own way, Casanova counted out loud with her. "Stop that moaning, you silly beast. I'm not going to put you down."

Thunder boomed again, then tapered off to a deep rumble. The thunder and lightning weren't as bad as before, though. They were moving on, followed by rain. It pounded the roof with such force she wondered if it was mixed with hail.

Conscious of the weight in her arms and the chill from the air conditioner, she was more than ready to return to the warmth of bed. Avery reached for the other half of the curtain to pull it closed. The next lightning strike was caught behind the rain clouds and lit only the sky. Her hand froze around the material. She'd just seen a shadow moving fast from the direction of the barn toward the house.

She yanked the curtain closed, leaving a gap just wide enough to peek through. Lightning again veined the sky, and the figure was still visible. It had horns and batlike wings that flapped in the wind. Avery rushed out to the leaky front porch with some foolish notion of identifying the figure and watched as it came closer and closer.

Then she reacted out of blind fear and pitched Casanova at him. The cat made sharp-claw contact, and there were howls of surprise and protest from both parties.

Avery recognized Logan's voice and exhaled in relief. "Oh, my." She dashed out in the rain to help pry the cat from Logan's chest. On closer inspection, she realized how she'd been fooled. The bat-wing appearance was caused by a rain poncho that reached his knees. And the curled brim of his cowboy hat looked like horns. "I thought you were the devil."

"And you threw the cat at me?" His voice was incredulous.

"I'm sorry. He's all I had." It was all so ridiculous that they both found themselves standing in the rain laughing. She was soaking wet and their hands were locked around a snarling, wiggling cat. They lost the struggle. Casanova leapt to the ground and took off for the house, only to be halted at the closed door. He was wet and his fur was sticking out in all directions. With as much dignity as he could muster, he turned and sat.

Avery hadn't felt so free and happy in years. Even the fact that she was soaked to the skin didn't bother her. Not, at least, until lightning flashed across the sky and she caught the look in Logan's eyes. Avery glanced down. The beige nightshirt was not only plastered to her body, it was almost transparent. She folded her arms across her chest.

"That doesn't hide much," he said. "And I've got a great imagination."

She recrossed her arms. "Well, you shouldn't look."

His voice was hoarse with desire. "That won't happen till I'm six feet under. You better get in before I forget you work for me."

"What were you doing out in the storm?"

"Making sure everything was secured and the horses were okay. Go inside, Avery, or I'll take your reluctance to leave me as an invitation."

Even though she really didn't want to go, she

turned and ran for the door. She scooped up Casanova and slipped inside. Before she closed the door, she watched Logan until he disappeared into the night. If he'd taken one step toward her, she knew she wouldn't have turned him away.

Her admission startled her. "I've really done it now, cat, the very thing I swore not to. I've gotten involved." She made sure the door was securely locked.

"It was the damn kiss," she said to Casanova as she toweled him dry. "I know, I know, you don't understand why he did it, but I do. He thought he'd scare me away." She set a wildly squirming cat on the bed, then quickly dried herself and changed her nightshirt. Shivering, she crawled between the covers, pulled Casanova next to her and began to scratch his stomach. He vibrated loudly with ecstasy.

"Logan needs help, Sir Cat, whether he knows it or not."

That damn, wonderful kiss had been a turning point. There'd been something in it that gave her hope. "Crazy, isn't it, Casanova?"

Maybe it was time she pulled her head out of the sand and took control of her life. She'd learned a lot in the past year. She'd learned to accept the loss of her family and friends. She'd faced public shame and disgrace. All she'd been through should have made her strong. Instead, she'd wallowed in self-pity, become crippled by hurt feelings and things, she realized now, she could never change. "I'll know when it's the right time and then I'll tell Logan every-thing."

Avery glanced at the clock. It was four-thirty in the morning and she was wide awake. Early hours and five-hour nights had become so ingrained in her in past months that she couldn't get used to sleeping like normal people. She folded her hands behind her head and stared at the ceiling. Rain still pummeled the roof like a thousand angry fists. Then those fists were hers and she beat back her demons until they disappeared. She was suddenly, and for the first time, crying for herself and that part of her she'd lost.

That kiss, she thought in disgust, then smiled dreamily, *it's changed everything.*

LOGAN STOOD at his bedroom window drying his hair and watching the window of the little house. When the lights went out, he turned away. What was the matter with him? Since the moment she arrived, his old heart had been tripping over itself.

Now he'd involved her in his problems, problems with no solution. He turned back to the window and his gaze moved to the buildings beyond. It didn't matter that it was too dark to see anything but outlines. He knew every inch of this place. Every tree. Every corner. He stayed by the window, watching until he was sure nothing moved that wasn't supposed to.

He threw the damp towel over the back of a chair and crawled naked into bed. Not very long ago he couldn't have cared less what happened to him. He'd only been going through the motions of living. Actually, he admitted, he might even have had a death wish—marking time, waiting for whatever force was turning his life upside down to claim him. But now he couldn't ignore what was happening. Closing his eyes, pretending that the acts of vengeance and violence no longer mattered, wasn't possible.

Whatever it took, he had to make sure Avery didn't

become a target in the crosshairs of whoever was trying to destroy him. He closed his eyes and, despite all his problems, smiled.

The day she'd walked into his life, everything had changed.

CHAPTER EIGHT

AVERY SAT ON THE TOP RAIL of the fence, watching in fascinated silence as Logan worked. He was astride Possum, looking impossibly big on the dainty dappled gray she'd fallen in love with. At one end of the enclosure were three cows, one just a calf. It was this calf that Possum was concentrating on. Every time it bawled and tried to reach its mother's side, Possum blocked its path.

The cow was more cunning than her offspring. She would fake a hop in one direction, then immediately jerk around to head in the other. But Possum outsmarted both cow and calf and kept them separated. While all this was going on, Logan sat perfectly still, never moving the reins to guide the horse. Logan and Possum seemed to be of one mind.

Avery almost lost her balance when Tanner climbed up on the railing next to her. "How does Possum know when the cow or calf is going to move?" she asked him. "She seems to know before they do."

"In a way she does. That's what Logan teaches horses—to read their minds." He grinned. "I'm serious. Watch the cow. She'll give her calf a signal, a move of her head, a twitch of her tail. That's why Possum's watching both of them so closely and why Logan has her slowly moving toward the cow."

Avery listened intently but kept her gaze on Logan. His hat was pulled low over his forehead, shading his eyes from the sun. There was a sensual quality in the way he sat so relaxed in the saddle, moving like an appendage of the horse, instead of a rider.

"Eventually Possum will cut the calf from the cow, drive them apart and into separate pens. Or she might keep the calf away while it's roped and tended to."

The scene brought back early childhood memories of Saturday mornings spent glued to the television with her sister, watching Westerns in breathless excitement.

Avery swallowed. She was experiencing that same breathless stir of excitement watching Logan.

"...expertly trained," Tanner continued, unaware he'd lost his audience for a moment. "A quarter horse can just about do his job without a rider. Night Rider's like that."

Avery made an effort to follow Tanner's conversation. "Night Rider?"

"A stud worth a bloody fortune, more so because he was bred, raised and trained by Monahan Farms. Most of our breeding stock comes out of him. Jamie named him after some old TV show he was crazy about." Tanner gave a long sad sigh before he went on. "Possum's a young horse and she's smart. She's going to bring in a hefty profit when Logan's finished training her."

"Hefty profit? Do you mean he's going to sell her?" Avery couldn't hide her dismay.

"That's what we do, Avery. Raise, train and sell horses."

Logan rode over and caught the last part of their conversation. He and Tanner shared an amused look before he said, "It'll be a while before she's ready to go on the market, though."

Avery stroked Possum's nose, then pulled a bag of carrots from her pocket and fed her some. Logan glanced over at Casanova, sitting expectantly on the fence post, his tail swishing back and forth and his bright eyes fixed on Avery.

"I think he's jealous, Tanner," Logan said, gesturing at the cat.

"The way he's taken to her, I'd be really worried if he was black," Tanner replied. "You don't need any more bad luck."

"Among other things," Logan said cryptically as he reined Possum around and started back toward the center of the paddock.

Avery gave an inward sigh. It had been almost two weeks since the night of the thunderstorm, and with each passing day Logan had put a little more distance between them. There were times when she wondered if he regretted the kiss. He'd said he hadn't, but she wondered if his explanation about Becky was really just his own rationalization. He was a hard man to read, she thought as she watched him ride.

Tanner gave Avery a firm poke in the ribs to get her attention. "I see you finally got yourself a decent pair of boots."

"Logan bought them." The words were out before she could stop them. She couldn't look at Tanner.

"Good for him."

"He said he wouldn't teach me how to ride in tennis shoes." She tried to keep the pride out of her voice as she glanced down at her beautiful black leather boots.

"You look pretty nifty in that hat, too."

She glared at him, knowing full well Tanner wanted her to say Logan had bought that for her, also. She refused, even though it was the truth.

"Keeps the sun off your face."

"Stop it, Tanner."

"Hey, it looks good on you. Just the right size, too. The straw's a summer hat—you'll need a good felt one for winter."

"If I'm still here then," she mumbled, and kept her eye on Logan and Possum.

"What's this? Look at him now, Avery. Hadn't you wondered why he never rode? And didn't you think it odd that a veterinarian, an animal lover like my brother, had no animals around except for a beat-up old cat and a few horses? Now he's back to riding and training. Just yesterday he asked me if old man May's bitch had had her litter of yellow Labs. He's always admired that dog, and when Jamie wanted one, all May's pups were promised, so they found Blackie."

"He won't let me help him."

"He's proud and thinks he can do everything himself. That's not just a big-brother thing, either—it's Logan. I envy him sometimes. For as long as I can remember, he's taken care of the weak and injured. It didn't matter whether it was animal or human. When we were just kids, he'd stay up all night with a sick bird or beat the stuffings out of the town bully for picking on someone. Then he'd patch up the bully. Logan has always known exactly what he wanted to be. I don't believe there's ever been any other profession for him but what he's doing."

"What about Pierce?"

Tanner frowned. "Pierce would do anything Logan

did. They were always in a kind of competition with
each other. Or at least Pierce was with Logan. Logan
just one-upped my brother at everything without trying.''

"They're not close like you and Logan?"

"Pierce is different. He's quiet. Dad says it's because he has a special talent. Still, he's hard to get a
handle on sometimes." Tanner shrugged. "And
there's the rivalry between the two—at least there
used to be. Lately they just seem to deliberately stay
out of each other's way. Pierce was furious when Logan pulled out of the clinic and left him to handle it
alone.''

Avery kept her eyes on Logan and Possum as they
worked the cattle. "Is Pierce married?"

"No. Why the sudden interest in Pierce?"

"Curiosity. What about you?"

"Me what?" Tanner asked.

"You're not married?"

"God, no."

Avery heard the finality in Tanner's answer. Logan
happened to be close enough to overhear, and he said,
"Tanner doesn't have the discipline to settle with one
woman."

"Not," Tanner snapped back, "with so many to
choose from."

Logan reined Possum in closer to Avery. "As you
might have noticed, peewee here is the family ladies'
man. His escapades keep us amused."

"I'd settle down in a minute with the right woman.
Trouble is, she just hasn't found me yet."

"What about Jessie?" Avery asked.

Tanner was the first to speak. "Have you lost your
mind? She's like a sister." His eyes narrowed with a

suspicious gaze at Avery and his brother. "Okay, what's going on here?"

Logan sternly calmed Possum's impatience, then said, "Avery's playing detective. I suspect she's pumping you for information." He chuckled as he rode toward the center of the ring.

"Is that why you asked about Pierce?" Tanner queried.

"Yes."

Tanner's handsome face settled into a fierce scowl. "Pierce is family. He wouldn't hurt Logan."

The statement was written in stone and not to be broached again. Avery wasn't wearing blinders anymore. She knew all too well what family members, those you love and trust, could do.

Logan passed close again. "Ask her who she thinks is responsible for what's going on."

Tanner stared at Avery. "Jessie," she said.

Tanner nearly fell off the fence rail laughing.

She seriously considered pushing him.

"You're joking. You are, aren't you?"

"No. She had motive and opportunity."

Logan circled by them again. "I told you she was playing detective."

Avery wasn't about to back down. "She's always around or has just left before something happens. I've seen it for myself. She hates me. She blames me for your not wanting her at the ranch so often."

"That has nothing to do with you," Logan said.

"I don't think Jessie sees it that way."

"Wait a minute," Tanner said. "You've lost me. Jess has always hung around here. Now you're implying she's jealous of you in a..." Words seemed to fail him.

Avery sighed. "Female jealousy because she's hot for Logan? Is that what you mean?"

Tanner flinched. "Dammit, she's…she's a kid, for heaven's sake."

Avery wondered how two grown men could be so deaf, dumb and blind. "You two see her as a kid, a child, because she grew up here."

"You refer to her as a girl," Logan said. "Isn't that the same?"

"No." Avery sighed. "I call her a lot of things, but I don't see her with the same eyes as you and your family do. Believe me, she's a woman. A woman in love with you, Logan. She's also a liar, spoiled, possessive and, in my opinion, unbalanced."

Logan pulled Possum to a halt beside the fence. "High-strung. Quick-tempered. But you're right—she does lie to get what she wants."

"Logan, believe me, I know her type. I've seen it firsthand, and I think I know what she's capable of doing."

"How do you know?"

"Because," she said, "except for their sex, my brother and Jessie are interchangeable. David is Daddy's only son. The only boy in a house of women. Daddy's pride and joy. He was pampered, spoiled and handed everything without having to work for it or earn it. He turned into a selfish, irresponsible, manipulative liar. And that was on his good days." Avery knew she was saying too much, but her pain ran too deep for her to check her words. "It didn't take long for David to turn into a cheat and a thief, and no one saw it coming."

Suddenly she realized how much she'd given away. Her face paled. She looked from Logan to Tanner, then jumped off the fence and headed for her house. Casanova glowered at the men, then leaped after Avery.

Tanner broke the silence first. "She said, 'house of women'. Does that mean she has a sister?"

"What?" Logan was distracted. Another piece of the puzzle of Avery Jensen fell into place.

"If her sister is anything like Avery, I'd like to meet her."

Logan's scowl deepened. "Is that all you think about?"

"No. And I just asked. Besides, I'm feeling in need of a woman."

"Well, go visit one of your girlfriends in San Antonio, but stay away from Avery."

"Aha!" Tanner laughed as he hopped off the fence and headed in the direction of his truck. "Careful, Logan," he called over his shoulder. "She's not one of your injured birds."

But she was. Tanner just couldn't see it.

Logan rode Possum to the barn, where Benton and Raul met him. "Thanks for coming by. You're sure you're not skipping a class?"

Raul flipped his long ponytail over his shoulder. "Well, it was only welding shop. Teach says it's too hot to light the torches, so he don't check attendance to see who's cutting. Besides, it don't matter. You know we'd do anything to help you, Doc. Maybe we can prove to that hard-assed sheriff we're not scum like he believes. So what's the skinny?"

Logan grinned. They were trying to be tough, but down deep they were just kids that got a raw deal. "You're sure your parents don't mind that you're spending your nights here?"

Benton and Raul exchanged looks that spoke volumes. "Naw," Benton said. "My parents are drunks. They don't know much of what goes on after nine."

Raul shook his head. "My mom's got a new boyfriend. He and I don't see eye-to-eye, know what I mean? I think she'd just as soon I didn't come home when he's there."

Logan swallowed around the lump in his throat. "Avery's going into town later to do some shopping. Will you give Tony and Tom a call and tell them to keep an eye on her?"

Benton plucked a toothpick from behind his ear and applied it to his teeth. "You really think she might be in some kind of danger?"

"Well, the trouble started up again after she arrived, so yes," Logan said. "I think there's going to be more trouble. This time, I'd like to head it off, or at least find out where it's coming from."

Raul wiped his arm across his sweaty forehead. "Things have been really quiet around here since the garage thing."

"That's usually when it starts again. A lull, then something worth remembering."

Raul whipped out the cellular phone Logan had given him. He'd given one to each of the boys so they could keep him posted and in contact with each other. Raul checked to make sure it was charged, then slipped it back in his jeans pocket. "I'll make myself useful at the garage. She goin' to take the blue monster?"

Logan nodded.

"Doc, that old thing's like driving a tank."

"That's the idea." He could see Raul didn't fully understand, but it made him feel better knowing that

Avery was in the twenty-year-old truck constructed of heavy-duty steel than in the more modern plastic-and-fiberglass trucks.

"I'll check old blue over, make sure nothing's been fiddled with."

"I'd appreciate that, thanks."

"Sure, Doc."

Logan gave Possum's reins to Benton as he watched Raul swagger across the yard. Logan didn't know whether he was doing the right thing or not. Heaven knows he'd tried everything else. Except for the boys, Tanner was the only person who knew what he was doing. There was going to be hell to pay when his dad found out he'd been excluded. But Mac, though he would never admit it, was getting old. His blood pressure was too high and he was prone to losing his temper. And Pierce? Logan stared at the ground. He hadn't made up his mind on that score.

"You want me to wash her down, Doc?" asked Benton. "She sure enjoys it."

Lost in thought as he was, it took Logan a moment to return to the present. Benton was still beside him and talking about Possum. "I'd appreciate it. And yeah, you're right. She loves the water." He started to turn away. "How'd you do on the algebra test?"

Benton abandoned his impassive posturing as a wide, boyish grin split his face. "A solid C. Can you believe? I've never made a C in my life. Raul got a B plus. The teacher made a fuss over it. Read the grades out loud, set us up as some sort of example. I tell you, Doc, it was embarrassing."

Logan was amused but kept his expression bland. The boy was thrilled, not just with the grade but the attention. A few weeks back, Logan had come home after an emergency call to find all four boys at his kitchen table, surrounded by bags of chips, soft drink bottles and open textbooks. Avery was tutoring Benton and Raul in algebra, helping Tom with economics and quizzing Tony for a spelling test.

"She's good with numbers."

Logan agreed. Avery had whipped his office and accounts into order in no time. She'd even broached the subject of what he should do with his money, advising him on the wisdom of a diversified investment portfolio, retirement plan, setting up a living trust and doing some estate planning. She'd been so animated and wound up, she'd forgotten to be careful about hiding her past.

After Avery straightened out his billing and accounts, he'd been concerned she wouldn't have enough work to keep her busy. He'd been almost as happy as the boys when she'd offered to help them with their studies. And just to make sure she didn't have too much free time on her hands, he'd started classes of his own. He was teaching her to ride.

They'd fallen into a routine. Every morning after breakfast, they'd walk to the barn together. He'd taught her how to groom Possum, how to clean a stall, lay fresh hay and attach the feed bags. Avery was kind and gentle with the animals, and when she was completely comfortable around them, he showed her how to saddle a horse and take care of the tack. He'd prolonged those lessons as long as he dared without arousing her suspicions that he just enjoyed being close to her. Last week he'd started teaching her how to ride. It was a new experience, and he hadn't realized how much touching was involved.

Logan was surprised out of his entertaining

thoughts by the sound of Avery's voice. He stepped deeper into the shadow of the barn so he could follow her progress across the lawn without being seen. Halfway there, she was stopped by Raul. Her laughter floated like butterfly wings on the summer breeze, making Logan smile at his own poetic notions. She'd changed into a flower-sprigged sundress, and he thought it strange that the sight of her shoulders and arms brown from the sun could stir his desire so. Or maybe it was the sway of her hips or her shapely legs. Maybe it was just Avery and the whole package that had him ogling her like a teenager. But damn, he wondered if he'd ever get the opportunity for another kiss.

He watched the old blue truck back out of the garage, and grinned. For his own reasons, he hadn't wanted her to go to Haven. Instead, the first time she needed to shop, he'd driven her over to the unique emporium and general store at Willow Creek, a town thirty minutes away. He'd sensed she'd been relieved. Now that the trouble had started up again, however, he didn't want her driving that far and insisted she take the ten-minute trip to Haven.

He watched the truck as it moved slowly down the driveway. Before she came to a stop at the gate, she disappeared from view, shielded by a stand of oak trees. Logan felt the sickness in the pit of his stomach as he struggled to block out remembered sounds: a blast of an eighteen-wheeler's horn, a scream of tires, the unforgettable impact of metal on metal.

He forced himself to take a deep breath. It was blissfully quiet except for the familiar noises of horses in the stalls and Benton's off-key whistle. Logan opened his eyes, surprised to find Raul standing in front of him, his expression one of sympathy.

"I—I called Tom," the youth reported. "He's hanging out at his father's barbershop. And Tony's sitting outside the courthouse. They got a good view of Main Street. Those guys are slick as owl grease. Avery won't even know they're there."

AVERY HAD A FEELING she was being followed the moment she parked the truck and saw Tom in the side mirror. He was supposed to be in school. Then, to confirm her suspicions, she saw his reflection in a dress-shop window two blocks from where she'd parked. He was spying on her! It was the only explanation.

How a gangly, six-foot teenager wearing a neon-red western shirt embroidered with yellow roses, and jeans tight enough to choke off the blood supply to the lower body, thought he could be inconspicuous was beyond her. She was about to confront him when she caught sight of Tony across the street. He was trying to make himself small by leaning sideways against a traffic light post.

There was little doubt they were following her. But just to test her theory, she jaywalked across the street, then quickly stopped. Avery faked a fascination with a display of cordless power drills in the window of Lowe's Hardware. The vast expanse of glass was like a mirror and revealed Tom's and Tony's attempt at stealthy maneuvers.

She would have laughed aloud at their antics, the nods and hand signals, if her feelings hadn't been hurt. She'd thought she'd developed a good relationship with the boys and couldn't understand why they were tailing her.

Then it hit her. *Logan.* He must have put them up to it, but why?

She didn't have time to worry about it. Avery glanced at her watch, then looked around. Now she understood Logan's amusement when she'd asked for directions to find her way around Haven. He'd said all she had to do was stand in the middle of Main Street. Actually she didn't need to stand in the middle of the street, but simply stand *anywhere* for a good view of the whole place.

A rather ugly three-story limestone courthouse, rough-hewn and turreted, stood in the center of town on a shady parklike square. Simply by crossing from one side of the street to the other, Avery could see all the major shops, stores, bank buildings and offices in Haven. She was two blocks from JoAnn's Tea Room where she was to meet Rosemary in only a few minutes.

Let the boys have their fun. She started up the street, keeping track of them in the windows of the passing stores. By the time she reached the door of the tea room, she was ready to burst with laughter. As sleuths they had a long way to go.

Avery hadn't expected to face a crowd.

When she opened the door, the first thing she was aware of was the welcome rush of cool air. The second, as she stepped inside, was how crowded with women the place was and how suddenly and completely the cacophony of chatter stopped. All eyes turned in her direction, and after an uncomfortable silence, the talking resumed, but lower and more reserved. And even though most of the curious had turned their faces away, Avery was the center of attention.

After all she'd been through during the past year, that she'd be intimidated by a group of women was ridiculous. But the fact remained it was one of those dreadful moments, and her feet seemed riveted to the ground. When she sensed someone attempting to move past her, she couldn't budge.

"I thought better of Logan Monahan, I really did," the stranger said, "keeping a woman so openly. His mama, bless her sweet soul, must be rolling over in her grave."

The comment let Avery know she was an object of condemnation in this town. Her accuser, a silver-haired biddy leaning heavily on a cane, was accompanied by a somewhat younger woman.

Avery wanted to curl up and die, to slink away, but pride kept her back straight. She stepped aside to let the women pass, then said sweetly, "Excuse me."

"She's attractive in an overblown way, Stella," the old woman grumbled to her companion, "but has no breeding. Not like the Middleton girl."

Avery's chin went up. The remark was intended for her ears, but the old gal's voice carried to a few other people. Finally Avery spotted Rosemary and zigzagged her way among the tables. As she sat down, she could tell by Rosemary's expression that she was furious. Avery opened her mouth to say something, but couldn't. She picked up the water glass and drank.

"I'm so sorry, Avery," Rosemary whispered.

"Who was that woman?"

"Wilhelmina Bauer-Steiner." Rosemary glanced around the room, making no attempt to hide her disgust. Those still staring looked away guiltily. "I deliberately asked you to meet me here because it's never crowded at lunchtime. But there was a DRT chapter meeting—Daughters of the Republic of Texas—and all the old girls and their offspring showed up because of the Fiesta. That's in San Antonio. Don't look so confused. I don't understand it all myself."

Avery noticed the continued sideways looks. She touched Rosemary's arm and said, "Don't make things harder on yourself by sitting with me. I should leave. You can come by the ranch."

"Don't be ridiculous. Sit down. I wouldn't budge if they put dynamite under my chair. Oh, they can dislike me all they want. And they can talk behind my back, but they'll never dare do anything *outwardly* to anger me. I know it and they know I know it."

Avery chuckled and watched as Rosemary relaxed. "Why? Have you learned where all their skeletons are hidden?"

"No—their wallets. If I've learned anything, it's that the rich enjoy staying that way." She grinned at Avery's puzzled expression. "The sterling citizens of Haven were the ones who all but begged my husband to relocate his practice here. They had to have another doctor around in order to keep their insurance and Medicare ratings. When we agreed, the town fathers and ladies made certain promises for perks. It's the reason we were able to buy a house twice what we could afford and join the golf and country club. Do you honestly think any of these narrow-minded, so-called good people would have allowed a black fam-

ily in their inner circle any other way? I don't think
so.''

Avery didn't know what to say, then realized that
Rosemary didn't need or want her sympathy.
"How're Annie and Sugar?"

Rosemary smiled. "You're changing the subject,
but I don't mind. Actually, one of the reasons I
wanted you to meet me in Haven was to stop the
gossip. Avery, you've been really kind to me and especially to Annie. The calls checking up on Sugar and
calming Annie down, your understanding every time
we brought Sugar back for Logan to look at just because the dog whined... Well, Annie thinks you're
pretty great, and so do I. That's why I'm probably
going to make an ass of myself and tell you a few
things.

"You just can't keep going into Willow Creek and
Hamlet to do your shopping. I know it's all very silly,
but it's small-town rivalry. They snip and fight over
state funds, highway taxes, road repairs, educational
funding—and God forbid, football, baseball and basketball. It's like an ancient family feud, handed down
from one generation to another.

"So, when you don't shop in Haven, it's a slap in
their faces. You're on shaky ground as it is, with Jessie Middleton mouthing off. If you're going to continue working for Logan, for the Monahans' sake,
spend his money and yours in Haven and do it with
a smile. Take the old girls' hard looks, be gracious,
and they'll come around as they get to know you, but
for heaven's sake, give them a chance."

It all sounded so easy. But life, Avery's life, was
anything but that. The hollowness in the pit of her
stomach made her all too aware that, except for Logan

and his family, she was alone. Oh, she had Denise and talked to her when she could, but it wasn't like having her here.

Avery had come to trust Rosemary, not because of a few visits or the times they'd had to chitchat while Logan examined Sugar. No, she'd asked Logan, Tanner and Mac about Rosemary. They'd all had nothing but praise for her and her husband.

And it wasn't Rosemary's determination to develop a friendship that held Avery back and made her nervous. She was, she admitted, starved for female company, but could she afford it? Maybe she'd been standoffish as long as she dared without arousing suspicion. Rosemary was talking and Avery struggled to pay attention.

"And I'm going to give you another piece of advice—whether you take it or not is up to you. Be really careful around the Middletons. Jessie's out for your blood. And for all Ross's soft-spoken, good-old-boy manners, never forget that he's a tough customer. It wouldn't surprise me in the least if there was a sheet and hood at the back of his closet."

They ordered lunch and passed time by talking about Annie's escapades. It wasn't until Rosemary mentioned Jamie that Avery found an opening to ask, "Did you know Logan's wife very well?"

Rosemary made a face, started to say something, stopped, then shrugged as if it no longer mattered. "To be perfectly honest, I don't think anyone really knew Becky Monahan. Not outside her immediate family. She was always warm and gracious. She laughed and joked and she never let anyone stay a stranger. And there's no doubt she loved Jamie."

"I hear a *but* in your voice, Rosemary," Avery said.

"You want my honest opinion?"

"Of course."

"She was a big phony. Oh, her family has money. Her dad is Lillian Health and Life Insurance. They have all kinds of subsidiaries—companies, hospitals, medical supplies, international pharmaceuticals. Lillian is Mr. Middleton's wife and Becky's mother. From what I've heard, she was from one of those upper-crust Kentucky bluegrass families. You know what I mean—with champion racehorses and the derbies. That was Becky's life—the racing circuit. She'd leave for months at a time with her parents and a string of horses. Becky was a social animal. Logan never was. I could tell you stories, things I'd seen and heard her do, but this isn't the place. Just believe me that underneath all her Texas charm there was a viciousness. It was almost an unspoken rule—or at least, everyone who knew her, knew better than to cross her."

A sheriff's car rolled down Main Street and Avery watched its slow process. "If the Middletons have so much money, why is Ross a small-town sheriff?"

"It makes him a big fish in a little pond, instead of a minnow in a lake, doesn't it? From what I gather, he and his father don't see eye-to-eye. As for Lillian Middleton, the gossip is she's always on shaky ground. Drugs and alcohol. Still, I feel sorry for her. After Becky and Jamie were killed, they had to put her in a private sanatorium.

"Avery, I'm not a busybody by nature, even though I know I sound like one right now. But you need to know that there are strange undercurrents between the Middletons and Logan. Be careful.''

The warning set like a lump of stone in Avery's midsection. When they left the tea room, Rosemary grasped her arm. ''Jeff and I are going to the Hoot and Scoot tonight for a night out. Why don't you meet us there?''

Avery laughed. ''What's the Hoot and Scoot?''

''A country-and-western dance hall two blocks off Main Street. You can't miss it. Come on, Avery, it's fun. Have a few beers, dance a little. Mostly, we watch the people. It's a real show and lots of fun.''

''You mean a hoot?''

Rosemary chuckled. ''Jeff's getting good at the Texas two-step. He'll teach you.''

''I don't think—''

''Don't say no just yet. Think about it. Jeff and I will be there about seven, and I'll watch for you. Hey! Bring Logan. He could probably use a night out, too.''

Rosemary didn't give Avery time to refuse. She waved and headed in the direction of her car. Avery started toward the truck, telling herself she had absolutely no intention of going dancing. She crossed the street, so lost in the idea of maybe going out and having a little fun that she almost passed Logan's truck—and the sheriff leaning against the hood.

''Good afternoon, Avery.''

''Sheriff.'' She couldn't think of anything else to say, and rummaged around in her purse for the keys. Her heart started beating wildly. Thank heaven the heat could serve as an excuse for the perspiration dotting her forehead.

''Did you and Rosemary enjoy your lunch?''

"It was very nice." Where were the damn keys? Avery raised her hand to shade her eyes as she looked at Ross. The realization that he was curious enough to know where she was having lunch and who with almost made her physically sick. Then she reminded herself she'd seen him pass the tea room.

He couldn't have missed Logan's truck, either. Then there was the old lady and her daughter who'd stormed out in a huff. More than likely he'd run into them and gotten an earful.

"Is Logan with you?" Ross asked.

She continued digging for the keys. "No, he was working with the horses, and I had to go to the store." Logan had told her that Ross Middleton was a lot smarter than he allowed anyone to see, and Rosemary's warning was still fresh in her mind. Avery was afraid he could sense her nervousness, and made an effort to calm down.

"It's good that he's taking an interest in things again. We've been worried about him. I guess we have you to thank for that."

"Me?" Ross's words were full of understanding and sympathy, but she noticed his smile didn't reach his eyes.

"Sure. Logan's been in a slump since Becky and Jamie were killed. You show up and suddenly he's taking on clients, gone back to training horses. We were all concerned that he just might take it into his head to follow Becky."

Whatever his motive for the little chat, Avery couldn't afford to offend him. "Logan seems to be dealing with the pain."

"Well, you'd know better than most."

His words were innocent enough, but she didn't care for his insinuation. "I beg your pardon?"

"I mean, you see him every day. After the accident he wouldn't let anyone help him, not even his own family. And of course, there're all these acts of violence. I hope you're being careful. It'd be just awful if anything happened to you."

Suddenly Avery had the feeling he was playing a game, and it made her angry. Her fingers finally touched the cool metal of the keys. She yanked them out and started for the door. Ross beat her to it. He opened it and held it wide until she'd climbed in. She knew he was drawing his little drama out when he shut the door, then double-checked to see that it was secure. Avery started the engine, but it seemed he wasn't ready to let her go. His hand rested on the window ledge.

"Has Logan said anything about going to the Fiesta ball? He missed last year, and Jess was mighty upset when he said he wasn't going this year, either."

"Logan hasn't said anything about a ball to me."

Ross nodded and moved as if he was leaving, then hesitated and said, "By the way, where did you say you were from? I thought it was Houston, but I must have misunderstood you."

Avery slipped the truck into reverse. "I lived in Houston for a while before I came here."

He was walking beside the truck, stopped the oncoming traffic to allow her to back out. He laughed and waved at people in the first car. "So where exactly are you from?"

Avery glanced behind her, stalling for time, but he wasn't going to let her get away without an answer. "Seattle, Sheriff."

Ross whistled. "Ma'am, you're far from home." He smiled and continued, "If you haven't had time to apply for a Texas driver's license, I'd be happy to walk you over to the courthouse and see that the girls there take good care of you. We wouldn't want you breaking the law, now would we?"

"Absolutely not. And I thank you for the offer, but I believe I still have some time, and besides, I have to go to the store."

"If you need help, don't be shy about asking."

"Thank you." She smiled. "It was nice chatting with you." She backed out into the street. Her nerves were in shreds. Her foot trembled and her muscles quivered so badly she didn't think she had enough strength to push down on the gas pedal.

Ross Middleton reminded her of a bulldog with a bone. He wasn't about to let go until he'd stripped it clean and exposed the marrow. She felt like that bone.

CHAPTER NINE

AVERY GLANCED in the rearview mirror to check on the grocery bags in the bed of the truck, then returned her attention to the road ahead. Grocery shopping had never been one of her favorite chores, but you couldn't tell it from the number of bags. The fact that she didn't have a clue as to what all she'd bought was testimony to her state. The sheriff had made her more than nervous; he'd scared her. Ross Middleton *knew* something.

Avery's hands tightened on the steering wheel. She wondered how easy she'd made his job. She'd always been a lousy liar, and that flaw might very well have put the sheriff in the catbird seat.

Maybe it was time, she told herself. Time to talk to Logan before Ross or anyone else did first. But the thought of what she'd say or how she'd even say it nearly drove her crazy.

As the miles rushed past, she wavered back and forth over whether or not to tell him. How would he react? What would his family think? They'd taken her in on trust and without a lot of questions.

Coming upon a sharp, dipping curve in the highway, she saw an oncoming car. It was straddling the center white line, flying at her like a bat out of hell. With her heart in her throat, Avery automatically slowed, then realized the car wasn't going to return to its lane. She jerked the truck to the right, then fought for control to keep the wheels on the road, instead of the soft shoulder.

The black Corvette convertible zipped by, barely missing her. As it blew past, she was able to register the blur of a white face and flying red hair. Avery spent a moment gathering her shattered nerves. Then, her heart still pounding, she lifted her foot off the brake and applied it to the gas. She glanced in the rearview mirror and fear lodged in her throat. The Corvette made a wild U-turn in the middle of the highway and began tearing after her, dust and gravel spewing in its wake.

An old truck and a brand-new sports car. Some contest. Avery watched as it came up behind her, close enough that she steeled herself for the slam of metal against metal. Instead, the Corvette veered sharply to the left and was suddenly beside her. Avery looked at Jessie Middleton's angry face and watched as the sports car inched closer.

The scare she'd just experienced and the dangerous game the girl was playing was enough for her to forget caution and lose control. For over a year she'd held every emotion in close check. Suddenly it was like someone had thrown a switch inside her.

Avery eased the truck onto the shoulder of the road and watched as the Corvette spun to a stop directly in front of her. She waited until Jessie was out of the car and walking toward the truck before she opened the door and got out herself. She didn't give the girl time to speak or vent her rage.

"You stupid little bitch! If you want to join your sister, that's your business, but have the decency to do it alone. Don't take any innocent bystanders with you.''

"It's all your fault Logan won't go to the Fiesta ball. He promised me months ago that he would.''

"Grow up, Jessie. Maybe he's just not in the mood for a ball.''

"No, he said he didn't think you'd enjoy it.''

Avery was momentarily stunned. ''But he never…'' She didn't finish as she realized Logan must have felt, for whatever reason, that he needed an excuse and she was the most expedient. She also realized something else. Jessie's frequent appearances at the ranch had all but stopped.

"Everything was just fine until you came here.''

"Dammit, Jessie, open your eyes. Nothing's been fine or right at the ranch for a long time. You need help, and if you don't get it soon, you're going to turn everybody who cares against you.''

"How dare you speak to me like that!''

"Oh, stop acting like a prima donna. Grow up.''

White faced and speechless, Jessie started to turn away, but Avery grabbed her arm. ''Listen to me, Jessie. If you don't make an effort to change, you're going to do something really crazy. You're going to step over the line, and when you do, you'll never be able to repair the damage you've done. What's worse, by then you'll be so far gone you'll let others take the blame for all the bad things you do. You'll destroy them, and ultimately yourself.''

She dropped Jessie's arm and watched as the girl ran to her car. Then Avery sagged against the side of the truck, feeling spent and sick. Well, she'd done it now. What had happened to her promise to stay as far away as possible from this family's troubles? And of all things, to start interfering with the sheriff's sister. *Cool move, Avery.* If she'd wanted to self-destruct, she'd gone about it in the fastest way possible.

A bead of sweat rolled down the side of her face, making her aware of the heat and the sun, and the fact that she was standing by the side of the highway. She crawled back into the truck and drove away.

The ranch had that deserted feel to it. No one stirred or showed up to help her haul the groceries in the house. She called out for Logan, then the boys, but there was no response. Later, as she was putting everything away, she spotted the note from Logan by the telephone. He'd been called away on an emergency. Avery held the paper in her hand and wondered if Jessie had talked to Logan before he left. She'd been coming from the direction of the ranch.

Casanova hopped up on the table. "If you're looking for chocolate, pal," she said, "forget it. But I do have some kitty treats for you." She opened a box and set out a few on a plate. "It says right here on the package that cats love these. You're a cat, so…"

Avery watched as Casanova sniffed them, then turned his nose up in disdain and walked away. She shook her head, then went to the fridge, poured herself a cold soft drink and collapsed in a chair at the kitchen table. Maybe Casanova wasn't really a cat. Maybe he was just a very small man in an ugly fur coat.

As if aware he was the subject of her thoughts, Casanova jumped up on her lap and pressed his nose into her chin. "Are you trying to sweet-talk me? Don't think you can twist me around your finger…foot…paw." Avery reached for her purse and as Casanova watched, she opened it and pulled out a giant bag of M&M's. The cat pounced and she just managed to yank it out of his reach. "One. It's all you get, and we won't tell anyone."

He protested.

"No, that's all." She carefully tore open the bag and peeked inside. "What color?" He howled and she set a red candy on the table then watched as he pushed it around. "Trying to make it last, are you? I know that trick, but I've got news for you—it doesn't work. When they're gone, they're gone."

Avery poured the rest of the candy in a jar, tightened the lid then placed it on top of her purse. She planted her elbows on the table, rested her chin on folded hands and watched the cat play.

"What am I going to do, Casanova? Logan's got this blind spot where Jessie's concerned and I think she's the cause of everything. She's always hanging around, lusting after Logan and giving me the evil eye. I know how jealousy and envy can eat away at a person until all they can think about is striking back.

"Jessie Middleton poisoned those horses, cat. Maybe the girl didn't realize how disastrous the results would be. Or maybe she did. Logan hurt her feelings. She struck back. When Logan showed the least bit of interest in me, Jessie took her temper out on the one thing that would hurt Logan equally—she destroyed Jamie's belongings. And do you know, Casanova, I believe she's been snooping around in my quarters.

"Jessie thinks there's something between me and Logan." Avery laughed, then immediately sobered. "It's not true, you know. Oh, I'll admit he did kiss me, and by the way, he's a great kisser." She absently played with Casanova's tail until he swatted her hand away.

"He's kind, too. But I get this feeling he's always laughing at me—not unkindly, though. And I'll grant you I like his sense of humor—his laugh, his warmth and the look in his eyes when he sees me. He's patient, Casanova. The way he's been teaching me to ride. 'Course, it's kind of nice the way he touches me," she said dreamily. "Not that he's out of line. But his hands do linger around my waist when he helps me into the saddle. I wonder—"

She stomped on the brakes of her imagination. "Just because he's sexy and I'll admit I'm attracted doesn't mean I'd act on that attraction. And it doesn't mean I have any deeper feelings for Logan than genuine concern and simple friendship. You believe me, don't you?"

Apparently not. Casanova leapt off her lap and crossed the room. Laughing, Avery picked up her purse and the jar. "We'd better hide this before Logan catches us."

Avery had just stepped on the porch of her house when she heard a car. She turned in time to see Logan's clinic truck round the corner of the house and stop. Benton and Raul piled out, and Avery waved in their general direction, unlocked the door and pushed it open. Casanova streaked between her legs, almost making her stumble.

"Ouch!" Casanova had just slashed at her ankles with his sharp claws. "What's the matter with you?"

Suddenly the cat began to growl. It was a deep sound, one she'd never heard him make before. His back arched and his fur stood on end. What on earth had happened to turn him into this spitting, vicious animal?

Avery moved quickly around him, then headed for the kitchen. When she reached the end of the counter, Casanova pounced on one of her feet. "Listen, you…" She tried to shake him off her foot, when from the center of the room she heard an ominous rattling sound. She looked, and what she saw horrified her.

A snake was coiled tightly in the middle of her living room, no more than a few feet away.

She screamed, loud and long, and at the same instant vaulted onto the counter. Casanova joined her, spitting and hissing. The snake's tail vibrated like a buzz saw. She screamed again.

THE FIRST SCREAM went through Logan like a cold blade of steel. He dropped what he was doing and charged in the direction of Avery's quarters, Benton and Raul at his heels. The scream came again as he hit the porch. He yanked the door open and saw immediately the cause of her terror.

"It's okay," he said calmly as he inched his way around the wall. "The snake's only upset by your inhospitality."

Avery took a long, shaky breath. "Not funny." The reptile turned its head in Logan's direction. "Be careful, Logan."

"Tap the counter with your foot. Get its attention."

"I can't, Logan. I can't move." She saw the boys standing in the doorway. "Don't come in here. There's a monstrous snake."

Their snickers weren't appreciated. She couldn't turn away, and watched in fascinated horror as Logan doffed his Stetson, took aim and threw it so it covered the snake.

Raul rushed forward, held the hat down, then tipped it to one side. He reached inside and pulled the snake out by his head. "It's just a youngster."

Avery nearly fainted. "Get it out of here." Her voice shook and she watched until she was sure the door was closed behind the boys before she collapsed on the counter.

Logan pushed the cat aside and gathered Avery in his arms. She was pale and cold, and he could feel her heart racing. All he could do was hold her until she stopped trembling. Slowly, she quieted.

Avery took a deep breath and leaned back. "That was one of the worse moments of my life."

"You've had others?"

He'd intended to make her laugh, she was sure, but his question hit its mark. If he only knew. Looking into his face, she noticed his brow was furrowed with worry and his mouth was a tight line of concern. But his eyes said something entirely different. She couldn't turn away and watched as his lips slowly lowered to hers.

It was a kiss that started out soft and tender, then quickly turned hungry. She didn't bother disguising her desire, and couldn't if she'd wanted to. His fingers tightened, holding her still as the kiss heated up. Desire flowed through her like liquid fire. She spread her hands across his back and pulled him closer. Muscles bunched under her touch. She would have let him take her there on the counter if he hadn't come to his senses first.

"This isn't the way it should happen." Logan's voice was rough with emotion. She made a beautiful picture sitting on the edge of the counter with her dress pulled up to her thighs and her legs locked around his waist. His words shattered the moment. Reality and embarrassment made her face flush with guilt. When she attempted to move, he wouldn't let her and said, "It wasn't as crazy a thing to happen as you might think."

"I didn't say it was," she snapped, trying to regain some of her dignity.

"But you were thinking it."

"No, actually I was wondering what it would be like to make love with you." She could see that she'd surprised and pleased him with her honesty. There was no coy protesting or apologizing.

"I've been wondering the same thing lately. But trust me, Avery, this isn't the place where I'd want something so special to happen."

"All right. I won't take your reluctance as an outright rejection."

Logan smiled. "Please don't. I've wanted you for a long time. But when it happens, I don't want to be rushed." He kissed the curve of her neck. "And I don't want a couple of teenage boys bursting in on us with a skinned snake. Or—"

"Jessie." Everyday life had a harsh way of insinuating itself and throwing cold water on the flame of desire. "She put the snake in here, Logan."

"You forgot to close your door and it crawled in, drawn by the cool. It's ridiculous to accuse Jess."

"Is it? Not only did I close the door, but it was locked."

"Jess wouldn't deliberately hurt someone."

Avery controlled her rush of anger and set about to convince him. "Is she afraid of snakes?"

"I've taught her not to be, but to be careful."

"Does she know how to handle them?"

"Yes."

"She was here before you got the emergency call, wasn't she?"

"Yes, but she left when I did."

"I met her on the highway, Logan, and Jessie was coming from the direction of the ranch. That was only about an hour before you and the boys drove up."

"We left around noon."

Avery shrugged. "She was coming from the ranch. Why would she go back if you weren't there?"

"I don't know. You say that was about an hour before I came back?"

"That's right. She almost ran me off the road in that sports car of hers. If that wasn't bad enough, she came back after me until I pulled off the highway. She was furious, blaming me because you wouldn't take her to the Fiesta ball."

"I told her I didn't want to put on a tuxedo and go to it." Logan touched Avery's face, stroked her cheek. "Damn her. She scared you? What else did she say?"

"She blames me, of course, for your inattentiveness lately."

"I've tried to discourage her from spending time here. Not because I thought she had anything to do with what's been going on, but because it's unhealthy. I know Jess isn't stable—she faked suicide a couple of times when she was younger because she didn't get her way. She's obsessed with Becky and Jamie's deaths and can't let go."

There was suddenly more than distance between them as Logan stepped back enough for Avery to pull her dress down. Avery wasn't about to stop, though. "I'm telling you, Logan. Her 'obsession' with Becky and Jamie is a sham. It's *you* she's obsessed with. Jamie is just an excuse to keep you where she wants you—in the past. If you learned to cope with your grief, then your connection with her would be severed. She knows this, Logan, and so should you."

"Of course I know that. I gave your suggestion some serious thought. You were right. Every time some disaster happened, Jessie had been here. And yes, she usually left in one of her dark moods. Avery, she comes and goes as she pleases. She has keys to the big house and this one.

"But it's still hard to believe she hates me so much. She was just a child, a baby really, when I married Becky. She lived with us when her parents were traveling."

"She doesn't hate you, Logan—that's the problem. She loves you and won't let you love anyone else." He was so silent and pale Avery hated to continue. "Logan, Jamie's dog would have gone with her willingly, wouldn't he?"

Logan looked like he might be sick. "Avery, I—"

"She's like a bomb waiting to explode, and I'm concerned for you."

"I've got things under control."

She gave a weary laugh. "Sure you do. Like having Tom and Tony follow me today."

"I thought their bragging was a little too good to be true. How quickly did you spot them?" Avery told him about the red shirt, and he chuckled.

"Why did you do it, Logan?"

"Everything has been aimed at me. But I had a bad feeling things were going to change." Logan stroked

Avery's cheek. "Are you upset with me for having you followed?"

"No. I just wish you'd told me." She debated whether to tell him Ross Middleton had stopped her, then decided it was best not to. Logan probably already knew, but she didn't want to lie about what the sheriff had said.

"How were Tom and Tony keeping in touch with you?" She shook her head when he pulled out a cellular phone from his pocket.

Suddenly she remembered Rosemary's invitation. An evening away from the ranch sounded too good to pass up. "Rosemary invited me, and you, too, if you want, to meet her and Jeff at the Hoot and Scoot this evening. I'd like to go."

"I don't think so, but you go. Really, take the truck. Have a good time. You need an evening away from this place."

"It wouldn't hurt for you to have a little fun, either. Come with me, Logan. I'm asking you on a date."

Logan picked his hat up off the floor and tapped it against his thigh. "The Hoot and Scoot isn't exactly what I had in mind for our first date. Enjoy yourself, Avery."

AVERY USED THE DAMP paper napkin wrapped around her beer bottle to wipe her forehead, then she took a long swallow of the cold liquid. She watched Jeff weave his way toward the bar for a refill of their drinks, then turned to Rosemary. "I'm afraid he's going to have some bruised toes in the morning."

"Nonsense. You were doing good out there."

"He's really into this country-and-western dancing."

Rosemary laughed. "For a man who never danced a step in his life until we moved here, yes." She gazed lovingly at her husband. "There's not much nightlife in Haven, so Jeff bought into the cliché, 'if you can't beat 'em, join 'em.' And it's good for him. It's good for us. A doctor's life is hard work—long hours, disappointments and full of senseless tragedy. Jeff's the best at what he does. That means he brings his work home and frets and worries. We come here once a week and the tensions fall away. I don't mind telling you it helps our sex life, too."

Avery was suddenly so envious she could have cried. To hide her feelings, she looked away. The Hoot and Scoot was as big as a city block. It was dim, but not so dim that you couldn't see a handsome face across the room. Millions of tiny colored lights rotated across the mirrored ceiling and reflected down on the dance floor. The live band was so loud the building actually shook.

Avery felt Rosemary elbow her in the ribs, and turned to her.

"Take a look at the end of the bar," she said.

Avery did and was surprised to see Logan. For a moment she couldn't breathe. Maybe it was the lighting or the way he was standing with one boot propped on the brass railing of the bar. Maybe it was the jeans and the form-fitting shirt. Or it could have been the way his Stetson was tilted low on his forehead. Of course, it might be the fact that he was staring straight at her. More than likely, all those things made her heart skip a couple of beats. He was so damn sexy. She noticed she wasn't the only one staring at him.

Rosemary's elbow again made contact with her ribs. "He's going to come over."

Avery felt like a kid as she watched Logan set his beer on the bar.

"Look. Look. I told you."

"Rosemary, please. You're going to break my ribs."

"Oh, boy. I always thought he was a hunk. Look at the way he moves. I wonder if it has something to do with riding horses. Maybe I could talk Jeff into taking lessons."

"Stop it. He'll hear you."

"I don't care." Rosemary laughed merrily.

Avery didn't, either. She couldn't take her eyes off Logan, and as he drew closer she didn't even try to pretend she wasn't happy to see him. The band began to play a slow song, and when he reached her he held out his hand.

He led her to the dance floor and she floated into his arms. "Jeff's been teaching me the cotton-eye Joe and the Texas two-step, but I'm not very good."

"Relax. I don't do anything fancy."

He held her lightly, and she moved effortlessly in his embrace. "I didn't know what to wear." She was babbling and took a deep breath. "I'm glad you came," she said. "What made you change your mind?"

Logan's eyes met hers and he smiled. She was wearing a soft denim dress that buttoned up the front and the new boots he'd bought her. "The thought of you in someone else's arms."

She swallowed, overwhelmed with happiness. "I'm glad."

"You've said that."

"This is silly. I'm as tongue-tied as a teenager and…"

"And feeling a bit awkward?"

"Yes."

"Like you were on your first date?" he offered.

"Yes."

"You keep saying yes in that breathy voice, and I'll have to throw you over my shoulder and take you home."

"What would people think?"

"That I was a lucky man. But right now all I really want to do is hold you close and dance."

They danced through four songs, and it didn't matter in the least that a couple were fast tunes. Avery closed her eyes and drifted along on a cloud of her own fantasies, content just to be held and to feel his body against hers. Not for the first time, she wondered how it would be making love with Logan. Her imagination jumped into full swing and she gazed into his eyes. What she saw made her smile. If there was ever a man who could read her mind, it was Logan.

"You think it's amusing?" he whispered. "That I can't hide how much I want you?" His breath caressed her ear.

There was no need to ask what he meant. She could *feel* it. Logan was in a dangerous mood. "I'm not laughing," she said. "I'm in the same fix, only with *me,* the feeling isn't so obvious."

"Oh, I don't know about that." He lightly touched her neck and felt the pulse that pounded in time with her heart. "I think…"

Whatever he was about to say hung between them. Avery saw the way his gaze shifted over her shoulder. His body language changed. She glanced back and, with a sinking heart, saw Jessie and Ross dancing toward them.

Logan cursed under his breath, whirled Avery around and reversed direction. The ploy didn't work. Ross was a master at dance-floor tag and at cutting in.

Avery was so busy trying to keep from stepping on Logan's feet she didn't pay much attention. Then she saw a hand tap Logan's shoulder and heard Ross's voice.

"Do you mind, buddy?"

Avery immediately protested. "Really, I'm a dreadful dancer."

"It didn't look like that to me," Jess said, the snap in her voice a good barometer of her mood. Foul.

Before Avery could protest again, Jessie wedged her body between them and Ross took hold of Avery's arm and swung her into his embrace. She barely managed to control her distaste.

It was an odd tableau, the two couples standing in the center of the dance floor, eyeing each other. She could feel the tension between the men as clearly as she felt Ross's arms lock around her.

Logan removed a long-neck beer bottle from Jess's fingers and gave it to Ross. "You're a fool for letting her drink."

"Hey, I watch out for Jess."

"And when you're not around and she's here at night, what then?" It didn't take an expert to see that Jess had had more to drink than she should.

"No one," Ross said, "is going to hurt my little sister." He shifted the beer bottle to the hand on Avery's back, then waltzed her away.

Avery deliberately stepped on his foot. "Slow down," she said. "I told you this is all new to me."

"Forgive me, sweetheart, but I get riled when he

interferes in how I run my life and my family's. I've always protected those I love."

An icy finger of dread touched her spine. She stepped on Ross's foot again, this time harder. "Sorry."

"Maybe Logan doesn't care, but I know Jess is at the ranch more than she should be. I blame him for that. He shouldn't lead her on."

"What?" She sensed danger. Ross was too cunning to be openly combative. It was a bad sign. Then she realized something more frightening. Ross, like Jessie, had had far too much to drink.

"Well, look at him, honey." He turned so Avery could see Logan and Jessie. The girl had glued herself to Logan like a leech.

"Jess keeps telling me she's a grown woman and I should butt out of her life, but I tell you I don't like the way he's all over her. Logan killed one sister. I won't see Jess follow the same road, or you, for that matter."

Avery was speechless. But only for a moment. Whatever she said, she knew she had to be careful. "What are you talking about?"

"Don't tell me you haven't realized it yet. I mean, you go through his books, do his billing, don't you? You see the money he's got. Logan killed Becky. Oh, he wasn't driving the car—that would have put him in danger. But he was responsible for Becky's hysterical frame of mind. My sister was a good driver. Hell, she could handle a trailer loaded with horses like a seasoned truck driver. And she worshiped Jamie. Becky would never put him in danger. Logan said she was upset. Hell, she had to be scared out of her mind not to see that eighteen-wheeler coming."

With every turn, Avery tried to keep track of Logan and Jessie. "You're the sheriff, Ross. If you believe Logan had more to do with Becky's death, then why didn't you do something about it?"

Ross stopped and glared at her. Avery wanted to shrink away from the look in his eyes, but managed to meet his gaze steadily. She was being manipulated, lied to with innuendos, but she couldn't figure out what Ross hoped to gain by it. But he had made a mistake. A year ago she'd been manipulated, lied to and made a fool of by a pro. She wasn't as gullible now.

"I'd like to sit down," she said.

Avery pried herself from his arms. Logan and a sullen Jessie met them on the way to the table. When they joined Rosemary and Jeff, the men shook hands with Jeff and exchanged a few pleasantries.

But the tension was so palpable that Rosemary and Jeff immediately headed for the dance floor. Avery sat down and felt like prey being eyed by a couple of vultures. She glanced at Logan, and the shake of his head was barely noticeable.

He leaned toward her and said in a low voice, "I'm leaving." Avery started to say something, but he squeezed her shoulder to keep her quiet. "If I stay there's going to be trouble. I don't want you in the middle of it."

She could have told him she already was, but before she could open her mouth, he was gone, with Jessie on his heels.

"I don't mind telling you, seeing the two of them going off together just doesn't sit right with me."

Avery glanced around to find Ross standing right behind her. "Maybe you should keep her on a tighter rein,'' she said to him, ''and while you're at it, take that death trap of a car away from her before she kills herself.''

Avery knew she'd gone too far. Ross's eyes blazed with anger. Then he smiled. Avery shivered as he looked around, then leaned down and whispered, ''Have you told Logan yet that you're a jailbird who spent eight months in a Seattle jail for embezzlement?''

CHAPTER TEN

AVERY DIDN'T REMEMBER leaving the Hoot and Scoot.

She couldn't recollect walking to the parking lot or getting in the truck. She was aware she was on the highway and heading in the direction of the ranch. When she started shaking uncontrollably, she managed to pull carefully onto the shoulder of the road. Coming to a complete stop, she rested her forehead against the steering wheel and closed her eyes.

Ross had dropped his bomb and walked away.

She clearly remembered her panic; then dread had set in and she'd gone numb. Did anyone else know? Who was Ross going to tell? God, to have her past come out in such a way that would embarrass and humiliate Logan and the Monahans was unthinkable. She knew Ross was playing with her. He had every intention of telling Logan, and everyone else, but in his own time—and for his own reasons.

The relationship between the Monahans and the Middletons was as volatile as her own family's. Ross had let her know he hated Logan. Whatever friendship they'd once shared was over. In Ross's mind, Logan might as well have shot Becky in cold blood and gotten away with murder. Strange, she thought, that there never seemed to be any forgiveness within families. Everything was black or white, with no shades of gray.

Avery threw back her head and laughed hysterically. *What goes around, comes around.* Hadn't that been Dad's favorite saying? The memories of her father brought back all the humiliation she'd suffered. *What now?* she asked herself. She'd traveled full circle and there was nowhere else to run. She'd fled once and she couldn't do it again, not until Logan knew everything.

Avery drove slowly up the driveway, noticing as she did that the big house was dark. As she parked the truck next to the garage, she glanced at her watch and was amazed to see that an hour had passed since Logan left the Hoot and Scoot. She leaned against the side of the truck, trying to screw up the courage to wake him.

No, she couldn't bring herself to do it—at least not yet. She needed time to think through exactly what to say. But she knew.

The truth.

Her feet faltered as she neared the fork in the path. One direction and she would wake him. The other... She hung her head with shame and turned toward her house, berating herself as a coward with each heavy step. The thought of Logan's face when she told him was too much to bear, especially after the evening they'd spent. Maybe in the cold light of day she'd find the backbone.

Avery came to a stop on the top step, alerted by the sound of metal against metal. She immediately recognized the squeak as the chains holding the porch swing and turned in the direction of the darkened corner. A tall shadow rose and moved toward her. "Logan."

The moonlight captured his face and accentuated the sadness in his gaze. "You must think I deserted you, and I'm sorry I left like that. But believe me, Avery, if I'd stayed, the whole scene would have turned ugly." The back of his fingers caressed her cheek. "I know Ross when he gets on one of his mean, destructive drunks and it's not pretty."

Avery clasped his hand, closed her eyes and kissed the open palm. "It doesn't matter."

"Yes, it does. I had such plans for tonight. I'm sorry." Logan gathered her in his arms, tilted her chin up with a single finger so she was looking at him, and said, "But the night's not over, is it?"

"No," she whispered. She couldn't tell him now, not when all she saw was the heat of desire in his eyes. He murmured her name and stroked her hair before she felt his lips touch hers. She opened up to the pressure of his persuasive tongue and savored the sweetness of the kiss. Avery swayed toward him, threaded her fingers through his hair, pulled his mouth closer and abandoned herself to passion.

Logan tangled his hands in her thick black mane of hair, then pulled back and rested his forehead against hers. "Let's go."

She grasped his hand and began pulling toward her front door. Logan balked. "What's the matter?" she asked.

He shook his head, unable to hide his aversion to the place. "Not here. Never here."

He led Avery across the yard to the main house. He kissed her in the kitchen until her knees gave way, then scooped her up in his arms and carried her up the stairs.

Just inside the bedroom door, he set her on her feet. This time it was Avery's turn to balk. It didn't matter if he hadn't been in love with his wife. This had been their room, where they'd made love.

Reading her mind, Logan said, "The master bedroom is there." He pointed at another closed door. "Everything in this room either belongs to my family or was bought after Becky died."

"Thank you for that."

Logan began kissing her, all the while inching them closer to the bed. "You don't realize it, but without even trying you make me happy," he murmured, then stood back to look at her.

She was bathed in the moonlight coming through the window and looked like a goddess. He reached out and began to unbutton the front of her dress.

Avery's breath caught each time his fingers brushed her flesh. She knew she was in love with Logan. The realization was stunning. She should stop him and tell him the truth about her past before they were both in too deep.

His lips nibbled at the curve of her neck. She felt his warm breath on her skin as the dress was pushed off her shoulders and fell soundlessly to the floor. Avery's hands came up to stop him, but Logan grasped them, misunderstanding. He said, "Let me undress you." Everything she wanted to say died a quick death.

When her bra and panties followed the dress and she was left standing before him with nothing on but her boots, she glanced down.

"Is there a graceful way to get out of these?" She

was vividly reminded of her struggles to get the new boots off earlier—the one-footed hops around the room or the wrestling match on the floor, all accompanied by grunts and groans.

Logan laughed, then gently pushed her backward onto the bed. He removed her boots easily. With that same skill he shucked his own boots, then stripped. But instead of joining her on the bed right way, Logan stood over her, his gaze feasting on every curve. "You're beautiful." His voice was hoarse with desire.

"You're easy on the eye, too."

He chuckled, picked up her foot and lightly ran his fingers up and down her leg. With each stroke he moved higher and higher until he was leaning over her, his hands on her breasts and his mouth on hers.

With an intensity that halted her breath and made her hands tremble, she absorbed his touch. She'd seen him tame a horse with his hands, and had wondered what it would be like to have those big, beautiful hands on her. His touch was pure witchery, making all her worries and thoughts drift away. Now she understood why those animals trusted him so much, why they anxiously waited for him to come to them. Her body no longer belonged to her....

"Don't look away from me, Avery."

It took a second for her sluggish brain to register his words, and another moment as she struggled out of the ethereal fog of passion. She didn't want to open her eyes and barely managed the feat. "Magic fingers," she whispered. "Say abracadabra and I'll turn into a horse and follow you anywhere."

Logan grinned, then hissed air through his teeth as her hand slipped between them and found him hard and ready. "I want you to know, I'm not taking what's happening between us lightly," he murmured. "I've wanted you from the first moment I looked up and saw you. I just wish we were somewhere special, with champagne and music...."

"I don't need those things, Logan. Being here with you is all I want. Do you know what I thought when I first saw you?"

"That I was some old, ugly man and you hoped to heaven I wasn't going to be your boss."

"No. I thought you were the sexiest man I'd ever seen." She clasped Logan's face between her hands and kissed him, savoring every sensation as he slid deep inside her body.

Avery floated on the giddy realization that they were two halves of a whole, fitting together with the perfection lovers were meant to. They shared their breaths, their movements. Every sensation was in unison. When she softly moaned his name, his lips whispered hers in return. Suddenly she could do nothing but cry out in intense pleasure, then in release. He quickly followed.

Spent and shaky, Logan propped himself up on one elbow. "I'm sorry that was so fast. It's been a while for me."

Her eyes brimming with tears, Avery threw her arms around his neck. "Me, too," she managed to say.

Logan flopped onto his back, carrying her with him. "Of course, there's nothing stopping us from doing it again, is there?"

She smiled. "Nothing at all."

SHE SHOULD HAVE BEEN asleep, but that luxury wasn't afforded to people who lied and kept secrets.

Guilt was like a haunting melody in her head. She'd been stunned by the bounty of emotions Logan had made her feel. It wasn't fair, she thought as she stared into space. It was just supposed to have been sex.

"I know you're not asleep, Avery." Logan tightened his arm around her, pulling her closer against him. "Are you sorry?"

That her actions would even make him ask was like a knife through her heart. It was time.

Avery switched on the bedside table lamp, rolled so she could face Logan. Then she took a deep breath.

"I was in jail eight months for embezzlement."

She hadn't planned to just blurt it out. She was supposed to lead up to it, with the explanations first, then she'd drop the bomb. All she could do now was wait, hearing only the drum of her heart in her ears. The silence seemed to go on forever, and she could no longer look at him.

"Who set you up?" he asked. "I know you didn't steal anything."

Her eyes opened wide with shock. She was overwhelmed, speechless. That he thought she was innocent without knowing the facts was more than she could take in. She burst into tears.

Logan pulled her against him and she began to cry harder, deep racking sobs that tore at his heart. "Please don't," he begged, but her sobs only increased. He held her close and was patient. So much pain. It seemed she would never stop.

Avery didn't know where all the tears had come from. When at last her sobs turned to sniffles, Logan gave her a handful of tissues. She blew her nose, a loud honking sound that made them both laugh. Then she gazed at Logan through eyes that were almost silver with emotion. "I'm sorry." Her voice quavered.

"Why? How long have you been holding all that in?"

"Forever, it seems." She wiped her eyes. "I didn't steal anything."

"I know that. Who set you up to take the fall?"

Fresh tears brimmed in her eyes, then slowly spilled over and down her cheeks. "David. My brother."

Logan swallowed the bile that rose in his throat. "Betrayal is hard to take from someone you trust," he said, "especially a family member." At least her suffering hadn't been caused by a lover or husband.

Logan's belief in her was so absolute that she gazed at him in awe, wondering what it was about her that he could take her on merely her word alone. There were no doubts, no questions in his eyes. She snuggled next to him and smiled when he slipped his arm under her head, grasped her shoulder and pulled her even closer. For the first time in a year she felt secure.

"You can tell me everything, Avery, or nothing at all. Either way, I believe you."

"I never lied, Logan. I am Avery Jensen, from Seattle, Washington. I was a tax attorney and an accountant specializing in estate law. All of my family's alive—father, brother and sister. But I'm as good as dead to them—at least to Dad and David. Emma's my little sister." Thinking of Emma as little, Avery grinned up at the ceiling. "Emma lives in Europe. Paris, actually.

"Dad disowned me when one of our clients

charged me with embezzlement. I was tried, convicted and jailed for eight months.'' She felt the weight of shame lifting.

''So how did your brother frame you?''

She sniffed. ''Right under my stupid nose, that's how. You see, my father's an attorney. He's the head of the law firm Jensen, Talbot, Kincaid and Jensen. David and I worked for him. Actually, the last Jensen name on the office door is David's, not mine. Dad didn't think I was partner material. I'm a girl, you know.''

Logan snorted in amusement and she grinned.

''David Henry Jensen Sr. is a throwback to the dark ages, Logan. David's two years younger than me. He never made the grades I did. He certainly never made the Law Review, but David was sent to the best college with all his expenses paid. Dad said he'd be wasting money on me. Sooner or later, I'd only quit to get married and have kids. Even if I did finish law school, I'd end up a liability because I'd have to take so much time off rearing children. So I got my education with scholarships and jobs.

''To make matters worse, David is spoiled rotten, a poor excuse for a human being. But he's Daddy's little boy, the only son, and could do no wrong. That's David's problem. Life and my father handed everything to him. Don't get me wrong. David's smart. A genius. That's probably the only reason he didn't get kicked out of college. But he spent most of his time drinking, gambling and running around. Dad knew this but chose to shrug it off. You know what I'm talking about, don't you? Those man things—a wink, a nudge, and the boys-will-be-boys attitude. My father ran through all the clichés, even when he put David in a drug rehab center.

"David got clean, and he made an effort to straighten up. He did what Dad wanted. He got married and had two children. About a year and a half ago, one of my clients suspected something wasn't right with his father's estate. The accounts didn't jibe to his satisfaction, so he had an outside audit done. They found a forty-thousand-dollar discrepancy. The money wasn't there, and they came back to me for an explanation. All the bank withdrawals and authorizations were done from my computer. I knew David was the only one who had access to my accounts. And he always needed money."

"I take it you confronted him and he lied and denied it all?"

"Oh, no. That's not David's style, Logan. He confessed. With tears and genuine sorrow, he begged for help. After all, he had a wife and children to think about. The guilt trip he could take you on...well, sometimes it's hard for an outsider to understand unless they have a family member like that. I guess after a lifetime of being browbeaten with the belief that poor David was always blameless and everything that happened to him wasn't his fault, I agreed to lend him the money to pay back. Then I did the dumbest thing of all. I listened to him, and I allowed him to talk me into letting him handle the client. He promised me he would be able to keep everything from Dad. The client would accept his money and simply change attorneys."

Logan groaned. "David didn't repay the money?"

"No. I told you David had a style all his own. About a month later my ex-client's new attorneys called to inquire when I would be replacing the remainder of the money. The *one hundred thousand dollars.*"

Logan cursed under his breath and held Avery tighter. "The little bastard. How did he think he could get away with it? All you had to do was tell your father and show him the files."

"I'm afraid it wasn't that simple. I did tell Dad, and of course David denied it all. My proof? Everything was done from *my* computer, with *my* password. The forty-thousand-dollar payment was from my account, and like a signed confession. David's name wasn't on anything. Even worse, my father didn't believe me. I don't know why I thought he would. The more I tried to convince him of David's duplicity, the more Dad turned his back on me.

"I was arrested and charged with embezzlement. It didn't matter that I had paid back every penny David had stolen. Because I was a lawyer, the DA's office decided to make an example of me. He set the bail so high I had to sell everything I owned. My house and car. I cashed in all my investments and retirement accounts to hire an attorney and make bail. The only good thing that came out of the whole ordeal was that I had a judge who believed me. But in the end, with David and my father denying everything, the judge had no choice. I was found guilty. You know the rest."

"You spent eight months in jail for something your brother did." He shook his head. "Good God. I'm sorry, Avery."

She couldn't say it was okay, because it wasn't. She shivered. "I swear, Logan, I could never do it again. Do you know those places are never silent?

There's noise of one sort or another all day and night.''

Logan stroked her soft cheek, then pushed her hair off her forehead. ''What happened when you got out? Did you go see your dad?''

''No. He sent me a polite note the week before I was to be released and told me he'd rather not see me at all. I never heard from David.''

''You came to Texas?'' As if a light went off he smiled and said, ''The friend in Houston?''

''Denise Kirk. We'd been friends since we were little. Her husband was transferred to Texas about two years ago. She and Earl wanted to help, but by then there was nothing they could do. I told her I was going to need a friend when I got out. I'm a skilled estate lawyer and certified tax accountant with no licence to practise either.''

''So you end up playing housekeeper, cook and secretary to me. I'm sad about what happened to you, but Avery, whatever forces brought you here did us both a favor.'' He kissed the top of her shoulder, then trailed kisses over the curve of her breast. In midkiss he stopped, saw her dreamy expression and grinned. ''My poor Avery,'' he whispered. ''You know, you could have told me the day you arrived.''

''Could I? What would you have had me say—hire me because I'm an ex-con looking for rehabilitation? By the way, my references are thieves, burglars, drug dealers and addicts. Oh, and let's not forgot the murderers—''

''Stop it.''

''How *could* I have told you when I was so deeply ashamed?''

''But you're innocent,'' he argued.

"Not until I can prove it, Logan. And to be perfectly honest, I don't see how that will ever happen. Besides, I'm too heartsick to fight that fight again."

"It doesn't matter. I'll fight your battles for you."

"You can't—" A passionate kiss cut off her protest and scrambled her thoughts. When Logan pulled away, she tried to keep her happiness from showing.

"Now what?" he asked.

"Did you mean what you said about wanting me from the start, or was that just bedroom talk?"

"Avery, I'm too old for games. I'm almost forty and I swear to you I never thought I could feel like this. That first day I saw you, it was like I was hit between the eyes. I was stunned." He saw the doubt in her eyes, captured her chin and forced her to look at him. "Listen. I was never in love with Becky. There was a chemistry between us, and we shared a history and some strong emotions. But she became my wife because she was pregnant with Jamie. Haven is a small town and my home. I'm a Monahan and could do no less than marry her. I'm not going to sugarcoat our relationship. We dated and did all the things young people with raging hormones do. Later, while I was in college, we still saw each other, but Becky spent a lot of time on the racing circuit with her family and their string of horses.

"We grew apart and quickly found out that we wanted totally different things. She wanted me to finish college, get my veterinary degree, marry her, then join the family, her family business. A resident horse doctor to travel with her and go to parties."

Avery smoothed the frown lines from his brow. "What about your dreams, Logan?"

He glanced around. "I'm no pushover and never

was. Becky talked and talked and planned, and when the time came, I just told her how I wanted to live my life in Haven with family and friends. I don't know if she sensed my growing disinterest in our relationship, or if she thought by getting pregnant it would somehow change my mind. It didn't. I don't regret Jamie, not one second of our time together. He was a wonderful child, and I'm partly to blame that Becky and I couldn't make it as a family. That night, the night of the accident, I had told her I was through and I wanted a divorce. I also made it clear I wanted custody of Jamie."

"You argued?"

"Violently," he said. "I'd never talked to her, to anyone, like that. My only defense was I had good reasons."

"You can't blame yourself for another's actions. I think we've both learned that the hard way."

"That's why you're always on me about Jess?"

"I see so much of my brother in her, Logan. It's scary. If she steps over that emotional edge, she's not going to fall alone." Avery knew Logan was listening to her, but she got the feeling that he had other issues on his mind. Maybe he still couldn't see it. No wonder. After all, his family were loving and well-adjusted.

Except, she thought, for the mysterious Pierce, and the unexplained coldness between him and Logan. Thinking back, she couldn't remember Logan speaking about Pierce much, and now she wondered about Logan's disinterest. Could Pierce have something to do with the attacks on Logan?

"I think you're right about Jess."

"What?" She'd been so lost in her thoughts that

she'd missed what he'd said. Her unspoken question about Pierce lingered like a bitter taste in her mouth. "What did you say?"

"Jess has more than a crush on me," Logan admitted. "I've tried to keep her away from the ranch as much as possible. And tonight...well, let's just say some of the things she said and did on the dance floor shocked me. God help me, but I don't know what to do. I can't go to her parents."

"Why not? They'd be the most likely to help her."

"Jess was a change-of-life baby. The Middletons weren't prepared for another child, and I don't think they particularly wanted her. She was raised by nannies, Ross, Becky and me. After Becky and Jamie's death, Lilly Middleton had a nervous breakdown and was hospitalized. She's only recently been out. Except for Becky and me, and sometimes Ross, Jess has pretty much been on her own since she was a little girl."

Avery recognized the pattern of Jessie's upbringing. Confusion, neglect, overindulgence, then severe discipline. Smothered with love, then ignored. Avery felt that familiar sinking feeling in the pit of her stomach. She had witnessed her father doing all of those things with David. Her brother's childhood would probably parallel Jessie's.

"I can't go to Ross," Logan was saying, "and tell him what we think about Jess, either."

At mention of the sheriff, Avery grasped Logan's hand so hard he yelped. "Sorry. I just thought of something. Logan, Ross knows about me being in jail. After you left, he asked me if you knew I was a jail-bird."

Logan sat up and swung his legs over the side of

the bed. With his back to Avery he cursed viciously, then glanced over his shoulder. She was staring at him in surprise, but then she smiled. He apologized for his temper. "My bark's worse than my bite."

"That was your dad's first warning to me about you," she admitted. "Ross will tell everyone, won't he?"

"You can bet on it."

She hesitated. "I'm so sorry."

"For what?"

"It's all well and good that you believe I'm innocent. But I've been in *jail*, Logan. I was indicted, tried and convicted for embezzling. No matter what I say or how many times I deny it, it won't change that fact. So I've got the stigma of a jailbird." Just saying the word aloud made her feel small. "I...I think it's best if I leave."

She thought she might shatter into a million pieces. Then she took a deep breath, pulled herself together. Leaving was the only right and honorable thing to do.

"You want to leave me?" Logan asked.

She gazed into his eyes. "No," she said. "But, Logan—" He tried to hush her with a kiss, but she pulled back. He just didn't understand what he was up against. "Do you know for those eight months I was in jail, my closest friend was a murderer? Alice stabbed her husband ten times while he slept. Of course, it didn't matter to the courts what he'd done to her and their daughter for years."

"Avery..."

"No, listen to this. I'm sure if Ross has his way everyone will know about me, anyway. It's ironic, don't you think, that my best friend was a murderer and my worst enemy wore the uniform of authority?

"Logan, until I'm cleared of David's crimes, there's no whitewashing it. I'm an ex-con. Don't say it won't affect you. Your family and friends will be mortified when they hear it. And they'll hate me."

"Avery, my family and friends will believe you. As for the others…to hell with them."

Avery shook her head. "It's not that simple, Logan. When all this happened to me I had a fiancé who professed undying devotion. At first he said he believed me. But after the publicity and the trial, he disappeared just like my family."

"If he, whoever he is, didn't believe you, then he didn't love you very much, did he?"

Avery fought to keep fresh tears at bay. Logan was too caught up in the moment to think rationally. When faced with the truth, when he saw the distaste in his family's faces, he'd change. She'd have to steel herself for the heartache to come.

Avery changed the subject. "What are we going to do about Ross? He hates you, you know."

Logan settled back down beside her. "I don't think Ross knows what he feels about me. We were friends once—before Becky. Then he was my brother-in-law and Jamie's uncle, making for a pretty powerful mix of emotions. You're right. He blames me. There were too many unanswered questions after the accident for Ross's liking. Questions that were personal, ones I would never answer. Not then and not now."

"Do you think Ross could be behind all the things happening around here? He told me you were the target of all the violence. That everything was personal and aimed at destroying you." If she expected an answer or a comment, she was disappointed. "But if that's so, why the snake in my house?" she murmured aloud. "And why would someone break in and go through my things?"

"What did you say?"

"I'm pretty sure someone's gone through my things a couple of times. I locked the door, Logan, so don't give me that look. Anyway, I don't have much, so I knew what had been moved. But they never found my release papers. I taped them to the back of the drawer in the bedside table."

"You should have told me. I've had the boys watching the place since the horse-poisoning incident. None of them said a thing about seeing anyone hanging around."

"They're not here all the time, though, are they?"

"You're right." He gazed at her and frowned. "There's something else. What?"

"Sometimes at night I've had the feeling of being watched. Not the boys." She laughed at how ridiculous she sounded. Logan wasn't smiling. "The boys aren't Peeping Toms. They wouldn't sneak up to my bedroom window. It was that sort of creepy feeling, and even Casanova was disturbed. And speaking of the boys, don't you think using a bunch of teenagers as would-be James Bonds is a little crazy?"

Logan chuckled. "Remember where you are. Ross is the law in Haven. His deputies are in his hip pocket. If I'd called in outside help, their presence would have been noted immediately. Tanner and I discussed it and we figured since the boys are here most of the time, why not use them? I don't mind telling you they take their sleuthing and protecting you and the ranch very seriously."

"So you do think it's Ross? Or Jessie? Or both?"

"Maybe. I don't know. All I know right now is

that whoever's doing it knows how I feel about you. That makes you a target.'' He gathered her in his arms. ''I've lost too much. Nothing and no one is going to hurt you.''

They both gave a start at the sound of something crashing to the floor in the kitchen directly below. Avery said, ''Someone's there, Logan.''

He was already pulling on his jeans. He eased open the drawer of the bedside table and pulled out a handgun.

She gasped.

''Stay here,'' he said, and quietly left the room.

Avery scrambled across the bed and searched the floor for her dress. Then she pulled it on, frantically doing up buttons, and followed Logan. She caught up with him on the landing and grasped the waist of his jeans.

''I told you to stay put,'' he whispered.

''I know.''

''Well?''

''What if you need me?''

''I won't.'' He reached behind him and pried her fingers off his jeans, then started down the stairs.

Avery took the few steps after him. She poked his bare back with a stiff finger. ''Is the gun loaded?''

''Yes. And the safety's off.''

''Good.'' She took another step. ''I learned some things in jail, you know. I can pick a lock in seconds and disable an alarm system.'' She was scared and babbling, but couldn't seem to stop. ''Of course, it's all theory, a kind of visual teaching. I've never actually done it.''

Logan swung around. He grasped Avery by the shoulders, then twisted her bodily so she was facing upstairs. "Go back to the bedroom," he ordered in a whisper. "Now."

Reluctantly, she did as he asked, but she stopped at the bedroom door and listened. A few seconds later she nearly jumped out of her skin when Logan shouted. Another crash sounded. Avery squeezed her eyes shut, then darted toward the bed, jumped in and pulled the covers up to her chin.

Logan stepped into the doorway of the bedroom. In one hand he held a clear glass jar full of M&M's. The same jar he'd taken from Avery earlier. In the other hand he held a spitting, growling, wildly slashing cat by the scuff of his neck. Casanova caught sight of Avery. In a split second he went limp in Logan's grasp, then let out a pathetic meow.

Logan pitched the cat on the bed and watched as it stalked across the covers, then settled on Avery's chest. Casanova immediately patted her cheek with a paw and kissed her nose.

"Avery," Logan said, "you have ruined my vicious mouser and turned him into a candy-stealing kitty-cat. Damn animal knocked the jar to the floor and was actually trying to get it open."

"The candy's mine. I've weaned him off them with kitty treats."

"And that's why he was trying to chew through glass?"

Avery stroked Casanova. "Poor baby's got a chocolate monkey on his back. It must run in the family." She quickly sobered. "Logan, we left him at the little house, so how did he get in here?"

Logan's amusement trickled away. "I locked the door earlier, but it was standing open when I found him. I know the damn cat can't unlock and open a door.''

The hairs on the back of Avery's neck stood up. ''Do you think someone was here? Whoever it was could have come upstairs, Logan.''

''I don't think he would have. As vocal as we were, anyone could have stood at the bottom of the stairs and caught an earful. If he—''

''Or *she*.'' Avery absently stroked Casanova.

''Right. If there were any uncertainties about our relationship, there won't be now.''

He moved toward the window that faced the front of the house and surveyed the landscape. The moon was bright and kept the deeper shadows at bay. There seemed to be nothing amiss. But by the stiffness of Logan's shoulders Avery could tell he was uneasy about something. When he returned to the bed, instead of climbing in beside her, he sat on the edge, picked up the telephone and dialed the barn.

Avery pushed a protesting cat off her lap and scooted over so she was sitting beside Logan. ''Who're you calling?''

''Benton and Raul are sleeping in the barn.'' He held up his hand and Avery listened to the one-sided conversation. It was obvious that the boys hadn't seen or heard anything.

''I want you and Raul to let all the horses out of the barn,'' Logan was saying. ''Open the paddock gates and run them toward the back of the property. Then you two leave. Tell Raul to drive the blue truck and keep it out at his place.'' Logan glanced sideways at Avery. ''Yes, she's with me, and we're leaving for the night. I'll lock the barn up tight before we go.''

Logan promised to call the boys as soon as they

got back. Then he hung up and kissed Avery. "Benton said Denise called you a couple of times this evening."

"I'll phone her back later." Denise had done so much for her and was so pleased with herself for finding the job that Avery didn't have the heart to tell her about the attacks at the ranch.

Logan pulled Avery to her feet and began unbuttoning the dress once again. "How about a shower? Together. Then we'll throw some clothes together and leave."

"Where are we going?"

"Fiesta San Antonio."

"Why, Logan?"

"Because suddenly I feel like we're exposed, and too isolated here. We'll be safer in a crowd. Besides, Tanner, Dad and Pierce are there. Maybe by now Tanner's found the answers we need. Like who is behind all these incidents."

CHAPTER ELEVEN

AVERY STARED THROUGH the window of the Range
Rover, keeping her face turned so Logan wouldn't see
how upset she was.

"I'm sorry," he said.

"It's a shock, that's all. I've never had anyone hate
me to that extent. Even David, for all his faults, didn't
actually hate me, I don't believe." Avery looked at
what she was wearing. It was the same denim dress
she'd had on earlier. That dress, her boots, a pair of
sneakers and a few underclothes were the sum total
of what was left of her belongings.

Logan squeezed her thigh and she sighed. She
didn't want to think about what they'd found, but it
was impossible to wipe the picture of chaos out of
her mind or shake the feeling of fear that kept her
hands locked together in her lap.

After they'd showered together, she'd dressed, then
waited while he packed. It was when they'd entered
the bedroom of the little house to collect her belongings for the trip that they'd made their horrible dis-
covery.

Everything she owned, every stitch of clothing, had
been cut and slashed. Her makeup and toiletries were
smashed on the bathroom floor. Even the bedding had
been yanked from the mattress and ripped. It was the
sheer malice of the destruction that was devastating.

Avery closed her eyes against the darkness rushing past the car window. When she turned to look at Logan, she noticed how the dim car lights accented his locked jaw and knotted muscles. She had to speak.

"It was a woman's kind of vengeance, Logan. Jessie must have come to the house and used her key. If we were as vocal as you say, she probably heard us, and there was no mistaking what was going on in your bedroom. I put her over the edge and she took her jealous rage and hatred out on my belongings."

"When we get to San Antonio and the stores open in the morning, I'll replace everything."

"That's not the point or the problem, Logan. Jessie's out of control and there's no telling what she might do next."

"I know one thing," Logan said. "She won't ever hurt you again."

Avery wanted to strangle him. "I can take care of myself. But you need to take off your blinders." She was too upset to argue and Logan was too angry to listen. That he was out for blood was an understatement. She hoped he didn't go off halfcocked. Jessie Middleton wasn't the only one to keep an eye on.

Suddenly Logan said, "You mentioned a sister. Emma? Where was she when you needed her?"

"I told you she lives in Paris. I called her before the trial, but I didn't tell her anything about David."

"For heaven's sake, why not? She's your sister. She had a right to know."

"You don't know anything about Emma." Avery knew how defensive she sounded.

"Explain it to me, then. My brothers would have been there for me."

"Sure they would. Because you weren't born into

a totally dysfunctional family. Emma's the baby, yet she's the most independent of any of us. You have to understand my mother died soon after she was born. Dad blamed Emma for that and never let her forget it. Emma is nothing like me. I was always the peace-maker. But Emma never allowed Dad to ignore her or brush her aside. They clashed at every turn. Or maybe the reason she and Dad didn't get along was because David and Emma hated each other and Dad was so fond of his son.

"As a child, Emma was artistically talented and a bundle of energy. For as long as I can remember, she dreamed of being an artist, a photographer or a dress designer. She succeeded in doing it all, extremely well and without any help from our father."

"Because of David?" Logan asked.

"Partly. When Emma was thirteen, she badgered Dad relentlessly until he paid for her to go to a special art school. A couple days before she was to start, he found a hundred dollars missing from the safe at home. Some of the money turned up in Emma's room."

"Let me guess," Logan said. "David stole it and set Emma up to take the fall?"

"Yes. He was jealous of her. I guess in his warped mind he believed she was getting something that should be his. Anyway, Emma and Dad had a huge fight. Emma doesn't back down when she thinks she's right. She went after David, told him she knew what he'd done, but he wouldn't confess. I tried to talk to Dad until I was exhausted, but he'd made up his mind there would be no art school, ever.

"Emma ran away from home that night. Two days later my mother's sister in Boston called to tell Dad that Emma was going to live with her. Then when Emma was seventeen she moved to Paris to live and work.''

''That still doesn't explain why she wasn't here for you.''

''Easy. I didn't tell her. She's happy, and there was nothing she could do, anyway. Why subject her to David's venom and Father's endless stream of bitterness? Besides, in the beginning I really thought I could prove David was to blame. When I realized the extent of his crime, it was too late.''

''But you never talked to her?''

Avery scowled into the darkness, then rested her head on Logan's shoulder. ''I did call her several times, but I could never reach her. I tried again when I reached Houston, but it was no use. There was something wrong with her telephone line.''

''And that doesn't bother you?''

''No. Yes. We've never lived in each other's pocket, but we've always stayed in contact. I'll try to call when we get back to the ranch.''

By the time the lights of San Antonio appeared, it was two o'clock in the morning. ''What *is* this little fiesta thing?'' Avery asked.

Logan laughed. ''Don't refer to it that way to anyone else or you'll be hanged for a Yankee. Fiesta's a ten-day celebration that honors Texas's victory over Mexico. A party full of pomp and pageantry. There're plenty of parades, floats on the river, street parties and private formal affairs. Music is everywhere, roving mariachi bands, people dancing in the streets day and night, sightseers and tourists.''

''Like the Mardi Gras in New Orleans?''

He shot her an amused glance. ''Don't make that

comparison in public, either. San Antonio likes to think Fiesta is far better than anything a bunch of mudbug-eating Cajuns could put on.''

By the time he'd explained a list of other pitfalls to avoid, her mood had changed. When he stopped in front of the Menger Hotel, Avery was laughing.

It was the wee hours of the morning, but if she'd expected the hotel to be deserted, she was mistaken. Granted, it wasn't a crush, but there were all sorts of people milling about the lobby—women in glittering gowns and men in tuxedos.

Logan waved to a few friends, but refused to stop. Avery tried not to notice the eyes that followed them across the lobby. The desk clerk greeted Logan by name, handed over a room key and told him that Tanner had been waiting for him.

Logan turned and surveyed the lobby. ''I know you're tired, but I'd rather you stay with me until I've talked to Tanner. And speak of the devil…''

Avery followed the direction of his gaze and smiled. Tanner, head and shoulders above everyone else, and gorgeous in a black tuxedo and diamond-studded shirt, was cornered by a pair of beauties who showed an indecent amount of skin. He looked bored until he spotted Logan. He grinned and straightened, then he saw Avery and his eyes widened. As Avery watched he gave each woman a charming smile, kissed their cheeks and headed across the marble floor.

Before Tanner opened his mouth to speak, Logan said, ''Give me the key to your room. You can bunk with Pierce tonight. I assume he's here?''

''Evening, Brother,'' Tanner said. ''Happy to see you, too. Avery, what a surprise.''

"Cut the crap. You knew I was coming," Logan said. When Tanner frowned, he slapped his brother on the back and apologized. "Sorry, but a lot's been going on. Let's go to the coffee shop."

On the way across the lobby Logan slipped Tanner's key to Avery. She understood propriety, but was disappointed nonetheless that Logan wasn't going to stay with her. There was something going on that Logan had neglected to tell her. Tanner, it seemed, had been expecting him. And Logan had more on his mind than Jessie and Ross Middleton. She decided to keep her mouth shut and listen.

Logan rubbed his face and filled Tanner in on what Jess had done to Avery's belongings. Avery noticed that Tanner was far too observant to miss the holes in the story of their night, but was wise enough to refrain from asking questions. Logan met his brother's questioning gaze and smiled.

Tanner's gaze bounced from Logan's face to Avery's too-bland expression. "Jess didn't show up at the ball tonight, Logan. Ross was here, though, and from his actions I'd say he was searching for her."

"Did you get in touch with Joaquin?" Logan asked.

"Yeah, I was able to track him down. He was visiting his grandfather over at the Van der Bollen place in Two Rivers. He said he'd make some calls for us." He glanced at his watch. "That was about ten. He's rushed because the agency called back in."

Avery forgot her vow to just listen. "What agency?"

"Treasury Department," Tanner said.

Avery gave a huff of disbelief as Tanner continued, "Joaquin's plane is parked here at the airport. He said if someone would come get him and drive him to the airport, he'd swing by here first and fill us in on what he found.''

Avery couldn't stand it. She was tired of being left out and ignored. ''Who is this Joaquin and what's he supposed to tell you?''

''I'm Joaquin, ma'am. Joaquin Brightstone. And I can tell Logan whether he's a target for retaliation.''

Avery twisted around in her chair so she could see the man standing directly behind her. *My, my,* she thought. Texas was a woman's paradise. The men were handsome and sexy. Maybe it was a combination of all those things, plus the impeccable manners, that made them so attractive.

But Joaquin was different from Logan and Tanner. Dangerous came to mind. Mysterious. She watched him as he grabbed a chair from a neighboring table and pulled it over. She doubted if there was a person in the coffee shop who hadn't been under the scrutiny of his dark green eyes.

She noticed Pierce Monahan and was surprised when he also joined them. When she realized Joaquin was speaking, she listened.

''I've checked with some of my contacts over at the U.S. Customs Service, Logan,'' Joaquin said. ''They told me you were clean. No one knew you and Pierce were involved in the sting operation.''

Avery reached under the table and squeezed Logan's thigh to get his attention. When he covered her hand with his and looked at her, she said, ''What's he talking about?'' She'd been a lawyer far too long not to have heard the sort of veiled talk circulating around the table. She also knew that when the government got involved, trouble usually wasn't far behind. Taking another look at Joaquin, she guessed what he was. "Are you some spy?" She scowled at the chuckles. "Okay, an undercover agent?"

"He's just a friend," Pierce answered.

Avery's eyes narrowed. "And pigs fly. Listen, whether anyone wants to hear it or not, I'm involved in this, too."

Pierce crossed his arms over his chest in a mute challenge.

Tanner ducked his head and concentrated on stirring his coffee.

Logan shrugged and smiled, then shocked everyone by saying, "She's right."

"I don't see…" Pierce began, then stopped when he caught Logan's hard stare.

"Well, let me tell you. I came this close—" she held two fingers a fraction of an inch apart "to getting bitten by a rattlesnake someone left as a present in the middle of my living room." She had their full attention and was going to play it for all it was worth, but caught a glimpse of Logan's laughing eyes. "It was huge to my way of thinking since I've never seen one before. *And* I don't have any other clothes except for what I'm wearing because someone took out his or her temper on my belongings." She looked from one brother to the other then to the guest and waited.

Joaquin rose from the table and said, "It doesn't matter who I am or where I work because I'm not involved. But I have contacts and friends, and they told me Logan and Pierce are safe. I've got a plane to catch." He glanced at his watch. "Give me five minutes, Pierce, and I'll meet you in the lobby."

She watched Joaquin as he walked away from the table and out the door. "Is anyone going to tell me?"

Logan placed his arm along the back of her chair and said, "A month after the accident, Pierce and I were approached by some federal agents to help them break up a smuggling ring that was moving their merchandise through San Antonio and Haven."

Avery was appalled. If he was involved in catching drug dealers, it would answer so many questions. "You got caught up in drugs?" All three men were suddenly laughing, but she didn't see the joke.

Logan was the first to sober. "The merchandise consisted of parrots, toucans and spider monkeys. Most of them are endangered and more die in transit than make it to their destination. A big operation can bring in as much as six-hundred-thousand dollars in one run. A baby spider monkey goes for an estimated five-thousand apiece on the black market. It's an awful business and when the U.S. Customs Service and the U.S. Fish and Wildlife Service asked for our help, we didn't hesitate to take care of the sick animals."

That she was getting an edited version of their involvement and the danger, Avery didn't doubt. "So you're sure that nothing that's been happening at the ranch has to do with the great bird and monkey sting?"

"Actually," Logan said, "it was called Operation Jungle Beat."

Avery left the brothers laughing together and headed for her room. She was tired and more than a little peeved at being the butt of the Monahans' jokes.

SAN ANTONIO'S River Walk was the Venice of the Southwest. At least that's what Logan tried his best to make her believe as they floated down the river. They'd decided to put all their problems aside and enjoy themselves. "Just close your eyes and imagine you're in a gondola and you're hearing violins instead of the mariachi band."

"It's too much of a stretch. Besides, those jalapeño peppers you talked me into tasting are still burning a hole in my stomach."

"Eating them was your own idea. I did warn you."

"Sure you did. What was it you said? Oh, yeah. 'They're a tad hot.' A deliberate understatement." They were sitting side by side on the padded bench at the back of the tourist boat. Avery rested her head on Logan's shoulder as they watched the passing crowds strolling along the banks of the river and crossing the arched stone bridges that spanned the water. A slight breeze held the promise of a cooler evening.

"I've been thinking about David, Father and Emma and how much we missed out on. I envy the closeness you have with your brothers, Logan. Betrayal is a million times worse when it's a member of your own family." Avery sighed, wishing the day would never end. She couldn't remember when she'd had so much fun or been so happy.

She'd awakened that morning to knocking on her hotel room door, only to open it and find Logan and Tanner, grinning like a pair of idiots and waving shopping bags. They'd decided she needed something cool and comfortable to wear if she was going to go shopping for new clothes. One pair of white linen walking-shorts and a loose-fitting blouse had turned into three outfits. Her boots were replaced by a pair of sandals. Logan had taken over the underwear purchase and she'd actually blushed when she pulled out the skimpy little nothings.

Tanner had purchased a straw hat for her to wear in the scorching sun. And Logan made sure she had a pair of sunglasses. Then after breakfast, she and Logan disappeared for the day and only returned at dusk to change clothes and slip off to have dinner by themselves.

"It's been a perfect day," she said, too lazy and comfortable to lift her head from his shoulder.

"The night could be even better."

There was no doubt of his meaning and she chuckled. "Do you really think we have enough energy?"

It was his turn for amusement. "With a little encouragement I think I could muster up enough to show you a few things."

She snuggled against his side. "When can we get off this then?"

"Well, if you're feeling adventurous—at the next bend in the river, the boat will swing wide and come so close to the walkway, all we have to do is jump."

It was easier said than done. If it hadn't been for a few helping hands from some people strolling along the River Walk, they would have ended up taking an evening swim.

They thanked their rescuers, then headed back to the hotel. Logan stopped and glanced around to get his bearings. "I hadn't realized we'd come this far from the hotel or that it was getting so late."

As the night lengthened, the kind and size of the crowd had changed from evening diners and lazy strollers to more rambunctious partiers.

"We'll never find a taxi." He grasped her hand firmly in his and said, "I know a shortcut. Stay close."

It didn't take more than a few minutes for Avery

to understand why Logan had such a crushing hold on her hand. They dodged. They sidestepped. They ducked into shop doorways and stepped off curbs into the street, all to escape the roving groups of revelers who staggered past. She was constantly jostled and sometimes she was shoved so she was behind Logan, but through it all, he never once let go of her.

Suddenly, Logan pushed her into another shop doorway. Avery sighed with relief. She'd been bumped and shoved until she felt sore.

Logan pulled Avery closer to his side as a loud group of young men went by. "This place has changed in the past couple of years. There used to be the greatest Mexican restaurant on the corner. This whole place looks as if it's been turned into one big nightclub."

Logan stepped from the protection of the doorway. A halo of murky light from the overhead lamps tinted their skin a sickly yellow. A door was held open, and the steady drone on the street was split apart by the riff of a bass guitar and the heavy beat of drums. Avery looked toward the source of the music, managing a quick glance over her shoulder at the party-goers behind the big plate-glass window of the night-club. Something caught her eye. She didn't have time to confirm all her suspicions, but she was sure of what she saw.

Logan had started down the street at a faster pace than before and any attempt at conversation would have been futile. But it gave her a moment to think. She'd seen Ross Middleton in the club. Though she wasn't positive the person Ross had been talking to was Pierce Monahan, she knew one other thing. Ross had seen her. At the moment she'd recognized him, he'd stared directly into her eyes.

Logan slowed and turned around enough so he could shout. "We're only a few blocks from the back of the Menger." Then his attention became fixed on something behind her.

Avery saw the concern on his face and glanced over her shoulder. She saw about ten young men headed toward them. Unlike the tourists and the drunks, they seemed to have a purpose to their direction. She didn't know why she felt a chill of dread but Logan must have felt it, too. He tugged on her hand, and they were soon moving much faster than before.

Twice she'd caught him looking back. The second time, she had time to look, too. The men were still behind them, and gaining fast. That unexplained queasy sensation she'd experienced had developed into full blown fear. "They're following us, aren't they, Logan?"

Instead of answering, he said, "When I say go, walk faster. We'll see how much distance we can put between us and them. Then when we get to the corner, take a sharp left and run like hell. It's a straight shot to the hotel."

She stayed glued to Logan's side and kept her attention divided between the sidewalk and the crowd. But she desperately wanted to look back and see for herself how close the gang was. Her imagination was working overtime, and she could swear she heard the threat in their careless laughter.

Her mouth went dry as she and Logan approached the corner. She was already breathless from fear and wondered if she had the strength to run. Ten more steps, she thought, her heart pounding like a jackhammer.

The corner was within reach. They veered left but their route of escape was cut off by a rowdy crowd. Surprise caused them to flounder and in the midst of drunken singing, Logan's grasp on Avery's hand was severed.

She was pushed backward, away from Logan. Elbowed, jarred and shoved, she was barely able to look around. The crowd was carrying her in the direction she and Logan had just come from, back toward the gang.

Avery tried to fight her way through the crowd of bodies, but soon realized that if she didn't want to be seriously hurt or trampled, she couldn't fight the partiers.

After a few crushed toes, she was finally able to assess her situation. The gang that had been following her and Logan was close enough to allow her to make out a few faces. She didn't like what she saw. These men weren't innocent partygoers or tourists. They weren't drunk or amused by the celebration going on around them.

There was a brief break in the crowd, and her eyes locked with one of the gang members. He spotted her immediately, and Avery was shocked to realize that he recognized her. His startled look told her more than she wanted to face at the moment. He knew her—and until she found Logan, or he found her, she was on her own. A man's shoulder slammed into her back, and she was almost knocked off her feet. Hot, sweaty and scared, she struggled to stay upright as the group moved toward a nightclub entrance. With a groan, she realized they were heading directly for the club where she'd seen Ross Middleton and Pierce Monahan.

Several of the men from the gang started bulldozing their way toward her. The people around her started to respond angrily to being roughly pushed and shoved. She had to do something, fast.

Avery ducked as low as she dared and twisted around, heading against the tide of the crowd in the direction of the corner where she'd been separated from Logan. An opening in the crush of bodies afforded her a clear view of a side street. She was tempted to take it. Could she afford to get caught in a dark alley? She didn't know San Antonio, and hadn't paid attention to street signs or the route Logan had taken. Logan had said the rear of the Menger Hotel was close to the corner.

Avery crab-walked through the crowd, dodging and ducking until she felt she'd made significant progress. But to determine her position, she had to make herself visible. She inhaled shakily and straightened to her full height. Three things happened at once, so fast that all she could do was react.

A hand grabbed her arm in a painful vise. Her name was spoken with a soft Spanish accent, as she was whirled roughly around. She recognized the swarthy man as one of the gang and let her fear and instincts take over. Instead of pulling away from his grip, she fell into it. In the same motion she drilled her clenched fist in his groin. Then, as her assailant doubled over, she slashed at his eyes with her fingernails.

Strike and move. Hit and run. She'd actually learned something useful in jail. If she hadn't been so scared, she would have laughed. Instead, she was a true pupil to her teachings and escaped so quickly she barely heard his scream.

Avery elbowed her way through the crowd, deaf to the shout of outrage from a man who had his toes bruised by a deliberate stomp of her heel.

She was free of the crowd and felt the cool air on her face. There were still tourists milling about, but they were easily dodged. Still, she sensed she wasn't clear. Skidding, she righted herself as she made a sharp left at the corner. She couldn't believe her luck. The street was well lighted and almost empty. She started to run, seeing shelter and safety within reach.

Then she was struck at waist level and fell hard against the unrelenting pavement. She landed on her side and the air was knocked out of her but she tried to roll away. All she could think of was that they'd outsmarted her. Somewhere in the distance she thought she heard a shout and the sound of a person running away. Suddenly, a voice was demanding that she talk.

"Avery, are you hurt?"

Struggling for breath, she managed to shake her head. The voice was familiar, but not the one she wanted to hear. She opened her eyes and found herself gazing up at Pierce Monahan.

"Logan's about a block away." He helped her to her feet, but refused to let go. "I've never seen him like that. He's frantic. What the hell happened?"

"He didn't tell you?" She glanced up and down the street. They were the object of a few stares, but there didn't seem to be anything in their scrutiny except curiosity.

"Tell me? There wasn't time."

Once she knew she could walk, she started toward the hotel. She didn't trust Pierce.

"I ran into Logan, literally, outside The Black Hat."

Avery glanced at him. "Is that the nightclub where I saw you talking to Ross Middleton?"

"Yes." Pierce pulled a cellular phone from his shirt pocket and pressed a number. "Logan, I found her. We're heading to the Menger."

Avery stiffened and despite the pain in her side, she started walking faster.

"No, she's not okay. Someone tried to hurt her."

"I'm all right." Avery relaxed and held out her hand. "Give me the phone." But he'd already folded it shut.

"Logan will be at the hotel by the time we get there. Now, you want to tell me what happened?"

"Why don't you finish your story?"

"What story? Oh, you mean how I ran into Logan? He grabbed me outside The Black Hat and told me he needed help finding you. That's all I know."

When they reached the back entrance of the Menger, Avery was so relieved to be safe she almost collapsed. Pierce held open the door, and she took a moment to right her clothes and dust off the dirt and grime from her fall. By the time they reached the lobby, reaction had set in and she was almost in tears. Avery quickly scanned the lobby, and when she spotted Logan, she ran into his open arms.

"Logan," she whispered, "I saw Pierce and Ross together just before those men came after us."

CHAPTER TWELVE

"OUCH, OUCH, OUCH!" Avery's breath hissed through clenched teeth like a vacuum cleaner. "Blow. Blow harder." She winced and tried to jerk her arm away as Logan continued to swab her scraped elbow with antiseptic. "Logan, what's that stuff you keep putting on me?"

"It's only a scratch and can't possibly hurt that much."

She bit her lip. "I have a low tolerance for pain. Is my hand okay?" She wiggled her fingers. "It's sore."

"Not as sore, I'd bet, as the guy that got your fist in his privates," Pierce said, and passed Logan a Band-Aid.

Tanner and Mac laughed.

Avery's smile was full of triumph. "I've never hit anyone before, but I must say it did feel good. I scratched his eyes, too. Did I tell you that?"

"About a hundred times," Tanner said soberly, then he and Mac started laughing again.

She watched Pierce and Logan as they worked together to patch her up. The brothers were completely in tune with each other. Logan never asked for a swab or medication that Pierce hadn't already anticipated. Maybe she'd been wrong about Pierce. He was, after all, Logan's brother, and they were such a close family. Logan and Pierce were veterinarians, had once shared a business. Yet… She couldn't nail down what bothered her except that, unlike Tanner, who was underfoot most of the time, Pierce seemed to be always absent. And Logan didn't talk about Pierce as he did Tanner. Maybe it was a sibling thing.

Avery flinched and jerked her knees sideways and out of reach of the hovering wet cotton ball. "Is that going to sting?"

"No," Logan said as he grasped her thigh and applied the medication. "It's going to hurt like the devil."

When she could breathe normally again, she wondered mulishly why these grown men found her pain so amusing. "If you're through, I'd like to go to the rest room and wash my face." Her knees hurt, her elbow stung, her shoulder throbbed and she was feeling especially vulnerable. She allowed Logan to help her to the door, and when they were out of earshot of the others, she whispered, "Are you going to tell them about me?" she whispered.

"Yes. I don't want them blindsided by Ross—or anyone else, for that matter."

"And you don't believe Pierce had anything to do with Ross and those men?"

"Go wash up. We'll talk about it as soon as you're ready."

From the moment he'd taken her in his arms in the hotel lobby and she'd told him what she'd seen, Logan hadn't allowed her to discuss it any further. He was too concerned about her injuries and making sure she wasn't hurt more than she appeared.

Avery heard the rumble of male voices and took her time freshening up. Logan believed her on good faith, but would his father and brothers? She'd dallied long enough and opened the door.

The silence was like a vise around her throat. Her steps faltered, then she forced herself to walk into the living room. Grasping the back of the couch, she held on, worked her way around to the front and sat down. Avery raised her eyes and looked from Tanner to Mac and finally to Pierce.

"I didn't do it," she said.

Mac was the first to speak. "The possibility never crossed our minds." Avery allowed him to take her hand. "Poor child. To have a low-down, snake-in-the-grass for a brother. And I'd like to get my hands on your father and shake him till his teeth rattle like pebbles in a tin can."

Avery glanced at Tanner and was relieved to see the kindness in his eyes matched Mac's. "If Logan told you everything, then you know I can't prove my innocence. The awful stigma of being a criminal, of being in jail, will stick with me for the rest of my life. It could be embarrassing for all of you if I stay in Haven."

"If you stay?" Logan asked. He gave Pierce a hard look. "Avery saw you and Ross together at the Black Hat. She says that Ross saw her, and it was right after that the gang started chasing us."

"I see." Pierce put the caps on bottles and picked up the soiled cotton swabs.

"She thinks you're in cahoots with Ross," Tanner said, and grinned when they all stared at him. "Well, it has to be that. Look at her. She's scared of Pierce."

It was true, Avery thought. She was afraid of Pierce, but couldn't understand exactly why.

Pierce ran his fingers through his hair and looked

away as everyone turned to stare at him. "Oh, for heaven's sake. Yes, I ran into Ross at the Black Hat. He asked if I was waiting for Logan and Avery. I think I told him you'd probably show up. He's well aware, as is everyone else, that Logan always drops by the Black Hat when he's in town."

Avery stared at Logan. "Do you?"

"Sure. We all make a point of going there. An old friend of ours, Clara Hartman, owns the place and books great rock and roll bands." His gaze never shifted from his brother's face. "But I thought you'd stopped seeing Clara a long time ago?"

"I just stopped by because I figured you'd show up there."

Avery felt the undercurrent of tension between Logan and Pierce, and said, "Then Ross must have been pretty sure Logan would be there tonight." She could have told Pierce he would have had a long wait because she and Logan had never had any intentions of going anywhere but to bed. But that was their secret. "How did you find Pierce?"

Logan clasped Avery's injured hand. As he examined it, he said, "When we were parted and you were swept away by the crowd, I knew I'd never catch up. So I decided to round the block and try a frontal attack on the group. I was halfway there when I ran into Pierce. I sent him back the way I'd come, in case you were able to get away and he'd find you."

"Did you get a good look at any of the men who were following you, especially the one who knocked you down?" Tanner asked.

"You mean the one I slugged?" Avery grinned with savage pleasure. "He was sort of swarthy. My height. Black hair and mean little eyes. He spoke with an accent." That got their attention.

"He said something to you? What?" Logan demanded.

"My name. Logan, he called me by name. That proves it wasn't a random attack, doesn't it? Then he said..." She closed her eyes, trying to remember. "No. He called me something. In Spanish. Pooter, I think it was."

"*Puta?*" Logan asked, his jaw knotted with anger.

"Yes. What does it mean?"

"Whore."

"That wasn't very nice," Avery said calmly. "I thought cowboys, especially Texans, were gentlemen down to their pointy boot toes." This was received with a few chuckles. She'd used, apparently, just enough outrage and mockery.

Logan rose to his feet, stuffed his hands in his jeans pockets and gazed out the window, seeing nothing in the darkness but his own reflection. "I thought if we came to town you'd be safe. Looks like I was wrong. But I tell you this, I'd rather fight whatever's coming on familiar ground. At least I'd have some control." He offered Avery his hand, then helped her up. She grimaced and he said, "You're going to be really sore tomorrow."

"We're going back to the ranch?"

"Yes. Pack your things and I'll go get my gear. Tanner, don't leave this room until I come for Avery. Pierce, Dad, come with me. The Monahans are about to declare war."

Avery didn't know how to act or what to think when Logan kissed her in front of everyone. Could she trust her feelings? What if her past was the instrument used to hurt Logan or his family? She'd have a hard time living with herself if that happened.

"YOU'RE STILL NOT SURE it's Ross and Jessie, are you, Logan?" They were seated in the kitchen of the big house. Avery handed him a screwdriver and watched as he began to change the lock on the door. Before they'd left San Antonio, Tanner had given Logan a heavy bag full of new dead-bolt locks to replace all those at the ranch house and her quarters.

"What are you grinning about?" He gave her a quick kiss and took the tool from her hand.

"Don't you think it's rather pointless to install locks on the little house if you won't let me stay there? And don't think you can dodge my question that easily, either."

"I like waking up with you beside me. But I don't want to share our bed with a cat." The object of their conversation wedged himself between them so he could investigate the contents of the bag and sniff every item on the floor. "And I'm not avoiding the subject of Ross. It's hard thinking someone I've known for years—hell, family—could hate me so much." Logan could have bitten his tongue as he realized what he'd said. "I'm sorry."

"It's all right. Most people don't have a David in their family. It's difficult to accept. But, Logan, surely you realize it has to be Ross, and probably Jessie, behind what's happened." She handed him a brass doorplate. "How are you going to stop him?"

"That's the problem. If I openly accuse Ross, he'll only deny it. He's the sheriff, after all, and a good one. Who in this town is going to believe it?"

"What about outside help? Like the police in San Antonio?"

"The Middleton money and name swing a lot of weight there. I doubt I'd get anyone to take me seriously."

"Joaquin? I bet he'd gladly lend a hand." Avery removed Casanova from the large bag, shook her finger at him and was answered by a grouchy growl. "Don't give me your sass, cat."

"Brightstone's unavailable. He made that clear at the hotel. No, I think we'll have to do this on our own."

"That means waiting until Ross or Jessie makes another move, doesn't it?"

"Right. But it'll be different this time. Tanner told Pierce where to pick up security cameras. Pierce and Dad will be here soon to install them."

"Do you think Ross will try to set fire to the new barn?"

"I'm not worried about the barn. I designed it. It's constructed of steel, brick and a slate roof. Except for the wood interior, it's pretty fireproof. And I can lock it up tighter than a bank safe. The horses and cattle are all out in the back pastures. I've told the boys not to come around until I've resolved this mess. I don't want them getting hurt." He leaned over and kissed her. "And since you're staying here with me, I can protect you."

"How do you think Ross has been getting away with it this far? It seems someone would have seen his car."

"Not really. Besides the main entrance, there are three other access roads to the ranch."

Casanova didn't like the power tools and yowled

louder than the drill. "Can you give him something to shut him up, Avery?"

She grabbed the box of kitty treats, shook a couple out on the floor. Predictably Casanova sniffed them, then marched disdainfully off.

Avery sighed. "Have you thought about what you're going to do if you catch Ross?"

Logan finished installing the lock, then stared off in the distance, thinking that he knew what he'd *like* to do. "Until you arrived, most everything was psychological warfare aimed at hurting me as much as possible. Maybe in the back of my mind, I blamed myself enough over the accident that the punishment seemed fitting. Only a demented mind would carry out this game of revenge."

"That's why you won't consider Jessie, isn't it?"

"Yes. She's unstable, but she just doesn't have it in her to poison horses, take Blackie or destroy anything of Jamie's."

"But you have to admit that putting a rattlesnake in my room and ruining my clothes is something Jessie would do."

"Yes. But I still don't think Jess is helping Ross, nor do I think she knows what he's been up to. Another thing about Jess, she can't keep a secret—never could—and everyone knows that. She'd have let slip what Ross was doing."

Logan finished cleaning up where he'd been working and glanced at Avery. "I think after Jess found us in bed, she must have mentioned it to Ross. His scheme to use the information he had on your background as a means to blackmail you into leaving wasn't going to work. When he realized you were someone I cared about, he had a way to deliver a deeper hurt. So he raised the stakes. Ross figured we'd go to the Black Hat—I always did, and Pierce was there to confirm that we'd probably show. He'd made a deal with the gang, and all they had to do was wait for a signal. But what Ross doesn't know is that everything changed when those men went after you on the street.''

''I wish I felt as confident as you. To use one of Mac's sayings, I think Ross Middleton is as slick as owl grease. Just look at what he's accomplished already and no one's caught him, much less thought he was involved. I'd feel a lot better if you had the police to back you up.''

Logan set his tools on the table, leaned against the counter and gathered Avery in his arms. ''I'm sorry.''

''For what?'' she asked, but had a feeling she really didn't want to hear what was coming.

''I've charged headlong into this, dragging you into my nightmare of a life without asking you once if you wanted to stay. My offer still stands. If you want to leave here, I'll give you the money.''

''I'm not going anywhere, Logan. And you didn't drag me into anything. Besides, I'd like a little payback myself.''

''And what about *us?* We haven't had time to talk about that, have we?'' He rested his hands on her shoulders and gazed into her eyes. ''I don't want to push you into anything, Avery. Maybe we're going too fast....''

She wasn't going to lie or say something she wasn't sure of just to keep from hurting his feelings. She'd been doing that all her life. ''To tell you the truth, Logan, a lot has happened to me in the last year. I don't trust my instincts much anymore. What I'm saying is I can't read your mind. I need you to tell me what you expect from this relationship.''

Logan held her tightly against his chest and chuckled. ''And here I thought if I told you how I felt so soon, I'd probably scare you off.'' He grasped her by the shoulders and held her at arm's length. ''Don't look so surprised. I explained about Becky—that I never really loved her. Well, in fact I've never been in love, period. My family always teased Tanner about falling in love. Every time we turned around, he'd flipped over some cute little thing. Tanner would laugh at me and say things like 'just you wait,' or 'one of these days you'll know what it's like.'

''You see, I never expected to feel like this. Actually, I didn't want to.'' He caressed Avery's cheek with his knuckles. ''Then one day I looked up and there was this black-haired woman looking at me with incredible gray eyes. I finally knew what Tanner was talking about—it was like getting hit between the eyes. For the first time in my life I was in love. Isn't it the craziest thing you've ever heard?''

''No,'' she whispered, unable to take her gaze from his face. There was a softness in his that kept her from making light of the situation or of saying something to cover her own doubts. Deep down inside she was uncertain enough that she cringed as she waited for the punch line, for the joke to be on her. It never came.

She wanted to weep with the joy of knowing Logan loved her for herself. It didn't matter that she'd been in prison or that her possessions were few. He didn't care that her family was like something out of a bad novel. It didn't matter that she was kindhearted to a fault or that she loved a beat-up old tomcat. Logan didn't mind that her hips were a little too rounded. When she tried to tell him how she felt, she couldn't get a word in. It was as if a dam had broken inside Logan and he was determined to get it all out at once.

"You can't imagine how ridiculous I felt," he said. "I'm too old to get sweaty palms." He shook his head, still amazed by the depth of his feelings. "I dreamed about you at night, and I would stand at my bedroom window like some Romeo and long to be with you. I love watching you move and listening to your laughter. I thought I'd gone mad, and the harder I denied how I felt, the more I realized how hard I'd fallen."

Logan pressed a gentle finger to her lips. "You don't have to say anything. I wanted you to know how I feel."

Avery could barely contain herself, but anything she wanted to say was stopped by the appearance of Pierce and Mac at the door.

"Where's Tanner?" Mac asked. "He was goin' to help rig up the cameras."

Pierce gravely inspected the new locks, testing their strength and smooth workings. He gave Logan a nod of approval, then said to Avery, "With those locks and the solid doors, I think you'll be safe. How're you feeling?"

"Sore." The more she was around Pierce, the more she thought she might have been wrong about him. He seemed to be genuinely concerned about her welfare. Then she realized what it was that bothered her—Logan's coolness to his brother, which was so out of character. She sensed Pierce was a man struggling to bridge the gap between himself and his older brother, and Logan's less than enthusiastic attitude puzzled her. He only seemed to tolerate Pierce's presence, not have any real affection for him.

While Logan and Pierce went out to begin installing the cameras around the barn, Mac kept her company in the kitchen. He made himself comfortable at the table, with the coffee Avery had poured him. When she took a seat across from him, he chuckled.

"What?" she asked.

"I'm a really good matchmaker, don't you think?"

She stared at him as comprehension dawned. "Is *that* what you were doing by hiring me? What if I'd turned out to be an old bag?"

"But you ain't. I told that lady in Houston I wanted someone young enough to brighten up this dismal place."

"You did?" Avery bit her lip. Denise hadn't told her that. Maybe there was something else her good friend hadn't bothered to tell her.

"Yep, and I told her about Logan and the tragedy he'd been through."

Denise seemed to have left out quite a lot. Avery wondered why.

"I made it clear that I didn't care much about looks—'course, you being a real looker only added honey to the pot—but whoever she sent had to have a sense of humor and a good heart."

"I beg your pardon?"

Mac chuckled. "Don't play with me, young lady. You know very well what I mean. You got a deep-seated kindness in you that no amount of ugliness or pain is going to destroy."

"My sister thinks I'm just chickenhearted. A soft touch. She calls me the Pollyanna of peacemakers."

"Hells bells, this sister of yours, she just don't

know you at all, does she? Maybe what she thinks of as weakness is that sweetness in you that glows from your pretty eyes. It would steal any man's heart. Stole mine. And my son, well, he's his old self again. You've made him happy. Now, I don't pretend to know what's going on between you two or how it'll end, and I ain't one to interfere in my son's personal life." Cocking his head to the side, he smiled when Avery laughed. "What I'm saying is, I know you're innocent of stealing, and it don't matter a fig what people say. Don't let your past stand in the way of your happiness. We Monahans are a tough lot, and we can handle whatever's thrown at us. As for a past—we have a few skeletons in our closet. I'll tell you about them someday."

WAITING FOR TANNER, Avery quickly came to realize, was something the members of his family were used to. They even laughed about his tardiness, attributing it to the fact that Tanner must have run into one of his old flames. They'd moved to the spacious living room so Logan and Pierce could lay out the instructions for connecting the security cameras to the monitors—which Tanner had in his truck.

"It's been two hours," Avery said. "Isn't anyone concerned that something might have happened?"

"He'll turn up. Always does." Mac said.

"It takes my brother," Pierce said good-naturedly, "a couple hours just to shower and shave. The only time he's ever moved faster than a casual stroll was when he played basketball."

Logan had been carefully studying the directions, and glanced up when Tanner's name was mentioned.

"He should have called by now, though. I gave him that damn cellular phone for that very purpose."

Avery looked over Logan's shoulder and scowled at the instructions that were spread out like a road map and just about as confusing. "Jeez. Are you sure you know how to do it?"

"Sure. If we had the monitors, we'd have it done—" he snapped his fingers "—like that."

"Logan, whose idea was this?"

"Tanner's. Why?"

Avery was trying to keep her voice serious as she continued to stare at the directions. "The cameras." She sobered when three sets of male eyes gazed at her. They all had that pitying look men get when women try to muscle in on what they consider their territory. "The cameras—do they work in the dark?"

"What?" Logan studied her a moment, confused, as if she was speaking a foreign language. Tanner had never really outgrown his harebrained ideas. Long experience should have taught Logan better than to get taken in. His scowl deepened.

Avery pointed to the bottom of the instruction sheet. "I've always made a habit of reading the fine print. It says right there that the security cameras will only work properly in well-lit areas. Most of Ross's work has been at night, hasn't it? I don't think—"

She stopped at the sound of the front door opening. When a tall woman stepped into the living room, Avery thought she was hallucinating.

"Emma!" she said, her voice husky with emotion. "Emma, is that really you?" She was too stunned to do more than stand up as her sister raced toward her and threw her arms around her. "Oh, Emma, it *is* you!"

"Why didn't you tell me how much trouble you were in? And who are all these people?"

"They're friends, Emma." Avery smiled. "And they know everything about me."

She felt Emma relax in her embrace, then felt her shaking. She pulled back and saw, to her astonishment, that her sister was crying.

"You should have told me about the trial and jail," Emma said on the high end of a loud hiccup.

Avery smiled again. Some things never changed. As a little girl Emma had considered crying a weakness, but her efforts to mask her emotions had found their own outlet. She always got the hiccups.

"I would have come. My God, sis, you were in that awful place and didn't tell me. Why?"

"I tried to call when I got out of jail, but your phone was disconnected." Avery broke away, took a step back and turned a critical eye on her sister. Emma was the beauty of the family. She was five foot eleven, with broad shoulders, a tiny waist and legs that went on forever. She was still as thin as a willow, but made of pure steel. Emma was the gladiator, the street fighter. When Emma was on the warpath, there was no such thing as taking prisoners.

Avery brushed back Emma's coal-black hair, which hung in thick, soft waves almost to her shoulders. Her sister looked tired. Worried. Her heather-gray eyes were dark and shadowed. Her usually luminous, milky complexion had an unhealthy pallor, and her clothes—cocoa silk blouse and matching linen slacks—were crumpled and wrinkled. "Are you okay? Are you sick?"

"Sick, yes. Sick at heart for what you went through."

"How'd you get here?" Suddenly she noticed Tanner standing by the entrance to the living room. She frowned. "Do you two know each other?"

"Yes," Tanner said.

Avery stiffened as she saw Tanner's white teeth flash, his mouth curve in one of his charming smiles. He was looking at Emma, his dark eyes roaming over every inch of her sister's body.

"No, we *don't* know each other," Emma snarled. "The cowboy in his bubba-mobile rear-ended me at a traffic light. The only traffic light, I might add, in town. Now how smart is that?"

Tanner straightened to his full six foot seven and looked down his nose at Emma. "If you hadn't slammed on your brakes at a green light while you decided which way you wanted to go, I wouldn't have hit you."

Emma had never been self-conscious of her height; if anything, she used it to her advantage. Avery bit her lip, wondering how many times in her life her sister had had to look up at a man. Then she noticed that the Monahans seemed fascinated by the exchange, as if watching two beautiful gods squabbling like children.

Knowing her sister and enough about Tanner to realize sparks were going to fly, Avery decided to intervene before things got ugly. She introduced Emma to Mac, Pierce and Logan, then motioned for her sister to take a seat beside her on the couch. "And you've already met Tanner Monahan." She could have kicked herself as the two glowered at each other.

"Is that his name?"

"You know very well it is. I introduced myself."

"Yes, with your bubba-mobile jammed into my bumper."

Emma turned her back on Tanner, dismissing him as if he didn't exist. Avery leapt in and asked, "So how did you find me?"

"After I left Seattle—"

"You saw Dad?"

"And David."

Logan, sitting on Avery's other side, settled an arm around her shoulders—a protective move no one missed. One of Emma's perfectly arched eyebrows rose in silent question, but Avery only smiled sweetly. When Casanova jumped on her lap and stared at Emma, her sister looked horrified.

"What kind of creature is that? And why is he giving me the evil eye?"

Avery introduced Casanova as if he was a member of the Monahan family. The cat, she noticed, was on his best behavior and answered with a low meow, but didn't budge from her lap, nor take his gaze off the new arrival. "He won't hurt you."

Logan laughed. "Unless you make any sort of threatening move toward Avery, or try and dislodge him from your bed, or touch her jar of M&M's..."

Emma looked confused and Avery came to her rescue. "Go on, tell me how you got here."

"Denise. I called Denise. I knew she'd be the only one who wouldn't lie to me. And if anyone knew where you were, she would." She reached for Avery's hand and jerked as Casanova swatted her.

"What's with that animal?" She glared at Casanova, who glared back. "I'm her sister, you silly beast." Emma didn't try to touch Avery again, however. "I want you to know I called you several times in the past few months, but your home telephone had been disconnected. Then I called the office, and Dad's secretary always had an excuse why I couldn't talk to him. When I finally got hold of David at home, he never once mentioned what had happened or that you were in jail. Of course, now I know he didn't want me to find out where you were. He knew I'd be on the first plane.''

"How *did* you find out?"

"I didn't, not until I got to Seattle and contacted some of your friends. By the way, I called Peter, and how you could ever have considered marrying that man is beyond me.''

"Who," Logan demanded, "is Peter?"

"Peter Kincaid," Emma offered with far too much glee. "Avery's fiancé.''

"*Ex*-fiancé," Avery said.

"The jerk," Emma said, before Avery could defend him. "He's the son of one of Dad's law partners and an associate of the firm. He dropped Avery the moment the scandal hit the newspapers, didn't he, Avery? Don't answer. I've already heard the grisly details.''

Avery would have told it in kinder terms, but her sister had summed up what had happened too neatly to try to gloss over the events. Trying to stop Emma once she'd warmed up to a subject was like trying to stop a moving train. Avery gave a quick shake of her head to warn Logan not to ask. She grasped his hand and whispered, "You'll get more than you bargained for. Let her run down some and I'll tell you.''

"When I read the back issues of the newspapers on the trial and all the charges and what you were convicted of, I tell you, it wasn't much of a stretch to know that David's evil hand was behind the mess."

Emma, it seemed, couldn't sit still any longer, and she jumped up and began to pace the floor.

"I went to the house and told Dad what a fool he was to ever believe you'd steal anything. That did about as much good as it always does when someone says anything against David. Nothing ever changes. Well, I fixed the golden boy."

Emma stopped and, smiled, and Avery saw that everyone was captivated. What they didn't see was the flash of fire in her eyes. Avery had heard those words before, that same declaration, and knew Emma had done something to match David's behavior. Avery surprised herself by laughing.

"I hope that whatever punishment you dealt your brother," Logan said, "will equal what he did to Avery."

"Oh, I think you can count on it," Tanner interjected. "Avery's little sister—"

"Emma," Emma snapped.

Tanner bowed. "*Emma* doesn't strike me as the forgiving type."

"Not," Emma said, "when someone hurts my sister." She eyed each man in the room as she returned to her seat on the sofa.

Avery frowned. Tanner seemed determined to needle her sister into losing her temper. And she sensed that Logan and the other Monahans were enjoying themselves too much. She poked him in the ribs as a warning not to encourage his brother.

Logan said, "Let Emma finish, will you, Tanner?"

"Thank you," Emma said.

"So what did you do?" Avery asked her.

"Do you remember Joe Fairaway?"

"Oh, no, Emma. What have you done?" She closed her eyes for a second before she glanced at Logan. "Joe was a childhood friend. He was also a computer hacker, and when he was about thirteen, the FBI caught him. Joe did a couple months in a juvenile jail. When he got out, the people he stole from hired him to set up their computer security. Anyway, Joe's one of those whiz kids. But, Emma, didn't Joe move to Ireland?"

"Yes, but I ran into him several times in Paris. We kind of rekindled our friendship. You'll love this, Avery. When I read all the details of the trial, I called Joe and he flew to Seattle. We broke into David's computers—the one in his office and the one at home. And guess what?"

"You found all the evidence of what he'd done to Avery?" Tanner asked.

"No. My brother's too clever to do something so stupid. But, sis, he's at it *again.* Stealing from Dad's clients. He thinks he's just too clever to get caught.

"Joe and I copied his files from the office and home. Before I left for Houston to find Denise, I delivered copies to your attorney, with a check to cover expenses. I made sure the five clients whose estates he's been pilfering got copies, and the district attorney. Then for good measure, I mailed a copy to the fraud division of the police."

Emma was obviously proud of herself, and Avery wouldn't have ruined her sister's moment of triumph for anything. She smiled, but deep down, despite the way her father had treated her, she couldn't help but feel sorry for the old man and how embarrassed and devastated he'd be when the truth was known.

"Thank you, Emma." She pushed Casanova off her lap, then turned and hugged her sister.

"I know you, Avery," said Emma. "You would just as soon I had left things as they were. But after all you've done for me, all the sacrifices you made to send me to Paris and the Sorbonne, how could I not fight your battles for you? Having your good name and your life ruined by David was just too much for me to bear. Look at it this way. Just as soon as this mess is cleared up, and it will be, you can pick up your old life. You can go home."

"Emma—" Avery kissed her sister's cheek "—I *am* home."

CHAPTER THIRTEEN

"YOU'RE NOT SERIOUS!" Emma gasped.

Avery was pleased at her sister's stunned expression. "Emma, you're bulldozing your way without knowing all the facts. Stop a moment. Take a deep breath. Now let it out and listen carefully. I *am* serious. I have no intention of ever going back to Seattle."

"But your life there? Don't you want to clear your name?"

"Of course I do."

"If you don't go back and face Dad and David down, they'll have won."

"It's not a matter of payback or winning, Emma dear. Don't you see? I don't want to be around them. No matter what's happened or what happens in the future, Dad will never change and neither will David. As a kid you were smarter and wiser than I was. You had them pegged for what they were, and you knew it would only get worse. So you had the courage to leave home. It's taken me longer to get the message, but I finally did. That's why I'm here. I belong here, Emma. Don't you see that?"

Avery realized for the first time how quiet Logan and the rest of his family were. Maybe she was ahead of herself. After all, Logan had said he loved her, but he hadn't made that leap from love to a lifetime together. "Even if I decided not to stay in Haven, I wouldn't go back to Seattle. And I'll tell you another shocker—I don't want to be a lawyer, either."

Emma placed her hand across Avery's forehead. "You're sick or something." She glared at Tanner as if he were to blame. "What has this place done to you, Avery? You nearly killed yourself getting that damn law degree."

"Maybe if you'd stop badgering her and listen for a change," Tanner offered, his charming smile slipping at the corners, "you might learn something."

Logan rose to his feet and motioned his nosy and fascinated family out of the room.

"Tanner," Mac said, "that means you, too. Join us in the kitchen, Son, before you get your eyes scratched out."

Avery clutched Logan's hand and gave it a hard tug. "I don't want them to leave. Please don't go, any of you. Emma, Tanner's right. You're not listening to me, and it's especially important. When I told Logan I'd been in jail for embezzlement, do you know what his first words were? He wanted to know who'd framed me. And Mac, Pierce and Tanner—they didn't believe it, either. Emma, my friends and business associates, some I'd known all my adult life, didn't have that kind of faith in me. You'd be surprised just how fast they turned their backs on me."

"Okay, I understand your bitterness, but is that any reason to stay here?"

Avery was fast losing her patience. "You still don't get it, Emma. I'm in love with Logan." The silence was so total she thought everyone could hear her heart stop. Truth, she realized, was only a slip of the tongue away.

Logan was the first to recover. He laughed, not nervously or with embarrassment, but a deep rolling sound of pure joy. "Finally," he said when he was able to speak. "I didn't think I'd ever get you to admit it." He clasped her face in his hands and kissed her slowly and sweetly.

When she could draw breath, Avery said dreamily, "If I remember correctly, you wouldn't let me do much talking."

"That's because I needed for you to be sure. You are, aren't you?"

"Oh, yes."

"I knew it!" Mac jumped up, circled behind the couch so he could kiss Avery on the cheek. Pierce nodded his approval, but Tanner stood aside and said, "I'll take my turn when she's more receptive to my congratulations."

Logan gave Tanner a hard look. "You'll take it now and forget about later."

"I don't understand," Emma said, drawing herself out of Tanner's way as he leaned across her to kiss Avery.

"Of course you don't." Tanner flashed her a winning smile. "You've obviously never been in love."

Avery was suddenly overwhelmed by her decision. Wasn't she the one who had found out the hard way that she couldn't trust her instincts? And what had happened to the decision she'd made that she would rather be alone—that that was better than giving her heart and having it crushed with lies and deceit? What had she done?

Logan saw the panic, smiled and whispered, "Don't worry, it'll all work out."

"But, Logan—"

"Avery!" Emma wasn't one to give up easily. "You can't throw your career away just like that. What would you do? Become a farmer's wife?"

"This is a ranch, and actually, Logan's a veterinarian. As for what I'd do? I've been tutoring four teenage boys and you know what? I love it. If I could ever prove my innocence, I'd like to be a teacher. If not, I'll go on tutoring."

"This is crazy. Remind me not to drink the water here. I know there's something strange in it. You surely can't mean to throw your life away?"

"Oh, Emma, I know you forget sometimes, but I *am* older than you, and that time in jail made me a whole lot wiser about what's important and what's not. There are things in life, Emma, that don't have to make sense. I love you dearly, and please don't be offended, but do me a favor and mind your own business."

Logan glanced at everyone, including Emma, and said, "Now all we have to do is live long enough to enjoy old age. That means stopping Ross from killing me and Avery."

Emma turned to him. "What did you say?"

LUNCH, despite Tanner's famous grilled cheese sandwiches and Logan's chocolate malts, turned out to be an ordeal. None of the lengthy explanations from Mac or reassurances from Pierce soothed Emma's fears. And once her sister heard the facts of what had happened and was still happening at the ranch, Avery knew Emma would be more determined than ever to get her away from here.

Logan was uncommonly silent through the heated arguments. When Emma finally ran out of objections,

Avery leaned against his shoulder and whispered, "It's not personal. Emma's only worried about me."

"She has a right to be. Hearing it all laid out in detail and in order makes me realize just how dangerous Ross is."

"But, Logan," Avery said, "you told me the only way to prove it's Ross is to catch him. We need solid, indisputable proof. Of course, the security cameras would have solved that problem, but…"

"What's that about cameras?" Tanner asked.

Logan gave his brother the foldout sheet of instructions and pointed to the bottom. "You need to read the small print. They won't work at night."

Tanner read it and didn't answer; instead, he dashed from the kitchen. When he returned, he cleared a spot on the table, deposited four cigar-size boxes and slowly opened one box.

The suspense was too much for Emma. She grabbed the box and tore off the wrapping, then held up a drab, olive-green cylinder the size of a soft-drink can. Attached to its side were two long thin wires.

Everyone studied the objects with puzzled expressions. Logan broke the silence. "It has military stamped all over it. That can mean only one thing— Joaquin Brightstone. He's the only person we know who has access to this sort of device." He glanced at Tanner. "I'm not even going to ask how these ended up in your hands."

"Good." Tanner's smile was full of triumph. "They're night-vision lenses for the cameras. Shame on all of you. Did you really think I'd overlook something so important?"

"Show-off," Mac grumbled.

Logan declined to comment, but rose instead,

picked up a box and prodded his reluctant brothers and Mac out of the kitchen.

Avery roped Emma into helping her clean the kitchen. Her sister was thoughtfully quiet, and when they finished, Emma sighed, then wrapped an arm around her.

"I love you, Avery, and if you're happy, then so am I."

"Good. Would you do me a favor and try to get along with Logan?"

"Sure, as long I know he loves you. But if I ever doubt his feelings, I swear, I'll tear him apart." They both laughed and Emma added, "He is a sexy devil, isn't he?"

"Who? Logan or Tanner?" Avery dodged the flying wet dishrag.

"Logan, of course. Buckskin Billy's a little too slick for my tastes. I bet he's so scared of commitment he measures his relationships in dog years." Their laughter trickled off as they realized Logan had caught the tail end of the conversation. When he agreed that their assessment of his brother was on the mark, they all had a good laugh.

Avery watched with interest as Emma set out to charm Logan. She couldn't help but think that her sister and Tanner were more alike than either would admit. But there was a change in Emma that bothered her, a chink in her usual self-assured brashness that Avery couldn't quite put her finger on.

Then she knew. Emma was hiding something. Why the word *fear* popped into her head, she couldn't say. But that was what it was. Emma was frightened and it had nothing to do with her, the Monahans or Ross Middleton.

Avery had always been able to get Emma to reveal her secrets. It just took a little time. But right now she judged it a good moment to leave Logan and Emma alone to get better acquainted. Avery spotted Casanova stalking the M&M's candy jar, scooped him up and headed toward the living room.

LOGAN WAITED until he was sure Avery was out of hearing before he spoke. "Let's get a few things straight. I love Avery. I'll never let anything or anyone harm her. I'll make her happy. That's the end of it, Emma. I don't owe you any explanations or excuses, and neither does Avery. It's obvious that you haven't seen your sister in some time. But I was a witness to her arrival, fresh out of jail, wounded in her soul and hurt beyond physical pain. And I've watched her slowly heal.

"I saw the sparkle return to her eyes and heard the first notes of joy in her laughter. I saw all that, and I know she's not only happy now but at peace with what happened before."

"You're right. Of course you're right." Emma sat, rested her elbows on the table and rubbed her face. "I nearly went crazy when I found out what David had done." She shrugged. "I don't expect you to understand."

Distracted by a noise behind her, Emma turned. Tanner had entered the kitchen. When he joined them, she didn't stop talking or make a snide remark. "You'll never know," she continued, "what Avery put up with when we were all kids. I tease her about being the peacemaker, but it's true. She lied for me. She took the blame for me, and even suffered father's heavy-handed punishment when it should have been me.'' She swiped at a tear.

''I don't even know if I can put it into words, but she did everything in her power to keep peace in that dysfunctional family. Did Avery tell you that after I ran away and was living with our aunt, she supported me? No, of course not. When my sister realized I was never coming home, she worked an extra job so I wouldn't be a burden on our aunt. Then when she found out I wanted to be a fashion designer and dreamed of going to Paris, she made it financially possible.

''Don't you see that this is the only time in our lives that I've been able to do anything for Avery? For once I could repay a little of what she's done for me.''

Logan touched Emma's shoulder. ''And all Avery has ever wanted in return was for you to find happiness.''

''That's what's made my guilt so hard to live with. Knowing how good-natured she is and how easy it was for David and Dad to take advantage of her, I still left. I deserted her.'' Emma eyed Tanner, braced for a mocking comment.

But it wasn't mocking. ''Then don't run out on her again,'' Tanner said. ''Stay here for a while. Help us do what we can to make her safe and happy.'' He glanced at Logan. ''My brother deserves someone like Avery in his life. We all do.''

AVERY HAD TRIED NOT TO eavesdrop, but it was impossible to shut out their words when they made no attempt to lower their voices. She listened to Emma and Logan as she stood in front of the bay window overlooking a wide sweep of pasture. The wildflowers and the grazing cattle were only blurs of color through her tears. They weren't tears of sorrow, however, but happiness. For the first time in a lifetime of doubts, she felt like a whole person. That was Logan's doing.

Crying for happiness was new to her, and she quickly blinked away tears. The scenery wobbled back into focus and then she saw a plume of dust billowing from between the trees that lined the road. "Logan. Logan, you'd better come here." As she spoke, she heard Mac and Pierce entering the kitchen. "All of you had better come here!" she shouted.

Dry mouthed, she watched a vehicle break from the deep shadows of the trees. Her stomach knotted with nerves. "It's the sheriff's car." She didn't hear Logan come up behind her, and jumped when he wrapped his arms around her. She felt the deep movement of his chest as he sighed.

"Don't get your hopes up. Just the fact that he's coming here doesn't mean he'll show his hand. But whatever's brought him here at that reckless speed, you can bet it's trouble. He's angry and it's going to be ugly."

"I know."

"I wish you didn't have to be here." Logan glanced over his shoulder at his family and Emma as they took up positions around the room. He'd warned them not to interfere no matter what Ross said. "Come on, you guys. You look like a bunch of junk-yard dogs spoiling for a fight. Settle down. It's no use letting him know we've been expecting him."

"Just not this early!" Tanner snapped back angrily.

Avery grinned. Tanner was out for blood. They all

were, herself included. Tanner, she figured, was more than a little peeved that he wasn't going to get to use his new toy. Mac appeared to be the calmest, but on closer inspection she saw the way a muscle in his jaw jumped. From the corner of her eye, she .caught a strange look pass between Logan and Pierce. As quickly as she was certain she'd seen coldness and rage in Logan's gaze, it was gone, and she wasn't sure what she'd witnessed. When Logan directed his attention elsewhere, she saw how pale and shaken Pierce appeared, and couldn't help but wonder what was going on.

She didn't have time to ponder the strange reactions. She only had time for one brief amusing thought—that no one ever knocked in this house—before the front door was shoved wide. She wished she could have shared the thought with Logan, then caught his wink and smiled. It was comforting to know he knew her so well.

She sobered with her first good look at Ross. If there was ever a man who shouldn't have been wearing a loaded weapon on his hip, it was him.

Avery was scared. The air around them seemed to crackle with tension.

"Good, you've got the whole family here, and the ladies, to see you off. Logan, you're under arrest." He smiled at their shock and surprise. "You have the right to remain…"

No one had expected the direction of Ross's assault, and paralysis gripped the room.

Logan was the first to speak. "Arrest? For what, Ross?"

The sheriff's jaw was set, his eyes unblinking and glassy.

"What's the charge?" Logan asked again.

Ross twisted around and called, "Jessie, come in here."

Avery was shocked at the deep purple bruise on the side of Jessie's face and her cut and swollen lip.

"For starters let's try assault," snarled Ross, "then maybe we'll try rape. If I can get her to admit it."

"Jess…" Logan took a step toward the girl, but she backed fearfully away.

"You have the right to an attorney—"

"I know you're mad, Ross, that someone could do that to Jess. I am, too. But you're not yourself or you'd know how crazy this is. I've never laid a hand on anyone and I'd certainly never harm Jess." Logan held out his hand to her as if to offer support. "Jess, who did that to you? When did it happen?"

Ross took a couple of steps closer to Logan. "When did it happen? Try night before last—here in this house. But you didn't have the guts to stick around and face what you'd done. Instead, you left. Left with your girlfriend so you could celebrate Fiesta." Ross shoved Logan backward, his move swift, like a striking snake.

He'd surprised Logan, but Logan recovered and stood his ground.

"When Jess wasn't at the ball," Ross continued, "I knew something was wrong. I looked all over San Antonio for her. She was hiding from me, Logan. And do you know why? To protect your sorry butt."

Avery was compelled to speak. "Jessie's lying, Ross. Look at her. She can't meet anyone's eyes."

Ross ignored Avery. His face was fiery with rage. "If you can't afford an attorney, one will be appointed."

Avery couldn't let the girl wreck both their lives. She knew what the stigma of being branded a criminal felt like, and what having been in jail could do. It didn't wash away.

"Don't do this, Jessie. Don't destroy Logan's life just because you're mad at me. Look around." She waved her arm. "You've known these people almost all your life. The Monahans love you. They've been good to you and only wanted what's best for you.

"If you go through with this lie, Jessie, you'll never be able to take it back. Don't be bullied into doing something you're going to regret." She didn't know why she felt sorry for Jessie. Maybe if someone had reached out a hand to David, things would have turned out differently.

"Hiding behind a woman's skirts now, Logan?"

Ross's laughter was harsh and mean. His attention shifted to Avery, and she flinched as if she'd been hit. She recognized the look of scorn and knew what was coming. Even though Logan and the rest of his family were aware of her past, it didn't make hearing the details spoken with such malice any less painful.

"Did you know your... What is she, Logan?"

There was a wealth of contempt in his question. Avery shivered.

"Oh, yeah," Ross said with a sneer. "She's your housekeeper. Did you know she's a jailbird?"

"We're all well aware of Avery's past, Ross," Mac said. "We also know she's innocent."

"And how do you know that? Because she told you? Trust me—" Ross snickered "—that's what all criminals say when they shut those cell doors. Did she tell you what she was in for? Embezzlement, stealing money from people's estates. How does that sit with you, Logan? You're sleeping with a common thief.''

Logan struck so fast Ross never saw the fist coming. Pandemonium broke out. Mac and Pierce rushed at Logan and Ross, locked together in a vicious struggle.

Tanner restrained Emma from jumping Ross from behind.

Avery figured the men could take care of themselves. Her attention was on Jessie, who stood to one side staring at her with wide, shocked eyes. Apparently her past was something Ross hadn't told his sister.

Picking up the nearest lamp, Avery smashed it to the floor. If she hadn't been so scared, she might have laughed as the whole tableau froze. All eyes turned toward her.

''Stop it this minute!'' she snapped, and jammed her fists on her hips. ''Grown men, acting no better than teenage thugs. This isn't getting us anywhere.''

Avery stood her ground until the men reluctantly parted and backed away from each other. Ross crossed his arms in a belligerent pose and tried to stare her down. She refused to be cowed, then surprised everyone by saying, ''Sheriff, how could you drag your sister here and humiliate her this way?''

''Would any one of you have believed me if you hadn't seen her and heard her accuse Logan?''

''This isn't about Jessie,'' Avery snarled, ''and you know it. I doubt that *you* even care who really hurt her.'' She paused. ''Maybe it was you.'' Ross's arms dropped to his sides and she tensed. ''Even if you hate Logan, you know he couldn't have done this. You *know* him, Ross.''

"I thought I did once."

"You still do, but first let's get to the bottom of this mess." She shifted her angry gaze to Jessie. "Night before last you came here, didn't you? You came to the house and you searched for Logan. Instead, you heard us together in bed. Isn't that right, Jessie?"

Jess bit her lip and her gaze shifted to a spot between her feet.

"But you didn't believe what you thought was happening, so you went upstairs. You stood outside the open door and listened and maybe watched. You were hurt and angry. Then, in a childish fit of jealous rage, you broke into my quarters and destroyed everything I owned. More than anything, you wanted to hurt Logan like he'd hurt you. Didn't you, Jess?"

"This has gone far enough," Ross growled. "You're under arrest, Logan."

"Damn you, Ross." Logan started toward him, but Mac stepped between them.

"Jess, gal," Mac said, "you're like a daughter to me. Whatever's the matter, whatever you need, I'll help you. You won't get into any trouble. I'll talk to your parents. They'll listen to me, you know they will. But don't do this. Don't destroy Logan's life with false accusations over feelings you don't understand. Tell Ross the truth."

Without meeting Mac's imploring gaze, Jessie shook her head.

Ross laughed, a self-satisfied sound.

Avery wasn't about to give up. Jessie had managed to end up as her brother's pawn, but Avery wasn't going to let Logan's reputation be ruined by these two vengeful people. She took a breath and forged on.

"Jess, your charges won't stick because I'll swear to a judge and God and anyone else who will listen that I've been with Logan day and night."

"Who'd believe a convicted criminal?" Ross asked.

Logan itched to smash the smirk off Ross's face. He took a step, but once again Mac restraining him.

Avery ignored Ross's comment and focused on Jessie. "Your brother's using you, Jessie. He knows Logan would never hurt you. Can't you see he's willing to use you for his own twisted reasons? Don't let him ruin your life, too. Look at Ross, Jessie, take a good long look. He's enjoying himself."

But Jessie still didn't lift her head, and Avery felt like she was talking to empty space.

Her hold was slipping and she shifted her attack back to Ross. "Jessie's battered face fit right in with your plans, didn't it? Maybe you even planned to blame everything you've done on Jessie. Most of the incidents were rather childish attempts at revenge, weren't they? Jessie would certainly look guilty. After all, she's just a high-strung, lovesick girl with an unhealthy obsession for Logan. Isn't that what you told me? Or did you mean that Jessie could take the blame for what you did and get away with it because she's unstable?"

"Ross," Jessie whispered to her brother, "what's she talking about?"

"Nothing, Jess. Don't listen to her lies." Ross looked at Logan. "As far as I'm concerned, you murdered Becky. Then you went after Jess. Do you think I'm so stupid I didn't see the way you looked at her? The way you've kept her hanging around you?"

Logan ignored Ross and spoke to Jessie. "Ask him

who's responsible for the vandalism at the clinic. The barn fire, Jess. Blackie's disappearance. The cut fences. The loose livestock. Fouled grain. The poisoned feed. Jamie's toys smashed, and the rattlesnake in Avery's quarters. A dozen other things aimed at hurting me. He wanted me to believe that the boys…'' he paused significantly ''or maybe even you caused them.''

''But I didn't!'' Jessie cried. ''I didn't do any of those awful things! You don't think I did them, do you, Logan? Oh, please,'' she begged. ''I did ruin her things and put the snake in the house. That's all. I'm sorry.''

It was pathetic how Jess gazed at Ross for help and guidance. Logan couldn't stand it. ''I know you didn't do those other things, Jess. But don't you see, Ross doesn't give a damn about you. He has his own plan for revenge and he's not through dealing his cards.'' Logan stared at her. ''The *truth,* Jess.''

Jessie covered her face with her hands and mumbled through her fingers, ''I don't know what's happening to me. I never meant to hurt anyone.'' She sobbed as she raised a tearstained face. ''He didn't do it, Ross. Logan didn't hurt me. It was Harper Smith.''

''You stupid bitch,'' Ross snarled. ''Shut your mouth.''

The time was right to deliver the final blow. Logan wanted to make Ross lose control and either admit his lies or say enough to push him closer to revealing himself. ''You see, Jess,'' Logan taunted, but he was looking at Ross, ''your brother doesn't want the truth. Then he'd have to admit he's been wrong all along and he might have to face what he's done.''

"I don't understand." Jessie looked at Ross with beseeching eyes. "What's he talking about?"

"I told you to shut up, Jess."

Logan couldn't afford to feel sorry for Jess. "Ross thinks I got away with murder, Jess. He knew that during the investigation of Becky's death, I didn't tell everything about what happened that night. Your sister wasn't a careless driver. He knew something serious had to have happened for Becky to be so distracted that she'd pull out in front of that eighteen-wheeler. The truth is, Becky and I argued and I told her I was going to file for divorce and take Jamie away from her."

"But why?" Jessie looked stunned.

"Because she'd been unfaithful too many times for me to ignore the last man she had an affair with."

Ross exploded in anger and charged at Logan. "You're a goddamn liar! My sister was no whore! She didn't sleep around!"

Logan grunted as a fist chopped him in the ribs. "Ross, open your eyes. Becky—" he jerked his head to the right and barely missed catching one on the jaw "—Becky wasn't a saint." He ached to hit Ross, but he had to finish what he had to say.

"Who? Who was she sleeping with?" Ross laughed, but there was no humor in the sound. "You can't name anyone, can you? What happened that night, Logan? Did you hit her like you hit Jess? Did she run because she was scared of you?"

They shoved each other. Logan said, "How many times do you think I heard gossip about her lovers when I was in San Antonio? She was a tramp."

Ross's sudden stillness made it obvious Logan had gone too far. The sheriff grabbed him by the throat.

Avery circled the struggling, grunting men, yelling at them to stop. She was only somewhat relieved when Logan managed to break Ross's crushing hold.

Ross's hatred was beyond understanding, but Logan seemed driven to inflame him even more. As the two continued, she beseeched Mac to help stop the fight.

"No," Mac said. "Let them play it out."

Mac held Avery at bay. At last he nodded toward Tanner and Pierce, and she saw the brothers step in, each grabbing a combatant and pulling him away. Mac supervised the exodus of Ross and Jessie from the house. Then the rest of the Monahans, including Mac, followed.

Exhausted and angry, Avery collapsed in the nearest chair. "Oh, hell, let them kill each other, I don't care." She felt Emma's comforting arm slip around her shoulders and struggled to control her emotions. Casanova leapt into her lap and immediately, and vocally, began commiserating with her.

"Did you *see* them, Emma?" Now that the danger of Logan and Ross beating each other to death had passed, she felt appalled by their caveman mentality. "Am I crazy, or were they enjoying themselves?"

"Like ducks in a cornfield, sis. You have to admit the whole thing was exhilarating, even amusing."

"How can you *say* that?"

"Those Monahan men just might be in the wrong profession. They should form a roving troubadour group or start an acting school."

Avery thought Emma had lost her mind. "What are you talking about? Are you saying it was all faked?"

"Most of it was planned, at least on the brothers' side. You needn't shake your head at me. I swear it was. You were too busy to see the little looks and nods, all the silent signals that passed between them. For a bunch of cowboys, the Monahans are sure full of surprises.'' Emma tapped Avery's chin. ''Close your mouth, sis. They're coming back.''

Avery examined each man as they came through the door. If they weren't outwardly jovial or slapping each other on the back, there was definitely an air of satisfaction about them.

Tanner was the first to speak. ''You were great, Avery. I tell you, when you smashed that lamp, it got everyone's attention.''

Avery stared at him and the rest of the Monahans. ''You sound like it was all a big game. Am I dumb? Or was this a man thing I was meant to miss?''

Logan shoved Tanner out of the way. He removed Casanova from her lap, then squatted by the side of Avery's chair. ''It was a last-minute plan and I really didn't have time to fill you in. We figured if Ross showed up and we had a confrontation, he would never admit what he'd done. He was going to need a shove. I've known him for a long time. When Ross loses his temper, he makes mistakes. So we decided the best way was to push all his buttons.''

''From his reaction, Logan, you pushed more than just buttons.''

''Yeah.'' He grinned, then sobered when he saw her scowl. ''But we didn't get what we wanted, though. Jess's condition and accusations threw me.''

''Threw us all,'' Mac said. ''Poor little thing.''

''Well, it was obvious,'' Emma interjected, ''that Jess is a fruitcake.''

''No,'' Mac said sadly. ''She's just unloved.''

Avery silently agreed. ''What I don't understand is

why Ross dragged her here.'' She waved away what Emma was about to say. "I heard what he said, but that wasn't true. She was so humiliated and ashamed. Then to have to admit she'd lied. Ross should be shot."

"Brothers!" Emma said in disgust.

Mac's jaw clenched and knotted. "That is the last time Ross uses that girl."

"Will someone tell me what he hoped to gain?" Emma asked.

Logan explained. "He thought he could push me over the edge so I'd confess what happened the night Becky died. Jess played right into his plans. Her condition and state of mind were powerful weapons as evidence for a case of rape against me."

"But it didn't work," Avery said. "In the end Jessie blew Ross's plan apart when she admitted she'd lied." She closed her eyes for a moment, then gazed at him, her expression troubled. "I think you've only made the problem worse."

"I know," Logan said. "Ross isn't through. I haven't paid for my sins yet."

Avery stood up and looked around. "What happens next? What do we do?"

"You? Nothing. When he returns this time, I'll be waiting for him. Everyone else leaves. You and Emma can go with Mac."

"No!" Avery and Emma declared in unison.

"No, Logan," Avery said. "I'm not leaving. Besides, if Ross is as smart and sneaky as you say, he'll know if we leave and realize you've set a trap. I agree your father and brothers should go. Ross might be watching. We'll just have to be extra careful." Avery listened patiently to all his arguments. But when Lo-

254 SAFE HAVEN

gan started doing a finger count, listing all the logical reasons for her departure, she picked up Casanova and left the room.

Emma followed Avery. Halfway out of the room, she turned to the men and said, ''I could have warned you what happens when she gets that sweet, sugar-wouldn't-melt-in-her-mouth expression. I could have warned you just how stubborn my sister can be when she's made up her mind. I *could* tell you—but I won't. It'll be too much fun watching you guys learn the hard way.''

CHAPTER FOURTEEN

LOGAN KISSED THE BASE of Avery's neck. "I love this warm spot, right here." She laughed as his lips moved on to nibble her earlobe. "And I love this spot." His lips trailed across the top of her breasts.

Flushed, disheveled and smiling, Avery raised her head. "There ought to be a law against feeling this way."

"What way?"

"Wonderful. Happy." She loosened her arms from around his neck and captured his face between her hands. "In love. There's something to be said about making up after an argument, too."

Logan chuckled. "What argument? I tried to talk some sense into you and you kept smiling and walking away. We have to talk about that. It's not fair, you know."

Her kiss halted anything else he might say. When she pulled away, she asked, "Fair? Who ever said love was fair? I hate having the cards stacked against me before I start." She ran her hands over his shoulders, then let her fingertips trail up and down his naked body. He had a beautiful physique, all hard muscle and smooth warm skin.

Logan's breath caught as her hand slipped between them. "I'm sorry I didn't tell you what we'd planned." He gazed into her eyes and, with his heart pounding against hers, said, ''I feel I might burst with so much love.''

She gave him a playful tweak and laughed when he gasped, then she wriggled out from under him.

''That's a brave move,'' he said, ''for someone as tempting as you are this very minute.''

''You *couldn't*. Not after what we just did.''

''You're right,'' he said, ''I don't rebound like I use to. At least, not right away.'' Logan rolled onto his back, slipped his arm under her shoulders and pulled her against him.

Avery sighed. For a day of disaster and an evening that started out badly, they'd certainly ended in the right place. ''Do you really believe Ross won't do anything tonight?''

''He'd be a fool to try. After this afternoon, he knows we're on to him. He'll be on guard and won't be stupid and tip his hand.''

''There's something that still bothers me, Logan. I know he blames you for Becky and Jamie's death. But I get this weird feeling there's more. He keeps accusing you of killing her. As if the accident was really your fault. Was he always so protective of Becky?''

''More like obsessive about her. They were close in age. Jess, remember, came years later, a late-in-life child for their parents. Becky was bright and beautiful, but even as a teenager she was wild. I always thought she was reckless. She loved danger and pushed the limits in just about everything she did. Ross was always there for her. Her protector. Her rock. He fought her battles and smoothed the way for anything she wanted.''

''What about their parents?''

"The Middletons were a cliché for ultra rich, self-absorbed couples. They followed the Thoroughbred racehorse circuit all over the world. That meant they weren't home most of the time and left Ross and Becky in the care of servants. I can't fault Ross for his protectiveness. If anyone hurt one of my brothers, I'd cut him off at the knees. Maybe it's different when your sibling's a sister. But Ross's devotion to Becky always made me uneasy. It seemed…unhealthy somehow."

Talking about the Middletons brought back bad memories, ones he'd just as soon forget. "All Ross sees is that Becky's dead, and there are too many unanswered questions about that night." Logan knew the answers but chose not to discuss them.

Avery was concerned that he was willing to put so much on the line. And for what? His pride? She didn't think so. Or was he protecting someone? "If Ross is so out of control, how can you be sure he won't come tonight?"

"What makes Ross so dangerous, Avery, is his cunning. Mix that with rage, alcohol, the pain of his loss and now his own humiliation, and I think he'll wait until we least expect it before he acts."

She heard the worry in his voice and turned on her side to face him. "And you still wanted me and Emma to leave the ranch today?"

"Precautions. I'd feel a lot better knowing you and your sister were with Dad. I knew after one look at your face that I'd never convince you to go. But I really thought Emma would see the logic of leaving and convince you. I guess the Jensen girls are more alike than I realized."

"She's butt-headed, too." Avery giggled when he

grunted in agreement. "But I wish she'd left with Mac."

"I don't like her staying out in the small house, either," Logan said. "Why wouldn't she allow Tanner and me to move the bed here? We could have set it up in one of the empty bedrooms."

Avery thought about Emma alone in the little house and agreed with Logan. "She said she wanted to stay out there. I think Emma has a problem she needs to work out. When she was troubled as a child, she'd go off by herself to figure out what she wanted to do."

"I know the feeling," Logan said. "I did the same thing."

"You still do. I've seen that look you get when you need to be by yourself and think. You have it now. What's worrying you?"

There was no good time to say what he had to say. The decision had been eating at him. How would Avery react? He didn't want to hurt her. "I'm almost ten years older than you, Avery. Most days, I feel like I'm pushing sixty, instead of forty. I want to marry you, but…" He hesitated. "But I don't want to forget Jamie, and I'm not sure I'll ever want another child."

She was thrilled that he wanted to marry her, but deeply saddened by the rest of his words. Her head was on his shoulder and she kept her face turned in profile so he wouldn't see her disappointment. "I don't want you to forget him, either. No child would ever replace Jamie in that special place you have for him in your heart."

"Can you accept not having children?"

He wanted promises she couldn't make, but she said, "I can live with whatever we're blessed with."

Let him hear what he needed to in her answer to ease his mind. Life, she'd learned, was always subject to change without warning.

She sensed a stillness in him suddenly and knew it had nothing to do with their discussion. "What's wrong?"

He motioned for her to be silent. "Did you hear that?" he whispered. Before she could answer, he flung back the covers and jumped out of bed. Avery scrambled up and followed him to the window, aware now of the sounds that had alerted Logan. A small crackling noise like you'd get by crumpling stiff tissue paper came from somewhere outside. To her growing horror she could see flickering lights.

"Call 911," Logan said as he grabbed his jeans and shirt off the back of the chair.

But Avery froze as she watched orange tongues of fire lick the sides of the mother-in-law house.

Logan grabbed her shoulder and shook her. "Call 911. *Now,* Avery."

"Emma!" she gasped. The name on her lips worked like a shock wave going through her. She grabbed the cordless phone and dialed. As she talked to the operator, she struggled to get her jeans and shirt on. Logan pulled on his boots and ran from the room. Avery was right behind him, holding the phone in the crook of her neck as she juggled her boots in one hand and fumbled with the buttons on her shirt.

Logan took the stairs three at a time, landing with a long jump at the bottom. He yelled over his shoulder, "Call Tanner. He'll know what to do."

They reached the kitchen and Avery dropped her boots, jamming her feet into them while she dialed Tanner's number. Logan, she saw, was already out the door. She suddenly felt sick and a little dizzy. The kitchen had a strange, foul odor, but she didn't have time to ponder it as she raced after Logan.

The night was alive with the sounds of fire, and the odor she'd noticed in the house was replaced by the smell of smoke and scorched wood. With her attention on the blaze, she almost forgot the phone clasped against her ear until Tanner answered. Avery stopped beside Logan. Horrified, they watched the flames snap and leap up the front and sides of the house. She heard Tanner's voice, and the only sound she made was a sobbing "Emma..." as the phone slipped from her fingers.

The flames streaked across the porch and snaked up the columns toward the roof. Avery couldn't move. Like serpent tongues, scarlet flames flicked up the walls, rising higher and higher. There was only one window in the bedroom, and it was now blocked by fire.

The speed of the conflagration stunned them both.

"Stay put," Logan ordered Avery. "I'm going in." Before she could try to stop him he charged the door.

He jumped over the fire on the porch steps. Turning his body sideways, using his shoulder as a battering ram, he crashed into the door. Wood cracked and splintered, then he was immediately engulfed by a thick curtain of smoke.

Avery was paralyzed with terror as she watched Logan disappear. One moment he was framed by the light of the fire, the next, he was gone. It was as if the flames had swallowed him whole. All she could do was stare and wait helplessly.

With the exception of the greedy blaze and her

pounding heart, time stood still. She measured the seconds she waited by counting how many times she repeated Logan and Emma's names. *Too long,* she thought. They'd been in the house too long to withstand the heat and smoke. No one, not even Logan, could hold his breath forever. Avery's knees felt rubbery, weak. She couldn't see the door anymore because of the smoke that billowed from every crevice. The windows were full of flames. Suddenly she heard the reverberating crash of glass shattering.

It was the most hideous sound she'd ever experienced. Her legs gave out from under her. She collapsed to the ground on her knees, hung her head and started to cry. How could the two people she loved most in the world be gone so quickly? Wrapping her arms around her body, she rocked back and forth, the pain too much to bear. Over the snap and crackle of the fire she heard running feet and voices coming from behind, but she couldn't move.

She didn't know what made her raise her head and fix all her attention on the burning house. She could have sworn she heard the sound of her name being called. Avery jumped to her feet just in time to see Logan, with Emma in his arms, stumble out of the house.

Then there were men everywhere. Mac and Tanner rushed to collect Emma from Logan's arms and Avery, seeing Emma in Tanner's capable care, rushed to Logan. She threw her arms around him, heedless of the steam rising from his clothes, which had been water soaked.

Avery held him, ignoring his deep fits of coughing and the way he clung to her for support. She searched his face. It was streaked with grime and soot, and his cheeks and forehead were red, but the burns looked no worse than a severe sunburn. His eyes were wide with shock, fear still lingering in their depths.

"I love you," she whispered. "Thank you for saving Emma. Now sit." When he stubbornly shook his head, she signaled Pierce and together they forced him to the ground beside Emma. "I called 911. An ambulance ought to be here soon."

She looked at her sister. "Oh, Emma," she said, seeing that her beautiful hair had been singed, one side up above her ear. That side of her face was an angry red. Emma was almost hysterical as she tried to explain what had happened.

"When I awoke, the place was already full of smoke. I couldn't see or breathe." Emma couldn't go on. She made a strange choking sound as if she were strangling.

"Where're the damn paramedics?" Tanner shouted, his voice cracking with frustration and fear.

Avery clutched Emma's arm as her sister fought for air. Then Pierce moved in, pushing Avery to one side. He knelt beside Emma, slapped her on the back a couple of times, then eased her, supported by his arm, into a half-sitting position. He covered her mouth with his and breathed for her until she inhaled huge gulps on her own.

Avery sagged against Logan with relief.

Emma glanced around, cleared her throat a couple of times. Her voice was as raspy as sandpaper and deep as a man's when she spoke. "Come on, sis. I'm alive and kicking." She gazed at Pierce as he gently let her go. "Don't get any ideas about that kiss." She squeezed his hand and smiled. Then Tanner shrugged out of his shirt and wrapped it around Emma's shoulders, covering what the transparent gown she wore didn't.

"What the hell happened?" Tanner and Mac asked at the same time.

Emma wiped her mouth with the hem of her gown. "That's what I'd like to know. One moment I'm sound asleep, the next I'm on all fours trying to crawl out of the room, but I couldn't find the doorway. That was such a little room, but I got all turned around. Actually—" she coughed again and struggled to regain her voice "—instead of the door I wound up in the damn bathroom. All I could think about was water, so I scrambled into the tub and turned on the shower."

Logan picked up the story. "The minute I broke through the front door, I dropped to the floor and had to feel my way around. I called out a couple of times, then finally heard her and knew where she was."

"Don't be jealous, Avery—" Emma tried to lighten the seriousness of the situation "—but Logan and I showered together. It wasn't much fun, though. The heat started making scalding steam. Logan said it was time to get out. We soaked ourselves one more time and he insisted on carrying me out, since I had no shoes."

Avery clung to Logan's hand and grabbed Emma's, as well. "If I lost either of you…" She burst into tears. Logan gathered her in his arms, stroking her back.

Finally they heard the wail of sirens. Avery's sobs ceased and she lifted her head. "How did the fire start?"

"I don't know yet," Logan said. "But I smelled gasoline. Ross's work, I expect. He must have thought Avery was still staying in the small house. And why not? No one introduced him to Emma earlier, so he didn't know she was her sister. He probably assumed Emma was just one of Tanner's ladies.''

Avery tuned out the words as she leaned against Logan and just listened to the rumble of his voice echo in his chest. She said a silent prayer of thanks.

The sirens grew louder as fire trucks raced up the drive. Within minutes the place was complete chaos. Firemen rushed around shouting orders. Waters hoses lay like engorged snakes on the ground. Mac and Tanner cornered the fire chief. The air was full of steam and smoke. Someone pulled Logan from her arms and she was shouldered out of the way as Emma and Logan were taken to the ambulance. She followed, waiting until she was sure they were going to be all right. Then she leaned against the side of the truck and closed her eyes. She didn't know how long she stood there, but finally became aware of Logan and a couple of men speaking.

"You were right, Logan," the fire chief said. "Someone torched the house. There's a clear circular pattern around it where gasoline was poured. Do you have any idea who did this?"

Logan was saved from answering by a paramedic, who saw his shivering and said, "Enough, Harry. Move aside so I can get this blanket around him and give him some oxygen. He's half-naked, singed and suffering from shock and reaction."

"I am not!" Logan snapped.

Avery smiled as she watched him being fussed over. Then she looked at Tanner and Mac, who were hovering around Emma. Avery knew she should be doing something, but couldn't figure out what. Then she realized they both needed some dry, clean clothes.

As she headed for the main house to get some, she realized one member of the family was missing. Casanova. The last she'd seen of him had been outside the bedroom door. Logan had shut him out. With all the excitement and confusion, it had been the best place for the pesky cat.

A flicker of light from the office window caught her attention. She grabbed a fireman by the arm and pointed. "There's something odd at that window." But by the time the fireman turned to look, the light was gone. "At least I thought I saw something," she said lamely, then hurried on toward the house, fighting a sinking feeling in the pit of her stomach.

The first thing that struck Avery when she opened the kitchen door was the putrid odor she remembered earlier. Now it was much stronger and she recognized it instantly. Gas. She began calling Casanova's name as she stepped farther into the kitchen, and the smell almost overpowered her.

She snatched a napkin off the counter to cover her mouth and nose. It was then she noticed the jar of M&M's. Instead of calling Casanova's name and taking the chance of inhaling more gas, she picked up the jar and rattled the candy. It was a sound she was sure Casanova could hear from two miles away. It never failed to bring him running.

Avery rushed through the kitchen toward the office, shaking the jar. The gas was overwhelming; her eyes watered and began to burn. An inner voice whispered danger, but she ignored it. She couldn't leave Casanova.

Everything around her changed. She was so light-headed, disoriented and dizzy she stumbled into the wall in the hallway and lost her mask. She tried to turn and leave, but her feet got tangled together and she fell hard against the wall. Baffled by her clumsiness, she gazed at her feet and saw a lump of orange-and-white fur.

''Oh, no,'' she managed to say between numb lips. Sliding down the wall, groggy and weak, she realized just what a dangerous position she was in. She gathered the limp body in her arms. The cat was barely breathing and she shook him hard. Fear of dying sent a surge of adrenaline through her, enough to clear her head. Avery gritted her teeth and struggled to her feet, then had one last coherent thought. *The flicker of light she'd seen was a small fire. Gas and fire—not a healthy combination.*

With Casanova clamped tightly to her chest, she stumbled toward the kitchen. All she could think about was what would happen when the gas reached the fire. Avery kicked open the back door and went out. After taking a huge gulp of fresh air, she screamed as loudly as she could, ''Gas!''

LOGAN SAT ON THE BACK of a fire truck while one of the paramedics, Penny Holden, applied an antibiotic cream to his face. There was a lull in the activity around the small house as everyone watched it collapse in on itself in a belch of steam and smoke.

''Do me a favor, Penny. Go see if Emma's okay, then tell the other woman I need to see her.''

Penny glanced around the end of the truck to where the ambulance was parked. ''What other woman, Logan?''

''What?''

. "Tanner and Mac are there with the woman you saved. That's it."

Logan pushed Penny's hand away and bounded to his feet. Avery should have been with Emma. For the rest of his life Logan would remember the sight of the woman he loved screaming and running from the house. From that point everything moved in slow motion.

Avery's screams and the sight of her frantic escape were overshadowed by a flash of blinding light behind her as the two-story Victorian house exploded. The shock wave of the blast lifted her into the air, then dropped her on the ground in a shower of sparks and flying debris.

Everyone was knocked off their feet.

Logan was the first to pick himself up, then run toward her. He fell to his knees. "Avery, are you okay?" Gently he rolled her over, then smiled as two pairs of angry eyes glared at him.

Avery sat up and held a droopy cat at arm's length so she could inspect him. When he meowed softly and she was convinced he was going to live, she hugged him to her chest again.

Logan led them both some distance away to be safe from flying embers. They all watched as the firemen turned their hoses on his home. He looked at the ruins. His life as he'd once known it had literally gone up in smoke.

Avery looked at him. "If Ross Middleton did this, I want you to find him and string him up by his family jewels. He's a sick, sick man, Logan. Whatever it takes, you have to stop him now. He almost killed everyone I love in one fell swoop." The cat meowed. "Even Casanova."

"I promise he'll pay."

"That's not good enough. You have to tell him the truth about the night Becky died. Whatever his reasons, he thinks you were responsible, Logan. I know you weren't. There's more to what happened than you're telling. I know it, and he sure as hell knows it. Ross will never give up. I can't afford to lose you and you can't lose any more of those you love. Stop him."

"It stops tonight, I swear."

Avery gingerly rested her head on Logan's bare shoulder, avoiding the patches of angry red marks as much as possible. "Oh, Logan, look at your house. There's nothing left."

"Yeah. Ross would really be pissed off if he knew he'd actually done me a favor. It's a beautiful sight, isn't it?" Avery looked at him in amazement. "I hated that house. It was old and smelled of age and decay and death. I'm glad it's gone. But now you, you're a different matter. What happened?"

She told him the story, concluding with, "Ross must have sneaked back into the house when we were in bed, killed the oven's pilot light and turned on the gas. I'm not sure when he started the tiny fire in the office, but…" She paused and shook her head. "He's really deranged, you know."

Logan got up off the ground, held out his hand to Avery and pulled her to her feet. He scratched the top of Casanova's head. "Let's go join the others."

Avery wondered how Emma, sitting on the open tailgate of the ambulance wrapped in a blanket, her face covered in soot and streaked with ointment, her hair singed, still managed to look beautiful. It didn't even matter that she was sucking from a plastic oxygen mask. Emma kept her male audience entertained with her witty comments about her rescue.

She grabbed Avery's hand when they reached her. "Thank God you're okay. Looks like we're both in the same situation now."

"What's that, sis?"

"Not a damn thing to call our own. Maybe it's an omen, Avery. It's time we both started anew."

"I already have."

Emma's eyes filled with tears. "You scared the hell of me, sis. Why did you go into that damn house in the first place? And please don't tell me you went for the devil-cat."

Avery didn't answer. She shifted Casanova's slack body and cradled him in one arm as she scratched his stomach to soothe him. Then she said, "You need to go to the hospital, Emma." She gazed at Logan, and in the light of the ambulance he looked worse than she'd first imagined. "Has anyone looked at you, besides smearing you with goo?" She realized Logan was only half listening. His attention was elsewhere. A sheriff's car pulled slowly to a stop and the deputy, a young man, climbed out, then strolled toward the group gathered by the ambulance, his eyes taking in the ruins of both houses. "My God, what happened here, Logan? Looks like a war zone."

"Where's Ross, Chris?"

Chris Monroe doffed his hat and scratched his head. "Ross is probably where he always is this time of year. At Fiesta."

"No. He was here earlier. I want to know where he is *right now*. And Jess—where's she?"

The deputy waved to one of the firemen and motioned him over. "What's the story here, Jerry? Were they careless or—"

Nothing else came out of the deputy's mouth. His eyes bulged and his face grew red. Tanner's hand was wrapped around his throat.

"As you can see," Tanner said coldly, "we've had a really bad evening here, Chris. Our fuses are short, so when my brother asks you a question, you damn well better answer him. Or I just might forget that you have to breathe." Tanner shook him twice to make his point, then released him.

Chris swallowed. "If Ross came back to Haven today, he never checked in with the office. And Ross wouldn't do that. He's called a couple of times to see how things were. And as for Jessie, well, I haven't seen or heard from her in days. I thought she was a princess or duchess or something at Fiesta. Imagine she'll be there all week, too."

"I want you to call Sheriff Dawson over at Willow Creek," Logan said, "and tell him he's needed here." He watched the war of emotions cross the deputy's face as he took in the scene of total destruction. Then he agreed and hurried toward his car.

"Will he do it, Son?" Mac asked. "It goes against everything Ross taught him."

"What choice does he have?" Logan tapped Tanner's arm and asked, "do you have your cell phone with you? Good. Call Dawson yourself and tell him about this, but wait until he gets here before you tell him about Ross."

"Logan?" Avery didn't like the sound of those orders. "Where will *you* be when Dawson gets here that you can't explain everything yourself?" She was exhausted, and Casanova suddenly felt as if he'd put on another twenty pounds. "And don't give me that look, like I don't need to know what you're up to, either."

"Why don't you go to the hospital with Emma? Dad and Pierce will go with you."

Avery shoved Casanova into Emma's arms. "Scratch his stomach and he'll be sweet. I don't need to go with Emma. She's a big girl. But I want to know what you're going to do, Logan."

"Well, I'm not going anywhere," Emma snapped as she gingerly appeased the cat by scratching him.

"Folks, this is the only ambulance working tonight and I've got to go," Penny Holden groused as she packed her gear. "Looks to me like none of you need to come to the hospital. The lady should see a doctor tomorrow, but she's okay. Just singed around the edges. So, is anyone coming or not?"

Emma was the first to speak up. "I'm not leaving without Avery, and she won't budge without Logan. And I don't see Mac or the brothers going, either."

"Okay," Logan said. "We'll all bunk in the barn."

They watched the taillights of the ambulance disappear. "At least the barn and garage didn't get torched," Pierce said. "I'll go get some flashlights and blankets from the trucks."

"I'll come with you," Tanner said. "I need to call Dawson."

"I'm plumb tuckered out," Mac said with a sigh. "I'm too old for this." He sat on the ground next to Emma. "You got a man stashed away and waiting for you in France?"

"No." Emma twitched the blanket over her legs. "Why?"

"No reason. Might as well stay around Haven

awhile with your sister, don't you think? Tanner and Pierce can help you get settled in.''

Avery bit her lip to keep from grinning. Mac was eyeing Emma with the zeal of a matchmaker with high hopes. Then she noticed that Logan's attention was elsewhere. ''Something wrong?''

Logan lifted his arm and winced. ''I ache from head to toe. I'm almost too tired to talk.'' He shivered in the cooling night air and closed his eyes for a moment.

''Logan, look!'' Avery pulled on his arm and pointed toward the barn. There was a flicker of orange by a large oak tree at the back of the building.

''Oh, my God, that does it!'' Logan started in that direction. ''Mac, stay here with Emma and Avery.''

''No!'' Avery screamed, and ran after him. Ross wasn't through with Logan, but he had made a huge mistake by coming back tonight. She yelled for Tanner and Pierce, but didn't slow her headlong rush. The look on Logan's face, the rage she saw, was enough to convince her he was out for blood.

If she never accomplished anything else in her life, she knew she had to stop Logan from doing something he would regret.

CHAPTER FIFTEEN

LOGAN DISAPPEARED into the inky shadows along the side of the barn, and Avery charged after him, only to slam into him as she rounded the corner. They grabbed at each other to keep their balance.

"Logan, I said I wanted Ross to pay, but please, please don't do anything crazy. Wait for the sheriff from Willow Creek to get here."

"He might not come, Avery, then what?" Logan had to pry her hand off his arm so he could dig the keys out of his pocket. He fumbled with the key ring as he searched for the right one. Then he missed the lock with the first couple of tries, but finally managed to unlock the door to the large, black metal box attached to the barn wall. Directly behind them flames shot up the trunk of the massive old tree and began to skip across the grass toward the barn.

"What if Ross decides to start taking potshots at us?" he asked. "Are you willing to let that happen?"

"No, of course not." She couldn't figure out what he was doing and stepped back to watch.

Logan threw a switch, then took hold of an iron wheel and gave it a full twist. Almost immediately a cooling mist of water fell on them. He laughed at Avery's bewilderment as she held out her hand and gazed up at the sky. "Cloudburst on demand," he said proudly.

She laughed. ''I'm impressed. You have a mighty powerful friend.''

''I never intend to lose my barn or livestock again, so I made damn sure it would withstand anything, including fire.'' They watched the sprinklers placed high in the oak trees and on the roof of the barn douse the fires. Steam hissed, and smoke twisted upward like ropes. Water began to stream off the roof. Logan turned off the sprinklers, then switched on the power generator. Floodlights lit the barn and surrounding area like a rocket on NASA's launch pad. From the outer fringes of the light, where the veil of darkness started, they heard a rustle in the brush. A shadow, tall and broad, rose from cover and ran.

''Stay put. Do you hear me, Avery? Don't follow me this time.''

''I won't move an inch,'' she lied.

Logan took a step toward the fleeing figure, but Avery grabbed his arm and dug her heels into the ground. All she could think to do was hold on until help arrived. For a moment she thought he was going to drag her along with him, but he stopped, and she pleaded, ''Not alone. Please, Logan.''

She heard Tanner and Pierce calling, and relinquished her death grip on Logan's arm. She should have known by his silence, the set of his jaw and his hard stare that no amount of pleading was going to stop Logan.

Then he was gone. He'd leapt across that line dividing light and darkness. In an instant he disappeared, as though the denseness of the night had simply absorbed every trace of him. She couldn't even hear the sound of his pursuit.

Avery ran to the edge of the light, staring, listening

for a sign that would tell her the location of two men stalking each other. Who was the hunter? Who was the prey? As much as she wanted to follow Logan, she couldn't make herself step into the blackness.

Tanner called their names and Avery raised her voice and answered. Her shoulders sagged with relief when she saw the beams of two flashlights bouncing and bobbing toward her. Tanner reached her first and she said, "He took off after Ross. Oh, Tanner, he's so mad he could kill!"

"Can't blame him, can you?"

"No. But… Oh, hell. I'm not going to stand here arguing with you while Logan is out there. Please," she begged, "you have to stop him before he does something crazy!"

"Stay with Pierce." Tanner shined his light at his brother and said, "Take her back to Dad."

Avery waited until Tanner disappeared. "Do you have any idea where they might be?" Except for the rapid rise and fall of her chest, she stood perfectly still under Pierce's assessing gaze. When he gave her a crooked grin, she relaxed.

"Ross would need transportation to get here," Pierce said. "That means he probably parked on one of the side roads. At this moment, if I were Ross, and Logan was tracking me in the dark, I'd head for my car as fast as I could and get the hell out of here."

"But it's so dark and they don't have flashlights!"

"Logan knows every inch of this place. He doesn't need to see to track someone. It's all sense and smell and knowing the nature of the beast."

"You got that right!" she said.

"What?"

"Ross is a beast. Come on, Pierce. I can't stand

here and wait.'' He seemed relieved, but he balked, obviously troubled. ''You can blame it on my butt-headedness—Logan'll understand that. Say you couldn't get me to wait with Mac and Emma.''

It didn't take much convincing. ''How fast can you move?'' Pierce asked.

She was exhausted, but the doubt in his tone made her grit her teeth. ''Don't worry. I'll keep up.''

''Stay behind me at all times. If I say drop, you hit the ground no matter where we are or what's happening, okay?''

As soon as she agreed, he took off at a lope. Pierce was a good guide. He moved fast and kept the beam of the flashlight on the ground so they could see where to put their feet. When she didn't think she could take another step, he must have sensed it, for he slowed to a walk.

''I don't hear anything, Pierce,'' she panted.

''That's good. You wouldn't hear Logan, anyway. He moves like a cat when he wants to. But I guarantee, if he's found Ross we'd hear them. Rest a second.''

''Thanks for what you did for Emma. I won't forget it.''

Pierce's serious gaze rested on Avery. ''I'm not so bad, after all, huh? It usually takes people time to warm to me. I want you to know I'd give my life for Logan and Tanner.''

With that he began moving again, and she fell into step behind him. After what seemed an hour, but could have only been a few minutes, she noticed they were going more or less in a straight line. ''Where are we?''

Pierce stopped and played the light over a five-strand barbed-wire fence. Stepping on the bottom two strands, he used his weight to push them down. Then he grabbed on the wire above and pulled up hard, creating a yawning space. He motioned for her to crawl through.

"There's a blacktop road a few feet away," he said. When they were standing on the side of the road, he added, "We'll head toward the highway and see what we come across."

"And if we don't find anything?"

"Then we turn around and go in the opposite direction."

It wasn't what she wanted to hear, but she had little choice in the matter. "Ross could already have made it back to his car by now and be long gone, couldn't he?"

"No. We'd have heard."

Pierce was moving at a jog down the middle of the road and she had to struggle to keep up. Soon she realized he was slowing down. She sensed a kind of gathering alertness about him as he looked around.

Avery, too, became more attuned to their surroundings. Without the shadows of trees, the night didn't seem so intensely dark. She could actually see beyond the illuminating arc from the flashlight.

Pierce started running more quickly again and she blindly followed, keeping as close as possible. Suddenly he halted, and she nearly ran into him. She fought to catch her breath. Her heart was pounding so hard she was afraid she'd keel over. She grabbed Pierce's arm for support and hung on until she realized he hadn't stopped out of any concern for her. His head cocked to one side, he was as alert as an animal seeking prey, listening intently to something beyond her hearing. Avery straightened, fighting off the urge to ask questions, and as she stood up she saw the silhouette of a man burst from the cover of the gully. Seconds later, another dark figure vaulted over the fence and trailed the fleeing man.

Avery was about to call Logan's name, but Pierce clamped his hand over her mouth. His face was close, and in the moonlight she saw his eyes flash with anger.

"Don't distract them," he whispered. "I'm not sure if Ross knows Logan's that close to him."

He removed his hand and she whispered, "What do we do?"

"Try and keep up. Make sure Ross doesn't double back and get the upper hand."

Keeping up didn't take quite so much effort. She and Pierce quickly rounded a sharp bend and the road ahead was awash with the headlights from two cars parked beside a beat-up old truck. Ross and Logan had both been startled by the blinding light, and it was then that Ross glanced behind him and saw Logan.

Avery watched Logan gain the last few feet between them. He dived at Ross, tackling the big man around the thighs. The sound of the impact as they hit the road was shocking. Then in a jumble of grunts, groans and curses, the tangle of flesh and bone began to take shape. Half-naked, his skin slick with sweat, Logan sat atop Ross. His fist, hard as iron, was drawn back, ready for another punch. Avery made the mistake of calling his name.

She caught the disgusted look Pierce shot her and almost swallowed her tongue keeping the next words from escaping. But the damage was done. Logan had been distracted. Ross shoved him off his chest, then slid far enough away to stagger to his feet. Logan stood up, too, and they faced each other. Both men were swaying with fatigue.

Avery became aware of Mac and Emma. There was another man there, too. He was small and thin, in the unmistakable uniform of a sheriff. They'd all come up from behind the headlights. Tanner stumbled out of the bushes at the side of the road looking decidedly worse for wear. No one made a move toward Logan or Ross.

"You son of a bitch, Ross," Logan growled. "Have you lost your mind? Forget every hideous thing you've done since the accident. Tonight you burned down my home and tried to kill me, Avery and her sister in the process. You can't deny it because you reek of gasoline. Tell me, Ross. When did you cross over the line and decide murdering innocent people to get back at me was acceptable?"

"My point exactly," Ross retorted. "Murdering innocent people. My sister would never have pulled out in front of that truck, not with Jamie in the car, unless she was running in fear for their lives. Running from you, Logan. What did you do to her that she was scared of staying in her own home? Why did she feel she had to grab Jamie in the middle of the night and leave? She didn't see that goddamn eighteen-wheeler. Why?" Ross stepped forward, his eyes wild with rage. "Was she so afraid you were coming after her that she never looked down the highway or saw the headlights?

"You all but called my sister a whore," he snarled. "But you're not going to answer any of my questions, are you? And you expect me to do nothing."

"Dammit, Ross, you're crazy," Logan retorted. "We've been over and over this and we do nothing but go around in circles. Get this through your head— your sister killed herself in a fit of rage and she took Jamie with her."

Ross shook his head like an injured bull, trying to determine his next avenue of attack. "I don't believe it was rage. I think it was fear. What did you do to her, Logan? You bastard, I saw their bodies and witnessed her autopsy, so I'd know for sure what happened. But she was so smashed up the coroner couldn't tell me if she'd been beaten up prior to the crash."

Logan struggled to keep the nightmare of memories at bay. He'd been the first on the scene. He'd seen it all. He'd held Jamie's lifeless body in his arms. That horrific picture would be with him forever.

"No comment, Logan? That's typical. You can't hide forever behind the lie that Becky was unfaithful. Do you know why? Because I won't let you. I'll hound you until the day you die—or I finally kill you. She ran from you because you beat her up, didn't you? *Didn't you?*"

"No." Logan clenched his fist and drew his arm back. He would find nothing more satisfying than to shatter the smirk on Ross's face.

Avery jumped between them. "You have to tell him the truth, Logan. Can't you see what it's done to him? Secrets don't work—they only come back to haunt you."

"Listen to her, Logan," Ross said.

Avery searched Logan's face, looking for some sign that he'd heard her. "Ross can't live with the doubts of her death. And he won't stop until you tell him the truth, no matter how hard it is."

"What a novelty—a smart woman," Ross jeered. "Listen to her, Logan. Come on, tell me your secrets." Ross's voice had dropped to a whisper and had a crazy singsong quality. "What did you do? Slap her around? Hit her with your fist? Perhaps I already know the truth. So what's it to be? Were you the unfaithful one? Maybe you seduced Jess. Did Becky walk in and find you with Jess? Time for the truth."

"Enough!" Pierce yelled, and everyone looked at him. But Pierce was staring at Logan. "You made me swear and I agreed, but I can't let this go on any longer."

"Shut up, Pierce," Logan snapped, and pointed past his brother's shoulder to where Mac and Emma were standing.

Wearily Pierce shook his head, then straightened as if to brace himself for a blow. He looked at Ross. "Becky didn't catch Logan with Jess."

"Dammit, Pierce," Logan said. "You've done enough. Don't rip what's left of our family apart, too."

Pierce ignored him. "Logan caught Becky and me on the couch in the little house the night of the accident."

There was utter silence for a moment. Everybody looked at Pierce as if he'd sprouted horns and a long, forked tail.

"Liar!" Ross yelled, and lunged at Pierce, but Logan and Tanner stopped him. "You goddamn Monahans stick together, don't you?"

"I'm sorry, Logan," Pierce said softly. "But if you'd let me confess after the accident, none of this would have happened. And maybe, just maybe, you could have forgiven me if you'd ever listened to my side of what happened. You have to listen this time, or I'll never be able to face anyone again, much less myself." He never took his eyes off Logan. "I'm so sorry."

"Liar!" Ross shouted again.

Pierce ignored Ross and kept talking to Logan. "That night...that night I came looking for *you*. I was walleyed drunk by the time I got there. I'd had a hellish day. I'd tried to save two of Portland's prize Appaloosas, but ended up having to put them down. Then I drove to San Antonio, to the Black Hat, to see Clara. She made it clear that she didn't want to see me anymore. I swear, Logan, the only reason I went to your place was to see you. We used to talk over our problems and, man, I needed you that night.

"By the time I got here I'd managed to drown most of my self-pity in booze. I was still carrying the bottle. Becky met me at the door. She told me you'd been called out on an emergency."

Avery watched Pierce close his eyes as if seeing what happened in his mind's eye. She wondered how many times since the accident he had relived what had happened.

"Becky took the bottle from me, but instead of pitching it, she drank what was left, then said she wanted to show me what she'd done to the little house. Her grand remodeling job, she called it. I don't remember getting there, nor do I know how I got out of my clothes. And I certainly don't remember Becky taking hers off. Logan, I swear by everything I hold dear, we didn't do anything else. I didn't, couldn't have done anything. I was too damn drunk."

Avery recognized the shock Pierce's confession caused and knew that the pact of silence the two men had made that awful night had never been broken—until now. Tanner, probably for the first time in his life, was speechless. Mac made no effort to hide the tears that rolled down his leathery cheeks. She knew Mac had raised his boys with a strong sense of morals, good manners and respect for women. His family had been shattered for the second time in too short a period. Avery was glad to see that Emma had her arm around the old man and was comforting him. The sheriff simply leaned against the hood of one of the cars and listened.

Ross, Avery noticed, wasn't totally convinced, but for the first time she saw doubt in his troubled gaze. She knew that Pierce had to complete his story. He had to tell it all now, or he and Logan would never find any peace.

"What happened next, Pierce?" she prodded.

"I don't know. All of a sudden Logan was standing in the doorway and Becky was screaming. I just lay there trying to figure out why Becky and I were naked. When it all sunk in, it was too late. I was going to explain, but I hesitated, and Logan thought the worst."

"With good reason," Tanner chimed in. "Becky tried to seduce me on numerous occasions." He glanced at Logan. "Don't give me that look of yours and glare at me. Did you think it was something I could just walk up and tell you about? 'Hey, Brother, your wife is hot for my body'? Not bloody likely."

"You're all in this together," Ross growled. "Becky wasn't like that."

"Yes, she was, Ross," Logan said, "and a whole

lot worse. How many times do you think I caught her with someone when I showed up unexpectedly?''

Avery tried to head off another shouting match. ''Finish telling what happened that night, Pierce.''

''They started arguing and I sobered up fast, real fast. Logan made it clear to Becky that he was fed up, that he was going to file for divorce and he wanted full custody of Jamie. Becky went nuts, screaming, yelling that he'd never humiliate her with a divorce.''

Pierce rubbed his haggard face, sighed and focused on Ross. ''Not once when they were arguing did Becky even mention Jamie. It was as if he didn't matter. She was only concerned about Logan leaving her and the divorce. Logan walked out and headed for the barn. Becky watched him go. She must have known it was over. She was crying and talking to herself, saying things like Logan only loved Jamie. If he didn't love her, she'd make damn sure he couldn't have Jamie.

''She ran to the big house and I went after Logan to explain my side of it. It couldn't have been more than fifteen minutes later that we heard her car start, then the crash. We both ran toward the sounds, but we were too late.''

Pierce's gaze dropped to a spot on the ground between his feet. His shoulders shook with emotion. When he could speak, he said, ''Logan made me promise I'd never tell a soul what happened. For Jamie's memory, he said. I agreed, but I wish to God I hadn't.'' He lifted his head and met Ross's shattered gaze. ''You see, I'm the one responsible for Becky's death. If only I hadn't shown up drunk. But that's a cop-out. Being drunk is no excuse, is it? If I hadn't…''

Logan hesitated for a moment, then placed his hand on Pierce's shoulder. Avery saw that touching his brother had opened a door, and Logan walked through. He would no longer condemn Pierce. He wouldn't blame himself. Logan embraced Pierce and slapped him on the back a couple of times before he released him.

Avery turned her attention to Ross, and it seemed to her that he'd finally faced the truth. He seemed to have shrunk in size and his eyes had a haunted look. His devotion and love for his sister had blinded him to her faults. Avery imagined Ross was devastated by the truth and that he could have been so wrong. Sheriff Dawson stepped forward, and as they watched, he handcuffed the sheriff of Haven.

"Ross," Logan called out as the sheriff and Ross were walking toward the patrol car. "Ross, did you kill Blackie?"

"Good Lord, no. I gave him to a family that lives over in Hill County. They have five kids who are crazy about him."

Logan nodded, obviously relieved. Then he laughed, and Ross and Sheriff Dawson stopped to look at him. "I believe you actually did me a favor by burning down that monster."

Ross managed a shaky smile. "You always did hate it, didn't you? Maybe you'll tell the judge I was an instrument of good fortune."

"Maybe I will."

Then Sheriff Dawson put Ross into his car and drove off.

Everyone stood in the middle of the road silently watching until the taillights of the car disappeared.

They were all dirty and weary. Avery looked at the ragtag bunch and thought, *Quite a family*.

AVERY GENTLY APPLIED ointment to the worst of the angry red patches of skin on Logan's back and shoulders. "You're pink all over, Logan. Are you sure it doesn't hurt?"

He flinched. "Just a couple of places. I've got a good idea what being poached feels like, though."

Avery wiped her hands off and glanced around. "I had no idea this place was so nice." They were in what she called the barn loft. Logan had turned it into living quarters. It was air-conditioned and fully furnished with a bedroom, huge living area and a bath. The only thing it lacked was a kitchen, but there was a small refrigerator and a coffee maker. All the comforts of home, which was what the place had been to Logan.

After Sheriff Dawson had left with Ross, they'd all returned to the ranch. Mac had been mostly silent on the ride back, but when they arrived, he'd insisted that Pierce take him home. Tanner decided he would stick around and help Logan. Avery thought his real reason was Emma. They'd all invaded Logan's private hideout, and once they'd showered, three of them had divided up the few of Logan's clean clothes that he kept there.

"I don't hear any voices coming from the living room." Avery helped Logan pull on his shirt. "Do you think they've killed each other?" When they'd left Emma and Tanner, there'd been a heated discussion going on as to who would sleep on the couch and who would get the air mattress on the floor. Emma had a knack for getting her way, but Tanner seemed impervious to her charms, her barbs and viper tongue.

"Last I heard, Tanner was offering to give her a new hairdo."

"Omigod. She didn't take him up on it, did she?"

"I'm not sure, but my brother was talking fast when I left them." He caught a glimpse of Avery and himself in the mirror and smiled. He was wearing the bottom half of an old pair of pajamas and a soft white shirt. Avery had on the top, and a pair of his cutoff gray sweats.

"You looked adorable with your hair hanging straight and still damp," he said. Her face was scrubbed clean and her cheeks were shiny. He kissed her lips softly, savoring the sweetness. "Let's go see if my brother is as good as he thinks he is."

They went into the living room, only to find it empty.

"Emma would never let Tanner get within three feet of her with a pair of scissors."

Logan tossed the pillows off the couch and collapsed, pulling Avery down beside him. "Let's talk about us."

She snuggled against him and curled her feet under her to keep her cold toes warm. "Okay. You start."

"Well, when do you want to get married? We should do it while Emma's here. She is staying, isn't she?"

"She hasn't said. Actually, she hasn't said much of anything."

"We'll have to decide where we want to live. We could stay with Tanner at the farm while we build our house. You don't have any objections about building here, do you? If you do, Avery, I'll sell out and find

us another piece of land. Maybe that would be best.
Start fresh and new someplace else. There's plenty of
land for sale around Haven.''

"Logan, take a breath and give me a chance to
answer.'' For a moment, though, she was unable to
speak. She'd seen many sides of Logan, but this one
was new. There was a happiness within him that
showed in his eyes. And when he smiled her breath
caught. ''I'd love to build our lives together here.''

Logan kissed her and would have done a whole lot
more except the door slammed open against the wall
and Emma and Tanner, sniping at each other, came
into the room.

Avery turned to see her sister juggling a large bowl
of popcorn, while Tanner carried a tray of cold drinks.
Emma was gorgeous in her designer silk pajamas.
Why shouldn't she be? Avery thought grumpily. Most
of her sister's clothes had been in the trunk of the
rental car. Then she noticed Emma's hair, or what was
left of it.

"Emma,'' she gasped. ''What have you done?''
Her sister's hair was only a couple of inches long.

"Buckskin Billy used the dog shears on me.'' She
fluffed her newly shorn locks, then blew the spiky
bangs off her forehead. ''Well, I couldn't go around
with lopsided hair.''

"The walking coat hanger here,'' Tanner interjected, ''loves it. I think I have a hidden talent.''

"Yes,'' Emma snapped, ''but don't let one success
go to that big head of yours. You wouldn't have done
it properly without me supervising the whole thing.''

Tanner snorted. ''Complaining, you mean.''

Emma ignored Tanner and set the bowl of popcorn
on the table. ''Hey, Logan, did you know if you put

together a couple of Bunsen burners they do a bang-up job of popping corn?''

Logan groaned and Avery laughed.

''Look what Tanner found. Show them, cowboy.''

Tanner emptied the pockets of his borrowed shirt. Candy bars rained down on the table.

''You raided my desk!'' Genuinely outraged, Logan reached over to keep several bars from landing on the floor. ''It was locked and I have the only key.''

Tanner grinned. ''When have you ever, in our lives, successfully kept anything from me?''

''Never,'' Logan grumbled.

Avery lost track of their good-natured ribbing as she looked around. ''Where's Casanova? I thought he followed you downstairs.''

''I locked the pest in a cage,'' Emma said.

Avery started to get up, but Logan grasped her by the waist and pulled her down. ''Emma's joking. If she'd tried, her arms would have been in shreds.''

Avery picked up a bag of M&M's and shook them. In a moment a garish orange and dirty-white cat streaked across the floor and landed in her lap. He touched his nose to hers, patted her cheek with his paw and howled softly.

''That is the worst case of sucking up I've ever seen,'' Tanner said. ''Look at that—he's glaring at me as if he knows what I'm saying.''

Avery ignored the laughter, then, as Logan took the bag of candy from her hand and tossed it on the table, said, ''He was gassed, then I nearly crushed him to death. He deserves a treat for his bravery.'' A little miffed and amused, she watched as Logan offered Casanova popcorn. Which the cat, of course, refused.

Everyone was suddenly starving and began to eat

the popcorn and candy. Once their initial hunger was sated, Avery asked, "What's going to happen to Ross?"

Logan didn't want to think about Ross. Certainly didn't want to talk about him. His sentiments were shared by Tanner and Emma. But Avery, apparently, was more tenderhearted.

"Will he go to jail?" she asked. Casanova stalked the bag of M&M's Logan had dropped on the table. She snatched them up but accidentally spilled two.

"For God's sake, sis!" said Emma. "I hope he spends the rest of his life behind bars. I was almost toast."

"But, Emma, he *loved* his sister." A large paw reached from under the table and blindly searched the surface. Avery speared the paw with the tip of her finger, held it down long enough for a pair of blue eyes to appear level with the edge of the tabletop. She shook her head.

"And David loved you," Emma snapped. "But that didn't stop him from doing what he did."

Avery nodded as she scooped up the errant candies and dropped them in Tanner's shirt pocket with the bag. "You're right, of course." She turned her gaze on Logan. "He needs someone to help him, though. And what about Jessie?"

"Considering her feelings for me, I don't think I could do her any good. But Dad said he'd take care of her, and he will. He'll make it his mission to see that she gets professional help. Unlike her parents and Ross, Dad does loves Jess, and she knows that. Don't worry, sweetheart, it'll work out. Dad will see to it. As for Ross, I'll talk to the judge, but I can't promise you anything. He almost killed you."

"Hey, what about me?" Emma said.

Tanner leaned close to Emma. "You're not that important—just the sister-in-law. Avery will always come first with my brother, even over us. That's the way it should be. You'd know that if you'd ever been in love."

Avery could sense a heated discussion coming on and whispered to Logan, "Let's take a walk."

Minutes later they were roaming around the paddocks and the paths in their nightclothes and boots, uncaring of how they looked. It was a beautiful night. The clouds had departed and a quarter moon looked close enough to hang something on. She could hear a horse whinny in the distance and another one answer.

"I love this place, Logan. It felt right the moment I walked up the drive that first day. Does that make sense?"

"More than you know," he said, slipping his arm around her shoulders and turning her so she was facing him. "I love you, Avery. My biggest problem is that I want everything for us yesterday. I want us married, our new home built and our life together starting now. So if I get impatient and you feel rushed, just tell me to slow down."

They strolled hand in hand back to the barn. Just as they mounted the stairs, they heard Tanner scream. For a moment they were paralyzed, meeting each other's eyes. Then Avery recognized the sound of terror and, from Logan's matching smile, so did he. They ran up the rest of the stairs.

Tanner was pinned to the wall and at his feet was a tiny, but dead, mouse. Seated beside the mouse was

Casanova. Emma was on the couch, laughing so hard she couldn't move.

Avery scooped Casanova up in her arms, plucked the bag of M&M's from Tanner's shirt pocket and walked away, leaving the mouse as she scolded Casanova.

"Avery, don't leave that thing there!" Tanner pleaded. "Logan, Brother, don't walk away." Tanner scowled at Emma. "Sweet sister-in-law to be…no, no. Don't you leave, too." He raised his voice. "People, I'm in need here!"

Avery glanced over her shoulder as she headed for the bedroom. She smiled and for a moment watched the people she loved as they shared laughter. She felt so full of love that she thought she might actually bubble over with happiness. For the first time in her life, Avery truly knew what loving someone meant. It meant being loved in return, unconditionally, with all flaws and quirks included.

She had indeed found a safe haven.

Heart of the West

A brand-new Harlequin continuity series
begins in July 1999
with

Husband for Hire
by
Susan Wiggs

*Beautician Twyla McCabe was Dear Abby
with a blow-dryer, listening to everyone else's
troubles. But now her well-meaning customers
have gone too far. No way was she attending
the Hell Creek High School Reunion with Rob
Carter, M.D. Who would believe a woman
who dyed hair for a living could be engaged
to such a hunk?*

Here's a preview!

CHAPTER ONE

"THIS ISN'T FOR the masquerade. This is for me."

"What's for you?"

"This."

Rob didn't move fast, but with a straightforward deliberation she found oddly thrilling. He gripped Twyla by the upper arms and pulled her to him, covering her mouth with his.

Dear God, a kiss. She couldn't remember the last time a man had kissed her. And what a kiss. It was everything a kiss should be—sweet, flavored with strawberries and wine and driven by an underlying passion that she felt surging up through him, creating an answering need in her. She rested her hands on his shoulders and let her mouth soften, open. He felt wonderful beneath her hands, his muscles firm, his skin warm, his mouth... She just wanted to drown in him, drown in the passion. If he was faking his ardor, he was damned good. When he stopped kissing her, she stepped back. Her disbelieving fingers went to her mouth, lightly touching her moist, swollen lips.

"That...wasn't in the notes," she objected weakly.

"I like to ad–lib every once in a while."

"I need to sit down." Walking backward, never taking her eyes off him, she groped behind her and found the Adirondack-style porch swing. *Get a grip,* she told herself. *It was only a kiss.*

"I think," he said mildly, "it's time you told me just why you were so reluctant to come back here for the reunion."

"And why I had to bring a fake fiancé as a shield?"

Very casually, he draped his arm along the back of the porch swing. "I'm all ears, Twyla. Why'd I have to practically hog-tie you to get you back here?"

HARLEQUIN®
SUPERROMANCE®

From July to September 1999—three special
Superromance® novels about people whose
New Millennium resolution is

By the Year 2000: CELEBRATE!

JULY 1999—*A Cop's Good Name* by Linda Markowiak
Joe Latham's only hope of saving his badge and his reputation is
to persuade lawyer Maggie Hannan to take his case. Only Maggie—
his ex-wife—knows him well enough to believe him.

AUGUST 1999—*Mr. Miracle* by Carolyn McSparren
Scotsman Jamey McLachlan's come to Tennessee to keep the
promise he made to his stepfather. But Victoria Jamerson stands
between him and his goal, and hurting Vic is the last thing he wants
to do.

SEPTEMBER 1999—*Talk to Me* by Jan Freed
To save her grandmother's business, Kara Taylor has to co-host a
TV show with her ex about the differing points of view between men
and women. A topic Kara and Travis know plenty about.

By the end of the year,
everyone will have something to celebrate!

HARLEQUIN®
Makes any time special ™

THE MACGREGORS OF OLD...

#1 *New York Times* bestselling author

NORA ROBERTS

has won readers' hearts with her enormously popular MacGregor family saga. Now read about the MacGregors' proud and passionate Scottish forebears in this romantic, tempestuous tale set against the bloody background of the historic battle of Culloden.

Coming in July 1999

REBELLION

One look at the ravishing red-haired beauty and Brigham Langston was captivated. But though Serena MacGregor had the face of an angel, she was a wildcat who spurned his advances with a rapier-sharp tongue. To hot-tempered Serena, Brigham was just another Englishman to be despised. But in the arms of the dashing and dangerous English lord, the proud Scottish beauty felt her hatred melting with the heat of their passion.

Available at your favorite retail outlet.

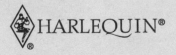

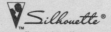